She tried to pull away, but his hands kept a firm grip on her hands. Her head remained downcast.

"Look at me, Rachel," he ordered.

Her hair, left in a loose braid, swung over one shoulder, leaving her nape bare.

Stryker looked down at the vulnerable strip of flesh. Skin like soft pink silk that never saw the light of day. He felt her tension under his fingertips and knew he was the cause of it. But he knew if he backed down now he would never learn the truth about her past.

"Look at me," he said gently.

Her face glanced upward. Only the slight trembling of her lower lip betrayed her inner turmoil as she stared back with eyes resembling dark purple pansies. Her cheeks betrayed a faint pink flush.

Could ghosts blush? Or cry?

Dear Reader,

Get ready for this month's romantic adrenaline rush from Silhouette Intimate Moments. First up, we have RITA® Award-winning author Kathleen Creighton's next STARRS OF THE WEST book, *Secret Agent Sam* (#1363), a high-speed, action-packed romance with a tough-as-nails heroine you'll never forget. RaeAnne Thayne delivers the next book in her emotional miniseries THE SEARCHERS, *Never Too Late* (#1364), which details a heroine's search for the truth about her mysterious past...and an unexpected detour in love.

As part of Karen Whiddon's intriguing series THE PACK—about humans who shape-shift into wolves—*One Eye Closed* (#1365) tells the story of a wife who is in danger and turns to the only man who can help: her enigmatic husband. Kylie Brant heats up our imagination in *The Business of Strangers* (#1366), where a beautiful amnesiac falls for the last man on earth she should love—a reputed enemy!

Linda Randall Wisdom enthralls us with *After the Midnight Hour* (#1367), a story of a heart-stopping detective's fierce attraction to a tormented woman...who was murdered by her husband a century ago! Can this impossible love overcome the bonds of time? And don't miss Loreth Anne White's *The Sheik Who Loved Me* (#1368), in which a dazzling spy falls for the sexy sheik she's supposed to be investigating. So, what will win out—duty or true love?

Live and love the excitement in Silhouette Intimate Moments, where emotion meets high-stakes romance. And be sure to join us next month for another stellar lineup.

Happy reading!

Patience Smith
Associate Senior Editor

Please address questions and book requests to:
Silhouette Reader Service
U.S.: 3010 Walden Ave., P.O. Box 1325, Buffalo, NY 14269
Canadian: P.O. Box 609, Fort Erie, Ont. L2A 5X3

After the Midnight Hour
LINDA RANDALL WISDOM

Silhouette®

INTIMATE MOMENTS™

Published by Silhouette Books

America's Publisher of Contemporary Romance

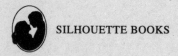 SILHOUETTE BOOKS

ISBN 0-373-27437-8

AFTER THE MIDNIGHT HOUR

Copyright © 2005 by Words of Wisdom

Visit Silhouette Books at www.eHarlequin.com

Printed in U.S.A.

Books by Linda Randall Wisdom

LINDA RANDALL WISDOM

grew up never imagining being anything other than a writer. In high school, her journalism instructor encouraged her fiction writing, but in college, her journalism adviser told her she wouldn't get anywhere in fiction writing while women were needed in the newspaper field. She wasn't totally derailed, just delayed for a while until the day she wrote her first two novels, *Dancer in the Shadows* and *Fourteen Karat Beauty,* which she sold to Silhouette Romance on her wedding anniversary in 1979. From that day on, she never looked back.

She lives in Southern California with her husband, a spoiled rotten terrier/Chihuahua mix named Bogie, who's also on her Web site, four parrots, five Siamese fighting fish and a tortoise named Florence. All of her pets have shown up in her books. She also likes to include at least one true incident in each book. Many of them have come from friends and prove that truth is stranger than fiction!

She can be contacted through her Web site www.occrwa.com/lindawisdom.

Many thanks to my editor, Susan Litman,
who keeps me on track, understands my insane moments
or at least pretends to <g>.

Prologue

"You're doing it again, Stryker."

"I am not."

"Yes, you are!"

"I'm just standing here having a drink!"

"Dammit, you've got your cop face on! What are you trying to do, put me out of business?"

Detective Jared Stryker pulled off the bar towel that had just been thrown at his face and dropped it on the bar. His expression was about as innocent as any bad boy's could be. Which meant he didn't look innocent at all.

"Darlin', I can't help looking like what I am." He rested his forearms on the bar's scarred surface. A half-empty bottle of beer sat in front of him. Since it had been sitting there for the past hour, it was obvious he wasn't there to drink.

A gray haze hovered over the pool tables, proof that no one obeyed the no-smoking laws in this place. That was why

Jared liked The Renegade. A longtime biker bar, it didn't serve frou-frou drinks. No candles decorated the scarred wood tables. No plants hung overhead, no Happy Hour specials and no tiny tacos and meatballs on a toothpick were offered to the clientele. If you didn't drink beer or whiskey you didn't belong here. And if you didn't ride in on a badass bike, or at least own a heavy-duty pickup truck, you might as well ride on past, because tourists weren't welcome.

The customers were also picky about their drinking partners. Jared Stryker might have a badge that declared him a cop—not one of their favorite types—but he owned one of the baddest of the bad Harleys made, and his pedigree hadn't allowed him to live the life of a good guy. He was grudgingly accepted.

Jared looked more bad boy than cop, just brushing the six-foot-two-inch mark, with sun-streaked brown hair that always looked a little shaggy, and deep, golden-brown eyes that belonged on a wildcat. The comparison was appropriate, since he preferred to walk on the side of danger.

A small scar zigzagged across one eyebrow and his nose had been broken more than once, but the imperfections only added to his appeal. Men noted he was an admirable foe, while women viewed him as the kind of man they wanted to bring home to Mom and Dad—when Mom and Dad were out of town.

He didn't hassle anyone for the sheer pleasure of doing it, and he didn't abuse his authority. If you left him alone, he'd leave you alone. If you made trouble, he made sure to set you straight.

He was also a close friend of Lea Raines, The Renegade's owner. Rumor among the scruffy clientele had it anyone giving Jared trouble for no good reason would be banned from the bar for life. So far, no one had tested that theory, along with the one that Lea kept a loaded shotgun behind the bar alongside her trusty Louisville Slugger baseball bat. There was no doubt she would use either if necessary.

Tonight was one of those nights where Jared wanted nothing more than to sit at the bar and enjoy his beer. A few women had broadly hinted he was more than welcome to come home with them, but he politely refused each invitation, much to their disappointment.

"So what really brings you out here if not the ambiance?" Lea asked as she efficiently parted a bottle from its cap and slid it down the bar to a waiting customer.

Jared hesitated before he picked up his beer and finished it. "It's my birthday, Lea."

Her eyes widened in pretend shock at his muttered announcement. "Really? And to think I thought that watch I gave you was for *my* birthday."

"You think you're such a smart-ass."

"Now that's the pot calling the kettle black." She took his now empty bottle and set a new one in front of him. "You're cut off after this one, lover. So tell me what else is bothering you besides being a year older."

He looked off into the distance as he confided, "Trust me, your watch was better received than the damn card my old man sent me."

Lea winced. She was familiar with Jared's history of being raised by an abusive parent. The only good thing that could be said about his father was that the man spent more time in prison than out. "Don't tell me. He signed it 'Love, Dad.'"

Dark golden-brown eyes narrowed with emotion Jared normally kept tamped down. He had no fond memories of his father and he would have been happier if he never heard from the man again.

"Maybe he wants me to know he's still in one piece? I don't know. Maybe he's feeling his age or got religion or something. He thinks sending me a card will make it all better."

"We both know that won't happen. He's not getting out of there, babe," she gently reminded him.

Jared looked off toward the pool tables that were set along one end of the tavern behind the small dance floor. He studied one man with dirty blond hair who wore old, faded jeans ripped at the knee and a black T-shirt that strained over a massive chest and bulging biceps. Fancy steel tips decorated the toes of his boots. Jared swore he could have been looking at his father fifteen years ago. Damn. More memories he didn't need. Some nights his shoulder ached from injuries his old man had inflicted.

He should have stayed home.

He would have preferred to sit at the bar and get roaring drunk. But since he knew Lea wouldn't let him use alcohol as balm as his father did it wasn't going to happen. Besides, he'd learned the hard way that alcohol only caused pain. Usually, his own.

Did his old man seriously think that Jared would forgive and forget his cruel treatment after all these years? The elder Stryker was in Pelican Bay for life because his temper had got out of hand and he'd beaten a man to death. After more than ten years he wanted to make amends. Jared didn't see it happening.

He considered it pure luck he wasn't sitting in the next cell.

"Jared?" He felt cool fingertips on his arm. He looked up to see Lea's look of concern. He managed a brief smile.

"I'm okay, babe." He reached for his jacket, which lay on the stool next to him, and shrugged it on.

She didn't look convinced. "Maybe you should stay here tonight. It's raining pretty hard out there. Mud and Harleys don't always go well together."

He knew the invitation was for the guest room, not to share her bed. He also knew she never invited a man to stay over. He wasn't the only one with issues.

Jared took a quick glance around the room. "Any reason why you want me to stick around?" he asked in a low voice, wondering if something was going on he wasn't aware of.

Lea shook her head. "No one's gotten out of hand lately. And the only thing I've heard are some rumors there might be a new meth lab nearby, but I haven't heard anything concrete. They're usually pretty careful about saying anything around me." Her rules about no drugs sold or consumed on the property were as strict as the ones she held for no fighting.

He nodded. "I wouldn't be surprised. A couple of county deputies had shut down that one lab a couple months ago. It's about time for another one to start up. As for gettin' home, don't worry. It's not the first time I've ridden home in the rain. Since I moved into the house I don't have as far to ride than if I had to go all the way into Sierra Vista." He leaned over the bar and dropped a kiss on her cheek. "Thanks for the watch."

"So you're doing it? You're really moving into the house?"

Jared nodded. "Tonight will be my first night staying there. I'm taking my vacation time to put the place into shape now that the plumbing and wiring is up to code. I'll just be up the road about five miles or so. We'll practically be neighbors," he joked.

"He's never coming back, you know," she repeated as he started to leave. "The judge put him in there for life, with no possibility of parole. He'll die in there."

Jared didn't show any reaction to her words. He'd walled himself off years ago when it came to the son of a bitch who'd fathered him.

He stepped outside of the building and stood for a moment, breathing in the clean night air that smelled of more rain coming.

It appeared to have stopped for the time being. He hoped it would hold off until he arrived home. Nothing worse than riding a motorcycle in the rain, where one slip on the road could do serious damage to a man's bike, not to mention his body. He sidestepped puddles as he headed for his wheels. "Whoever said it never rains in California never lived up this way," he muttered.

Jared was so deep in thought he didn't sense he wasn't alone until it was too late. Before he could react, something connected with the back of his head and he fell to his knees. Nothing more than sheer willpower kept him conscious.

"Keep him down," a rough voice ordered as a booted foot planted itself in the vicinity of his right kidney.

Jared swore out loud and lashed out at his attackers, grinning when he got one of them in the crotch. But his victory was short-lived when his retaliation earned him another blow to the skull.

His head was spinning when he was picked up and thrown into the back of a van, which took off the moment the door was slammed shut, tires spinning in the mud. After that, his existence was nothing more than punches and kicks from what felt like ten men, but was probably only two or three. He absently noted a familiar chemical smell in addition to the usual smell of unwashed male, beer and cigarette smoke.

These guys were definitely not leaders of the community. What seemed like hours later the van stopped and he was carried into a building. He could barely see out one swollen eye, but he instantly recognized the surroundings.

Happy birthday to me, floated through his mind before blackness took over.

Chapter 1

The crippling pain working its way through his body was unrelenting. He couldn't understand how it had happened. For years he'd managed to avoid too much damage to his person. He was no longer ten, and his abusive old man was spending the rest of his miserable life in prison. He was in the habit of stalking danger, not attracting it.

Jared opened his eyes a mere slit and discovered dawn was just breaking.

"Okay, Doc, you can just put me out of my misery now," he groaned.

"There is no way to bring a doctor here to treat your injuries." The matter-of-fact Hispanic voice spoke words that weren't at all soothing to his ears or to his peace of mind. "But I would not worry, *señor*. You seem to have a hard head that can take much. I think you will be fine."

"Oh hell. I feel like I'm going to die." He immediately passed out again.

Jared had no idea how much time went by between when the voice invaded his nightmare and the moment his eyes opened again.

The room was growing dark—it looked as if night was just falling. Mindful of the tornado whirling inside his head, he carefully turned his neck to get a better look. A candle flickering nearby allowed him to get a better look at the woman who knelt by his side. His fuzzy brain noted that her delicate features could have graced an old-fashioned cameo.

Now he knew he had to be dead. The woman who'd spoken to him before was older and Hispanic. He wasn't going to complain about *this* hallucination one bit. She was a soothing sight to his battered self.

The cannons from the *1812 Overture* were shooting off inside his skull, his stomach felt as if it wanted to empty its contents, and last but not least, his jaw and chest throbbed with almost unbearable pain. Just another typical night in the life of Jared Stryker.

He peered through the dim light to study his Florence Nightingale. He guessed her to be in her early- to mid-twenties, with dark brown hair coiled neatly on top of her head. Her delicate features formed a face so beautiful that just looking at her made him feel better than any amount of aspirin could have accomplished. Even with the muzzy sensation going on inside his head, he couldn't help wondering why she was wearing a heavy cotton dress with one of those bustle things on her lower back. She looked as if she had just come from the local Frontier Days celebration, except the western-style festival wasn't for another two months. But the dress did show off a slender figure and looked as if it was the same deep purple color as her eyes. Delicate lace edging the cuffs and collar was the only hint of femininity to the severe tailoring that clothed the slight form. He also noticed that her big eyes appeared to hold a great deal of sorrow for one so young.

He coughed, then winced as the grinding pain squeezed his ribs and stole his breath away. It took him a few minutes to think coherently again. "What happened...?"

"Some men left you here. I gather you were beaten," she murmured.

"Yeah, nice of them, wasn't it?" he rasped. "Especially since they were the ones who did the beating."

Her expression changed from one of concern to one of alarm. "I know they were rough when they handled you, but I had no idea they were the guilty ones."

"Not something they'd admit to just anyone, I'm sure." He looked up at her because he couldn't imagine looking at anything prettier. "They didn't see you, did they?" He knew if they had she wouldn't be here with him, but he still felt the need to ask.

She shook her head. "They were swift in leaving here."

"Good thing they didn't try anything with you. I would have had to whip their asses if they had." He winced as he tried to shift position. She shook her head and immediately reached down to help him.

A light exotic fragrance teased his nostrils as she drew closer.

"So tell me, beautiful angel, what are you doing here?" he asked.

"Shh." She laid her hand on his brow. "You must stay quiet. You need to rest. Don't worry, you're safe here."

He tried to smile at the idea of this sprite of a woman assuring him he was safe, but he could feel fatigue start to take over. He wanted to tell her that, no offense, but he doubted she could protect a fly. As for the word *safe,* his vocabulary didn't include it. But he couldn't find fault with her suggestion about the resting part. Not when sleep seemed like an excellent idea. He felt the gentle touch of her hand, cool and soft on his brow. He closed his eyes and succumbed to sleep.

The next time Jared opened his eyes the pinkish-gray light of dawn was shining through the dirty windows, depositing faint bars of light across the dusty floor. Before he tried moving a muscle, he took a mental inventory of his injuries and decided he'd live, after all. He felt a few twinges, but no severe pain that meant something serious was going on. He didn't need to look around to know the room was empty except for him.

Now that he could see the room more clearly, he knew exactly where he was. The khaki-green canvas duffel bag sitting in a corner of the room was the same one he'd left there that fateful afternoon before he'd headed out to The Renegade. The stack of CDs and DVDs lying nearby were also his. For the past week he'd slowly but steadily been moving his few possessions into the aging house he'd inherited from the mother he barely remembered. Curtainless windows that obviously hadn't been washed in years allowed little light into the room—which was probably a blessing. That way he couldn't fully see the balls of dust covering the floor, but he noticed for the area he'd been lying in had been swept clean.

"Hello?" His voice sounded rusty to his ears. Judging from the pain still crushing his chest, he'd hazard a good guess he had a couple of cracked ribs. He knew as long as he didn't laugh, sneeze, cough or breathe too hard he'd be fine. It wasn't anything he hadn't experienced before.

"You are awake again."

The Hispanic woman approaching him was the exact opposite of the angel of mercy who'd looked after him the previous night. She was dressed in a brown, shapeless, ankle-length dress that looked as if it was made from a rough material. Her waist-length, graying black hair was pulled back in a loose braid. She squatted by his prone body, surveying him with black eyes that he swore saw all the way down to his lack of underwear.

"Who are you?" he asked.

At first, she looked as if she wouldn't answer his question.

"I am Maya," she said, her voice powerful with pride of who she was.

"So, Maya, what are you doing here?"

"You will live," she pronounced, not sounding all that pleased with the idea—and, he noted, evading his question.

"Sorry I'm going to ruin your day." He glanced past her. "So where's your friend?"

She ignored his question and straightened up. "Can you stand?" She held out her hands.

With her assistance he was able to slowly rise to his feet. He hissed out a few harsh curses as the pain in his chest hit him, so hard his vision momentarily blurred. Once he could see clearly again, he took a better look at his surroundings. He considered it ironic that his attackers had deposited him in his own house. Now the question was, how did the woman get in here when he knew he kept the doors locked? And what were they doing here? He had found trash left by squatters, and teenagers who wanted some privacy, because the house hadn't been well secured. The first thing he'd done was install heavy-duty locks on the doors and windows.

"Mind telling me how you got in here?" he asked, feeling the breath-stealing pain of injured ribs. "But then, the idiots who dumped me here obviously got inside, so maybe the locks I installed aren't that good, after all. If you're here to steal, don't worry about me. After the way they worked me over there's no way I can fight you. Take what you want and go." He pressed an arm against his chest as if the pressure would keep the pain away.

"You do not have to worry about us, *niño*," she said flatly. "As for you, I think you look well enough to go now."

Jared tried to ignore the pain that had turned into his new not so best friend.

"Let's see," he said. "I don't feel the need to hurl, I'm not seeing double and my legs can hold me upright. I'd say I feel well enough to walk around as long as there's nothing more involved."

The woman's manner was less than subtle as she looked at the open doorway, then back at him. She picked up his leather jacket, which had doubled as his pillow, and handed it to him.

Jared started to laugh and managed to stop just in time. He knew that if he did his ribs would punish him with pain that would suck the life out of him. He thought about reminding her that they were standing inside *his* house and *she* was the uninvited visitor, but he sensed the revelation wouldn't bother her one bit. She'd still show him the door.

"Wow, you really have a gift for diplomacy," he muttered, as he took one cautious step, then another. He looked around. "I'd like to thank your friend." He wanted to do more than just thank her. He wanted to get another look at the delicate beauty, to make sure she was real and not a figment of a pain-fueled imagination. He wanted to find out her name. Most of all, he wanted to know how she'd ended up in his house.

The woman lifted her chin in a haughty manner worthy of

an ancient queen. Nostrils flared as if she'd just discovered a strange smell. "I will tell her you are all right."

His own nose wrinkled. He swore a faint exotic scent seemed to wrap around him. He thought he'd smelled it before, but his head still felt too muddled to give a rock solid answer.

"Thanks for taking care of me," he told the woman.

"De nada." Her gaze flickered toward the door again. There was no denying she wanted him gone *now*.

Jared winced as he slowly pulled on his jacket and walked to the doorway.

"You don't need to come back, *señor*. We will be gone." The woman spoke as if she sensed the direction of his thoughts.

"Maybe I better explain something to you. This is *my* house. I live here, even if it doesn't look like it right now. I don't want to leave the two of you out here unprotected. If you'll let me help you, I can make sure you have a safe place to go," he replied earnestly. "You helped me out. Let me help you."

"That is not your worry, *señor*." She effectively dismissed him. "We take care of ourselves."

Jared shook his head at the woman's stubborn nature as he slowly made his way down the dirt drive leading to the main road. He wasn't looking forward to the walk back to The Renegade. As he limped away, he felt the old woman's eyes boring into his back as if she wanted to make sure he left the property. He stopped once and turned around to study the house, which now legally belonged to him.

Thanks to the paperwork he'd been given, he knew the property had belonged to his mother, who was a descendant of Caleb Bingham, one of the founders of Sierra Vista. He'd inherited a ranch house and fifty acres of what had once been a working Thoroughbred horse ranch. Until then, he'd had no idea he was related to one of Sierra Vista's leading citizens. He'd only known that he was the son of one of its less desirable ones.

The lawyer also explained that Jared's mother had stipulated that if she died before Jared's thirtieth birthday, the land be held in trust until that date. Jared didn't need to be told why she'd made that condition. She wanted to make sure his father wouldn't get his hands on it. Jared knew his father would have sold the land in a heartbeat to have plenty of whiskey on hand.

Jared would have preferred the woman had thought to take him with her years ago, instead of leaving him property now. But he knew his father only too well. His dad's mean-as-a-snake temper meant she'd probably had to run for her life and didn't stop to think that she was abandoning her kid to a hell on earth.

If he believed in fate, Jared would say it was happenstance that he'd inherited the property he had visited so much as a kid. Back then, stories circulated about Caleb Bingham, that his spirit haunted the house and property, protecting his hidden treasure—and anyone old Caleb caught would be pulled down into hell. Young Jared had already considered himself in hell. Facing a frightening ghost was easier than facing his drunken old man.

He knew little else about Caleb Bingham other than what he'd learned in school.

The man had built the two-story ranch house in the early 1870s. Since it boasted seven bedrooms, there was no doubt he had planned on having a large family, even though he died childless, with the property passing to a relative living in the East. Surprisingly, the ranch remained pretty much intact over the years, except for small parcels being sold off from time to time by whatever descendant owned the land at the time. The remaining acreage held the house, the barn and several corrals. More property than Jared could conceive of ever utilizing.

He knew the place held a lot of history, and not just because of the rumors of Caleb Bingham's restless ghost. Local legend claimed there was a key hidden somewhere—a key that had something to do with a treasure. Specifics about the key and the treasure were never revealed, which only kept the legend living on and more than one person coming out in hopes of finding a fortune hidden somewhere on the property. So far, they'd all come up empty-handed. Jared wrote the stories off as odd ramblings from folks who wanted to sound self-important.

The first thing Jared had done was go through the house and decide what he would do with the interior. He planned to use the parlor as a den, since he doubted he'd ever be formal enough to require a living room. He figured he could turn the study into a home office. He also had plans to update the old-fashioned kitchen, which was complete with a cast-iron, wood-burning stove. He decided this was the perfect time to tap into his vacation time and work on the renovations.

Jared was already very familiar with the house. As a boy he'd sought out the place as a sanctuary from his abusive father. The times he'd crept in there, he'd never encountered Caleb's ghost, but he imagined that an unseen *someone* watched over him the nights he'd spent in the empty building. He considered it ironic that the house he'd once considered a sanctuary was now his.

He glanced up as a movement on the second story caught his attention. The tattered sheets hanging haphazardly in an upstairs window fluttered as if a breeze had caught them. Except there was no breeze and he could see that the window wasn't open.

"Maybe I've got a ghost, after all," he muttered to himself. "Or Ms. Personality is making sure I'm leaving."

It was still early in the day, so there was no traffic as he walked down the road toward The Renegade. He made sure to walk against traffic on the dirt shoulder, so no vehicle coming around the curve could catch him unawares.

Right now, his primary concern was retrieving his bike. He hoped the bastards that trashed him had left his ride alone. If he found one mark or scratch on his Harley, he was going to be really pissed.

He checked his jeans and jacket pockets. He wasn't surprised to discover his wallet had been emptied of all cash, but he was suspicious that his attackers had left behind his credit cards along with his expensive new watch and the keys to his bike.

"They probably checked my credit limit and decided they weren't worth lifting," he muttered to himself, looking down at the toes of his boots kicking up clouds of dirt. "Sure, Stryker, do yourself a favor and save money by moving into the house you inherited. There's no reason to pay rent on an apartment you only sleep in to begin with, when you have that big old house you can live in instead. What you should have remembered is that a big old house that's been abandoned for years means serious repairs. For all you know, you'll probably be spending the rest of your life making that place habitable."

He found The Renegade's parking lot empty and silent, since the bar was closed at this hour. He looked toward the second floor, where Lea had fixed up an apartment for herself. He noticed the upstairs windows were closed and there was no sign she was awake. He headed for the rear of the building. When he rounded the corner he saw his bike parked under an overhang by the barn that housed Lea's truck. A canvas tarp covered the motorcycle.

He smiled as he uncovered the Harley and found it unblemished.

"Bless you, Lea," he murmured, digging into his jeans pocket and pulling out his keys.

When he got back to his apartment, he'd call and thank her. He would also suggest she keep an eye out for men sporting raw knuckles from a fight—not all that rare in The Renegade—and anyone who still might be walking funny after Jared did his bit to make sure the bastard wouldn't be fathering children anytime soon. Right now, he had something else on his mind. Well, some*one* else, really. The engine rumbled a well-tuned roar and he made his way out of the parking lot. He was soon on the road. The chill morning air felt good on his face as he rode down the road toward the turnoff that led to the ranch.

Jared carefully made his way back up the dirt driveway toward the ranch house. He made a mental note to arrange to have the road graded for easier navigation. He stopped at the end of the drive to study the house before him, and the outbuildings nearby. The first thing he noticed was that, considering the two-story building's age, it had held up pretty well, which said a lot for the craftsmanship back then, though the lack of greenery around the building gave it a sad air of abandonment. He imagined it with a fresh coat of paint slapped on the exterior, maybe a few chairs set by the front door on the wraparound porch, and lush green grass planted around the house. He even thought it might be a good idea to set up a backboard and basketball net at the rear, so he could unwind by shooting hoops.

An unwelcome pang touched him. Jared only had to look at the house to know it was meant for a family. He easily imagined the man of the house mowing the lawn, while the wife tended a flower garden and the kids raced around.

Instead of that picture-perfect family, the house had got him, and he wouldn't consider himself any prize. He was a cop who didn't trust anyone enough to have any kind of long-term relationship, a man who didn't have any hopes of finding married bliss. Sadly, there would be no wife tending a flower garden or kids running around. There would be just him.

For a house he had never occupied, it held a lot of memories for him. He couldn't count the number of times he'd ridden his bicycle out here and spent the night, positive his father couldn't find him. The elder Stryker might have had a cruel streak, but he was also leery of anything he didn't understand. For some reason he had a superstitious streak a mile wide. All the ghost stories kept the man far away from the Diamond B property.

The first time Jared found himself at the house he couldn't have been more than six years old, a scared little kid who only knew he needed to get far away from his drunken angry father and his swinging fists. Night was falling as Jared stumbled upon the dark, empty house. Even then he'd known the place was reputed to be haunted, but anger coupled with fear of his dad outweighed the idea that a ghostly Caleb could drag him to hell. After that first night, Jared returned to the house anytime he needed a refuge, because he had convinced himself it was the only place he was safe.

"Look at the bright side of living out here," he told himself now. "You won't have to listen to the neighbors next door when they're fighting. You won't have any unhappy wives calling up with the excuse they thought someone was trying to break into their apartment when their husbands aren't home. No angry husbands accusing me of boffing their wives when they aren't home. No listening to oversexed teenagers fooling around in the swimming pool in the middle of the night."

He slowly circled the building before parking his bike in the rear. He unlocked the back door and walked inside. As he passed through each room he could sense the emptiness. A couple of times he lifted his head as he caught the distinctive scent of jasmine drifting in the air. He turned around to study every shadowy corner, but he found nothing there. Yet he still had the sense he wasn't alone, even after a thorough exploration of the house proved he was indeed the only one there.

A quick search of the barn and outlying buildings revealed nothing more than the usual trash he was sure had been left behind by teenagers.

"What they lack in imagination for a romantic spot, they make up for in smarts. I'll give them credit for practicing safe sex," he muttered to himself as he found more than a few discarded condom wrappers lying on the ground.

Jared climbed back on his bike and headed for his apartment. Once there, he swallowed a couple of aspirin, wrapped some tape around his aching ribs, shed the rest of his clothing and fell into his bed.

His last thought before sleep overtook him was the memory of a woman's face and haunting violet eyes looking down on him.

"Nice that you could join us, Stryker. I hope we didn't interrupt anything important while you were off doing God knows what. Or did you decide to begin your vacation a few days early and forget to tell us you wouldn't be coming in?"

Jared winced at Lieutenant Sam Adam's sarcasm. The man had a tongue that could flay one of his detectives in record time. Since he was involved in filling a mug with coffee, Jared didn't turn around until the mug was filled to the top. Right now, he was in need of a mega caffeine jolt. He'd count his wounds later.

His superior's gaze narrowed when he viewed his damaged face. Jared knew what he saw. He'd already seen it all in the mirror that morning when he'd tried—and failed—to shave after he took his shower.

His face sported a beauty of a black eye, a jaw showing an explosion of black and purple and a split lower lip. He knew he wasn't a pretty sight, and wouldn't win any awards at a beauty pageant.

"The good thing is they left the family jewels intact," he said cheerfully. "Actually, I am on my vacation time now. I just stopped by to pick up a few things from my locker."

Lieutenant Adams's expression didn't change. "Interesting, Stryker. I don't recall seeing an assault report cross my desk this morning, yet you look as if someone used you for a punching bag."

"You didn't receive additional reading material because there wasn't all that much to report. The guys who jumped me didn't exactly leave a calling card. Plus it was out on county land." Which meant it was under the county sheriff's jurisdiction and not the Sierra Vista Police Department's.

By no trace of expression revealed the lieutenant's opinion of the county sheriff, although Jared had heard rumors that Sam Adams once stated a blind and deaf Labrador retriever could do the job better.

"Did you at least go for medical aid?"

Jared shook his head. He wasn't going to mention the two mysterious women who'd taken care of him. "Since it wasn't anything serious, I went the self-prescribing route. After I took some aspirin, got some sleep and took a hot shower, I felt almost human again."

Adams narrowed his gaze. "Did you leave any damage?"

"Not as much as I would have liked. They jumped me from

behind." He really hated to admit he'd been taken by surprise. "But I did what I could to make sure they remember me."

The lieutenant shook his head. "You must have pissed someone off real good. Not that that's a new thing with you. Seems a lot of people get pissed off with you for one reason or another."

Jared gave his superior his best angelic gaze. "I have trouble believing that, Lieutenant. Why, everyone knows I'm as pure as the driven snow."

Adams's retort to that was graphic in the extreme.

"You're not planning on tracking anyone down during this free time of yours, are you?"

"As much as I might like to return the favor, it ain't gonna happen. No, I'm going to do the homeowner bit and spend my vacation getting my house into shape. I thought if I plan to live in it, I'd better make it more habitable."

"Just do us all a favor, Stryker, and stay out of trouble," the lieutenant advised. "As you said, you'll be living out under county jurisdiction. And we all know the sheriff isn't a patient and understanding man like I am. Nor is he that friendly with Sierra Vista's finest."

Jared swallowed the grin that threatened to erupt at the idea of the harsh-featured man standing before him ever being patient, much less understanding.

"It just goes to show you haven't seen my house. Believe me, I'll be too busy out there playing carpenter to have free time to get into any kind of trouble. I understand there's nothing more fulfilling than taking care of one's home." He lifted his mug to his lips and winced as the hot liquid assaulted his cut lip.

Adams studied his battered face, heaved a deep sigh and walked off.

"Tell me something, Stryker. How many women offered to soothe your battered brow?" Detective Dylan Parker asked as he stopped by Jared's desk a minute later.

He thought of the angel with the Southern drawl as he replied, "Just one. Jealous?"

"Hell, no. Well, yeah, because even with you looking like a train wreck, you still had it easier than me. You haven't lived until you've spent the past three days listening to Bradshaw bill and coo all these sweet nothings, and I do mean sweet nothings, to her husband on the phone. Since she got married, the woman is totally ruined for work. Ow!" He clapped his hand over the back of his neck. He whipped around and glared at the blond woman who stood behind him. She flashed him a sunny smile as she bent down and picked up the rubber band she'd just shot at his neck.

"Be a good boy, Parker, and tell your little friend you can't play any longer because you have homework to do." She held up a sheaf of papers.

Jared's injured lip protested his faint grin. He'd always considered the duo good entertainment.

Celeste Dante looked past Dylan and studied Jared's face. She winced at the painful sight. "Don't tell me. You spent the evening at The Renegade. You know, Stryker, most people go to a bar to relax and have a drink, maybe even dance. They don't go to get in a fight.'"

He nodded. "Yeah, I've heard that. I guess you don't have this kind of fun at Dante's Café." He mentioned the trendy restaurant and bar owned by Celeste's husband. Celeste and Luc Dante had met when Celeste and Dylan investigated a series of rapes in which the restaurant had been the link between the victims. Sadly, the rapist turned out to be Luc's partner and closest friend. Since the man pleaded guilty, he'd been sentenced to prison without going to trial, and had spared the victims the agony of having to relive their attacks. Celeste and Luc had married shortly after the case was closed.

"The only reason you like going out there is that you don't have to worry about tipping the bartender. Try to stay in one piece, okay? Come, Parker. Time to show off your hunt-and-peck method on a keyboard." She walked off with a grumbling Dylan on her heels.

As Jared left the station, he looked around. He hadn't taken any vacation time until he was pretty much forced to. He knew he was going to miss the place and wouldn't feel right until he was back doing what he did best.

When he arrived at the property later that day, the first thing he noticed was the quiet. This time he intended to survey in more detail what needed to be done. He wandered through the outbuildings, then checked the house to see what he'd require in the way of supplies. It didn't take him long to realize he needed everything. Suddenly, he paused, when a faint breeze touched his face. He breathed in the scent of jasmine. He spun on his heel, but saw nothing.

Funny. For a moment he could have sworn someone was in the room with him. A strange sensation skittered down his spine. An image of the violet-eyed angel with the kissable mouth drifted through his mind.

"Well, mystery lady, I guess you moved on, after all," he murmured, as he walked back outside and headed for his Harley.

Maya stood at the upstairs window, where she could watch Jared steer his motorcycle down the rutted road. She'd managed to avoid his finding her by hiding quietly in the attic when he looked through the upstairs rooms. She smiled as she felt a faint breeze caress her cheeks.

"He is handsome, *niña,* in a rough way," she said. "But I think he is a man with too much darkness in his heart. Not the kind of darkness that was in Señor Caleb's, but it is still a darkness that gives the man pain. He talks of living here, but he will not stay, just as others have not stayed. In the end we will be safe, as we always have been."

The double-wide trailer was partially hidden among a thick stand of trees. The exterior looked as if it hadn't been washed down in months, while inside, the rooms were filthy and smelled strongly of chemicals. But the five equally disgusting inhabitants didn't notice, or care, about the dirt. They were too busy drinking beer and using the illegal concoctions they sold on the sly.

"I tell you that cop knows something," one of the men growled, sprawling on a battered couch that had seen better days. "Did you see how he watched us that night? Why else would he be hanging around The Renegade so much, unless he thought he might have something on us? We don't need a cop sniffing around, now that we've got this setup going so well."

"Maybe he's down there a lot because of Lea. I heard the two have something going." The bearded man leered. "I gotta say I wouldn't mind having a piece of that. That woman is pure prime female." He scratched his bare chest.

The first man scowled at him "Can't you get your brain out of your pants for more than five seconds? We have other things to worry about. We're going to have to keep an eye on that cop. If he starts nosing around up here, we'll have to make sure he doesn't find anything."

"We shoulda finished the job that night," another of the men stated. "We coulda killed him and taken that sweet bike of his. No one would have suspected us."

"Are you nuts? Killing a cop is an automatic death penalty," yet another pointed out. "I'm not doin' anything that could put me on death row."

"Better him dead than us sitting in jail," the first man grumbled.

The leader leaned over the side of the couch and picked up a can of beer, a menacing grin on his face. "Don't worry. If he does try to screw with us, we'll make sure to finish the job next time. No way I'll let him bring us down now."

Chapter 2

The job turned out to be easier than Jared first thought. He rented a truck for his possessions with a trailer hitched behind to haul his Harley. Since he had little to move, he hadn't asked for help, though Jared wouldn't have thought to ask even if he needed it—he was used to doing everything himself.

As he pushed the dolly holding his television up the ramp he'd set up at the front door, he again had the unsettling feeling he wasn't alone. Once he got inside, he looked around, but as always, he didn't find anything. He blamed the strange sensation on the soft breeze that seemed to hover around him. He still couldn't understand why he smelled jasmine when there weren't any jasmine bushes on the property. So far, all he had growing around the house were weeds. He recalled he'd smelled that scent when the mysterious angel was near him. He wondered if he wasn't hanging on to the memory because he wasn't able to see the real thing.

He didn't find the sense of not feeling alone in the house alarming or suspicious. It even brought back memories of when he was a kid and hid out here all those nights his old man was on a drunk. How many days and nights had he spent in this building, feeling that same gentle breeze wrapped around him, inhaling the exotic scent? He hadn't known what the fragrance was until Lea, one of the times she came out here with him, identified it. After that, the young Jared considered the exotic fragrance as a sort of security blanket.

"Everyone insists this place is haunted," he said out loud, maneuvering the television into a corner. "Although I never thought of ole Caleb liking jasmine."

It was late by the time Jared finished moving in his meager assortment of furniture and returned the rental truck. After wolfing down the hamburger and fries he'd brought back with him, he snagged the last bottle of beer from the cooler and walked outside, moving along the sagging fence that separated his land from the main road. He leaned against a rotting post, hoping it was strong enough to support his weight, and sipped the yeasty brew, tipping his head back and staring up at the dark night sky with its faint sprinkling of stars. As he looked toward the nearby hills, he noticed faint bits of light high up on the wooded slopes. Once summer arrived, he'd probably see more lights up there, as vacation homes were opened.

Jared knew the mountainous area was dotted with custom-built vacation cabins. He'd also heard rumors about men living up there in small shacks. Men who didn't want to be found by anyone. For one reason or another they distrusted everything to be found in the outside world. They preferred being off by themselves, and the local residents were happy to leave them alone.

Jared could understand the men's feelings. Most of the time he, too, was content to be left alone. Which meant he'd been pretty solitary most of his life.

He'd had no idea he would ever inherit property, not to mention a ranch like this. Though much of the extensive acreage had been sold off, there was still enough land left to make a man feel like a king. And all his because his mother was descended from Caleb Bingham's brother, who'd inherited the property after Bingham's death. Jared briefly wondered if it *was* old Caleb who haunted the house and the land. There had been a lot of stories about the violent way the man died, so it would be logical he'd return to haunt the place.

"If he thinks I'll solve his murder, he's got another think coming," Jared muttered to himself. "I'm off duty."

He strained his ears, but the surrounding countryside was quiet, except for the sounds of insects. With the evening breeze blowing toward him he could hear the faint strains of music coming from The Renegade, about five miles down the road. There were no sounds he associated with living in town, no rumble of vehicles driving past or the blare of a car alarm assaulting the air. He almost missed listening to his neighbors having their nightly argument, followed by equally noisy making up. Here, there was nothing to pierce the stillness that surrounded him. If anything was unsettling, it was the tranquility. Jared Stryker's vocabulary didn't include the word *tranquil*.

He looked back toward the house. The faint glow coming from the camp lantern he'd left in the front room was a welcoming beacon. For a moment he swore he could see a figure standing at one of the windows upstairs, and briefly thought of the woman he couldn't seem to get out of his thoughts.

"Ghosts," he chuckled. "You're seeing ghosts." He tipped his beer upward and polished it off, then swung the bottle gently between his fingertips.

"It's peaceful here," he murmured, just to hear something other than his breathing. "Too bad mystery lady isn't around. She could have told me her story of why she was out here. I wouldn't mind just looking at her." He chuckled again. "Hell, if I don't want to go crazy talking to myself I better think about getting a dog. Talking to a dog is allowed."

He straightened up and ambled back to the house.

"I hope I've taken enough time off to do all this," he muttered, shaking out his sleeping bag and laying it on the floor he'd tried to sweep free of as much dirt as possible. He'd wrestle the bed upstairs in the morning when he had more energy.

As he turned off the camp lantern, plunging the room into darkness, he heard faint sounds coming from overhead. He was immediately on his feet.

"Better not be rats," he stated, keeping his weapon in one hand and a flashlight in the other as he stealthily made his way to the stairs. He climbed upward and silently navigated the hallway. The sounds had stopped, but he had a good idea what room they'd come from. The minute he appeared in the open doorway he quickly lowered his weapon. If he didn't know better he'd think he was dreaming.

His mysterious angel stood in the middle of the room. One hand was pressed against her throat as her wary gaze fixed on him, then slowly lowered to the gun in his hand.

"What the hell…?" Catching the direction of her gaze, he pocketed his weapon.

Her eyes grew even larger. "I am sorry," she whispered.

He had no idea how she'd got here without him hearing her,

or why she was back. At the moment, it didn't matter, because he'd hoped for another chance to see her.

"Don't be. This is better than my having to shoot a rat," he said, noting her nervous expression. "We meet again," he joked, secretly pleased to see her again even if he couldn't understand how she got in the house without him hearing her.

She nodded, still looking as if he'd said the wrong thing.

"You look better than you did before," she commented.

"The ribs still hurt, but I can move around better." Shining the beam of the flashlight at her, he looked her over, noting she wore the same old-fashioned dress she'd worn that night. He wondered if she belonged to one of those strict sects that believed a woman should be covered from neck to ankles. Considering the slight curves the dress revealed, he thought it was a crime. But it was her eyes and mouth that caught his attention. He'd never seen eyes of such a deep purple or such a soft bow-shaped mouth that begged to be kissed. He shifted from one leg to the other, hoping he wasn't about to embarrass himself. "I never did get your name."

She looked wary. "My name? Why do you want to know that?"

"You're in my house. I figure that gives me the right to ask."

She edged her way toward the window. Jared wasn't worried that she would escape. He doubted the window would even budge without the use of a screwdriver to pry it open. Not to mention they were on the second floor, so she wouldn't have anywhere to run.

"When did it become your house?" she whispered, looking even more panicked. "No one has lived here for a long time."

"Maybe no one lived here but ghosts, but that's changed," he teased. "I inherited the house and decided it was time I move in."

Her eyes remained huge. "I see."

"So do I get to hear your name?" he gently pressed.

"My name is Rachel," she murmured in her dulcet Southern drawl.

"Rachel. I'm Stryker." He took a deep breath. "Look, no offense, but you can't stay here. I told your friend that if the two of you need a place to stay, I can get you into a shelter in town."

A loud splattering sound startled them: raindrops that intensified to a steady downpour. Jared looked up praying the roof was in as good a shape as the roofing contractor claimed it was. Otherwise, he could end up spending the night in a wet sleeping bag.

"Don't worry, I wouldn't send you out into the rain," he stated.

A wry expression crossed her face. "I will be gone tomorrow," she assured him.

He suddenly felt like a royal jerk. "I mean it. I'll help you find something. Believe it or not, I do have connections."

Rachel shook her head. "You do not need to worry about me. I have a place to go to."

"There's no beds up here," he pointed out. "I've got an air mattress under my sleeping bag. You're welcome to use it."

"I don't sleep very much at night," she replied. She remained where she was, her hands loosely clasped in front of her body.

Jared was reluctant to leave her, but Rachel insisted he go to sleep, and assured him she would be fine. Still, over her protests, he carried the air mattress up the stairs to the room where he'd found her, and left it there with a blanket and one of his pillows. For now he wouldn't be too worried about her. She didn't look the type to carry off his possessions. Not that it didn't mean he wouldn't sleep with one eye open.

Once he was settled in his sleeping bag, and just as sleep captured him, he was positive the gentle scent of jasmine surrounded him. He even imagined he felt the slightest touch of cool fingertips against his forehead.

Even in sleep, his lips formed a word. *Angel.*

"Why have you brought all these things?"

Jared never considered himself a morning person—probably why he never minded working the graveyard shift. He wasn't happy that someone was shaking him none too gently.

Out of habit he reached for his weapon, which he kept under his pillow. He drew his hand back when he realized the Hispanic woman he'd seen before was standing over him like a dark angel. Her hands were braced on her hips and her face was screwed up in a scowl that would send most men running for the hills. Luckily, he wasn't most men.

"What the hell are you doing?" His voice came out the rough rasp of a man just jolted out of a deep sleep. His mood wasn't improved by the fact that it looked to be the crack of dawn. "I said the two of you could stay here last night. I didn't say I needed a wake-up call!"

"You do not have a lot of food in the kitchen. How do you expect me to make you breakfast if you have so little food?"

Jared rolled over onto his side and slowly sat up. He rubbed his face with his palms, and felt the bristles from his morning beard abrade them. His hair was likely sticking up in unruly spikes, but that was the least of his worries.

"Why the hell would you make me breakfast?" He could feel his whole being whimpering for coffee.

She ignored his question as she looked around. "You bring in things. Why?"

Jared got slowly to his feet. He might tower over the petite woman by more than a foot, but it was clear who was in charge, and it wasn't him.

"Like I told you before, this is my house. I'll be living here from now on." His head snapped up, his nostrils flaring in re-action to a scent that wafted past him. Why did the scent of jasmine keep teasing him? He didn't notice the sharp look the woman gave him. "Now answer my question. Why would you make me breakfast and why are you here?" He looked past her. "Where's Rachel?"

The woman sniffed with disdain. "That is three questions. I will make you breakfast because how else would you eat? You were kind to my Rachel last night, so I will cook for you this morning. But I see that the little food you have is not good for you. As for *la niña* Rachel, she is not here."

Jared was having trouble assimilating her words other than her announcement that Rachel wasn't there. She had told him she'd be gone in the morning. He just hadn't expected her to keep her promise so literally. He'd thought he would have a chance to see her again when he woke up.

"Your offer to cook is nice, but not necessary. Besides, the stove can't be hooked up until the gas company comes back out to inspect it. For now, all I've got is my camp stove."

"Why do you worry about a gas stove when there is a stove in there?" She pointed.

Jared laughed as he thought of the wood-burning stove that sat in one corner of the kitchen. "That old relic? I don't even think an antique dealer would buy that piece of junk."

She looked horrified. "You do not need to sell it. All it needs is a good cleaning. You get me things to clean with and I will take care of the stove. You work outside, I will work in-side." She paused. Her eyes narrowed. "If you let us stay."

He felt as if he was being played. "What about your friend? Does she cook and clean, too?"

Maya looked him square in the eye. "I will do the cooking and cleaning. She is not here right now."

The woman was lying. She was good, but Jared saw through her. There was no way she could pass the lie detector in his brain.

He looked around the room, which had more than its share of cobwebs, dirt and the remnants of squatters. Cleaning had never been one of his favorite chores. It was easier to buy paper plates than wash them. He scrubbed enough to keep mildew off the bathroom shower walls and to ensure bugs didn't invade his space, but that was about it. The idea that Maya was willing to help clean these disastrous rooms was appealing. And if he let her stay, he suspected he just might see the mysterious Rachel again.

"Lady, I'm a cop. I don't make a lot of money. Hiring you means I'd be an employer and have to pay taxes, plus I'd have to come up with benefits for you. I'd need your social to make it all official," he said. "Do you realize how much paperwork we're talking about? Trust me, it's more than enough to give me a headache. Which is why I don't need anyone taking care of the house."

She gave him a blank look. "My social what?"

"Your social security number. So that one day you can retire on all the money you'd make off me."

Maya shook her head. "I do not need money. Just a place to sleep." She looked him up and down. "You need someone who will make you good food and make sure you wear clean clothes."

He held up his hands, positive he wasn't going to win this argument. Damn, he never lost an argument! "Fine. Give me a list of what you need and I'll pick it up when I go into town." He'd planned on purchasing cleaning supplies, anyway. Not that he was about to tell her that. His old man's idea of cleaning had been throwing out the empty beer cans that accumulated in the kitchen.

Maya rolled her eyes. "Do you think I can read and write? I will tell you what I need and you will write it." It was an order, not a request.

Jared wasn't surprised by her admission. He knew many migrant workers moving through the state didn't bother with formal schooling since they had their very survival to think about. Looking at the woman's proud demeanor, he also knew he would never doubt her intelligence in pure street smarts. He found some paper, wrote down what she told him she needed, then settled for finger combing his hair and putting on clean socks before heading out.

"Do not forget I need a mop!" she called after him as he settled on his bike.

His shoulders slumped. "With the list you gave me, I shouldn't have returned the rental truck."

Maya remained in the doorway as Jared disappeared from view. "He is gone."

A gentle breeze caressed her cheeks. She smiled at the loving touch against her skin.

"He knows you are here, *chica,* even if he does not understand. You must be more careful."

She walked away, not expecting an answer. After all, how can a breeze speak?

Three hours later, Jared was grumbling that Maya's supplies would put him in the poorhouse as he unloaded them from his bike. He showed her how to use the camp stove and explained that he'd plug in the microwave oven later that day. Maya looked at him as if he was insane after he'd answered her questions about the device.

Jared then fled for the outdoors. Something told him the woman wouldn't think twice about putting him to work inside if he stuck around. Sure, he'd intended to clean up the interior. Just not yet.

Maya redeemed herself at noontime when she called him in for a lunch of hearty stew and homemade biscuits.

"This definitely beats fast food," he complimented her.

She frowned. "Is what you cooked before?"

"Careful, Maya, people will think you've lived in a cave for the past hundred years."

She offered a humorless smile as she returned to her chores.

"You never did say where your friend is," Jared stated, resisting the urge to look around.

"No, I did not."

"Where did you two go? Did you stay at one of the shelters in town?" He didn't want to admit he'd gone by there, but no one had seen anyone fitting the descriptions he had given the workers.

Her face could have been carved from stone. "It is a large country."

Jared waited for further explanations and soon realized she wasn't going to say anything more.

"I'm going out to see how much of the fence I'll need to replace," he said when he'd finished eating.

"A gentle wind could knock it down. You will have to replace all of it and put in new posts," she told him as he left. "I will have dinner ready when you return." She walked to the open doorway and watched Jared wade through the weeds covering what had once been a lush green lawn. She smiled at the faint breeze brushing across her cheeks.

"He will not be back until dark. I will fix enough dinner for two."

After so many years Rachel shouldn't still feel the isolation so keenly. Or feel so affected by it. Over time, memories of commonplace actions faded, until they seemed nothing more than dreams. She couldn't recall the feel of the morning sun on her cheeks, or completely remember the sounds of the men working around the barn and in the corrals. Or the homey clucking of chickens in their pen, their calls rising when the cook, Elena, went outside to feed them.

She missed the nights hearing one of the barn hands, Diego, singing songs in his native tongue. Songs of a love she had never experienced. There were other memories that weren't as pleasant. Those she would have joyfully forgotten, but they refused to leave. A woman's voice that was dark and cruel still haunted her at odd times. She shuddered at the memory of rough hands holding her down so harshly they left bruises on her delicate skin. Those times she experienced a visceral fear that was embedded so deep within her that it never left her being. On the heels of that memory was one of the day she'd faced death and instead, ended up in a world that had no beginning and no end.

Now she felt nothing, as if she was wrapped entirely in cotton wool. The walls formed a prison she was doomed never to escape unless she could find the key to her freedom. She knew if she hadn't had Maya with her all these years she would surely have gone insane.

The closest Rachel could come to the outdoors was to hover at a window and look outside. She'd done just that, watching Jared walk around the buildings before he headed across a field she remembered had once been filled with Thoroughbred horses. Horses grazing on rich grass that had been planted to provide them with the best food money could buy. The house, built with quality lumber, had been meant to last years, and the furniture that once filled it had been brought all the way from New York City because Caleb wanted the very best. The library had been filled with books that were never opened, since he couldn't read and refused to allow his wife to use them, resenting the fact that she could. He wanted the trappings of knowledge and prosperity so his business associates would assume he had qualities he didn't. He wanted them to envy everything he had, including his beautiful wife. She wondered if any of those men had known what really went on in this house. Or if they would have cared.

She wondered if Jared would care about what had gone on in this house all those years ago. She remembered the nights when the angry young boy would come out here to escape his own beatings. She'd never seen him cry. Many times he hadn't even said a word. He would pace the floor or sometimes sit huddled in a corner, anger rolling off him in dark waves. She'd seen a boy who hated the world grow into a lonely and bitter man. She remembered the cuts and bruises on his face and body, testaments to the violence he must have endured. She prayed the boy's anger hadn't blackened the man's soul the way it had Caleb's.

Caleb's dark nature and obsession with things beyond his control had ultimately caused her death. Then it gave her a shadowy existence that would never end.

Damn that woman, Jared thought as he studied the sagging fencing. Maya was right. He would have to replace all the posts.

He stopped and squatted down on his heels. Out of habit, he didn't use his fingertips to pick up what he saw lying on the ground, but dug a screwdriver out of his back pocket and used the tip to sort though the pieces of papers. The familiar sweet smell of marijuana wafted upward.

"No surprise there."

He stood up and glanced around, again having that feeling of being watched. When he looked toward the hills he thought he saw a flash of light among the trees. Logic told him the flash didn't necessarily mean binoculars trained on him, but his sixth sense also told him the spark of light didn't come from the sun hitting a window, either.

It was late afternoon by the time a weary Jared made his way back to the house. His thoughts were centered on a much needed hot shower and then collapsing in his bed. He picked up his pace when a rich aroma reached his nose.

"How did you do that?" He stared at the pots bubbling on top of the stove he had planned to toss out onto the trash pile. Now it looked so clean he wondered if the woman had spent all afternoon scrubbing the black iron surface.

Maya sniffed. "A good cleaning is all it needed. It was always a very good stove. Wash your hands."

"You act as if you know that stove."

"This stove I know," she said cryptically.

"Do I have time for a quick shower?"

She nodded. "Go."

Jared went upstairs and showered in record time, eager to find out if the food tasted as good as it smelled.

"I hope my hands are clean enough for you," he announced, walking back into the kitchen.

"Maya pretends to be very stern, but she is actually very sweet."

Jared spun around so fast he almost skidded on the wood floor. His angel stood a short distance away. The expression on her face was wary, as if she'd bolt if he even breathed wrong.

"Hi." *Good going, you smooth talker, you.*

"Hello," she said softly.

Jared tried to unscramble his brains. "Rachel, right?"

Her smile lit up her delicate features. "Yes."

He thought how the name suited her. He noted that her dress was the same one she'd worn the last time he saw her, while his ear relished the musical drawl of the Deep South in her speech.

"Where have you been lately?" he asked.

Her smile wiped pretty much all thought from his brain as she walked over to the table with a plate in each hand. "These plates are not very sturdy."

"They're sturdy enough. The best thing about paper plates is that they don't need washing," he admitted. "I've never been much on fancy housewares in my kitchen. I'm rarely in there enough to care."

She smiled. "Maya said you need a proper table."

Jared chuckled. "Maya seems to think I need a lot of things. That woman is bossy with a capital *B*."

Jared's taste buds fairly screamed as he looked at the pork chops, fried potatoes and corn bread Rachel placed on the table. He ate with a hunger he hadn't felt for a long time. He slowed down when he noticed Rachel eating with dainty bites, as if she savored each mouthful.

"When was the last time you ate?"

Rachel stopped, carefully put her utensils down and folded her hands in her lap.

"Actually, I do not require a great deal of food," she murmured.

"Women and their diets," he muttered. "You'd be better off eating more." He stared at her until she shifted uneasily under his intense gaze.

"Is Maya always so bossy?" he asked, to break the tension.

"Sometimes she's worse," she whispered with a hint of a smile. "But she has a big heart and enjoys caring for people."

"She sure knows how to cook, I'll give her that." He took his third piece of corn bread.

After dinner, Rachel led the way to the front room, as if she was the hostess and he was the visitor.

Jared looked at the scarred wooden floor, which was much cleaner than it had been that morning. Considering the amount of dirt ground into the wood he was amazed to see it actually shine. The scent of lemon and beeswax told him just how busy Maya had been that day. He chuckled when he saw that his two easy chairs had been arranged on either side of his big-screen TV.

"She obviously doesn't think I'll be watching football this fall," he commented. He gestured toward one of the chairs and waited for Rachel to be seated before he sat down.

She sank down gingerly in one of the chairs. Her ankles were crossed, hands placed demurely in her lap and her back ramrod straight.

"Someone would think you were in the military." Jared sat back in a more comfortable posture. "Take it easy, Rachel."

She appeared to relax a little in her chair.

"You said your name is Stryker?" she said.

He nodded. "That's right."

"Is that your first or last name?" she asked.

"My last name. I don't bother with my first."

"If someone wished to use your first name, what would they call you?" Rachel persisted.

"It depends on who it is. Some people usually call me something a lot more graphic." He chuckled. "My first name is Jared."

She smiled. "But you refer to yourself by your last name. Don't you like being called Jared?"

His mood darkened with memories best left undisturbed. "It's just a name I don't like to be associated with."

Rachel's smile dimmed. "You did not have a pleasant childhood." She made it more a statement than a question.

"Trust me, that's another topic better left alone." He speared her with a glance. "Unless you're willing to tell me *your* story."

Her eyes darkened with unhappy memories. "My story is very simple. I was raised in Atlanta, Georgia, and my husband brought me out here after we were married."

That piece of news wasn't something Jared expected to hear. He barely knew the woman, yet he felt a sinking sensation in his stomach at the idea that she was taken. But that brought up more questions. He couldn't imagine any man being fool enough to abandon her. "So you're married. Where is your husband now?"

She looked away. "He is dead," she whispered.

Jared usually believed a person who didn't look at him directly was lying, but he didn't think that was the case this time. There was a sorrow in her eyes, but he'd bet his Harley that sorrow had nothing to do with her dead husband. He had a hunch she hadn't had a happy marriage. Maya's protective nature about her spoke of a close alliance between the two women. Was their closeness forged by a shared tragedy?

Where did that idea come from? Usually his suspicious nature would wonder if she'd had something to do with her husband's death. He'd seen sweet-faced women who looked as if a breeze could blow them away think nothing of using a knife or a gun on their spouses.

He mentally shook his head to clear his thoughts.

He turned to Rachel, studying her face. He didn't care that she quickly appeared uneasy under his scrutiny. He wanted to memorize her features before she disappeared on him again.

Her dark hair was such a rich shade that calling it brown would be a gross mistake. Gold highlights gave it a shimmering effect he didn't think came from any salon. She wore her hair in a simple braid draped over her shoulder. Her dress might be old-fashioned, but it was spotless. For someone who was apparently homeless she was clean and neatly dressed. What fascinated him the most, though, were her eyes. He'd seen that deep luminous violet color on only one other woman, in the movies. She took his breath away.

"How many people have told you you have eyes like Elizabeth Taylor?" he asked.

She looked puzzled. "Who?"

"Hey, I'm not that old," he said wryly. "Look, no offense, but I don't think you and your friend can stay here much longer. This place is barely habitable for me and, well, I'm not in the market for roommates. I'd be more than happy to make some calls and find the two of you a place to stay."

"That is a very kind offer, but we do not need you to find a place for us," Rachel said. "We have always been able to take care of ourselves."

He still had trouble believing her. Deep down, he felt as if there was a lot more to her story than she cared to reveal. He knew if he had any common sense, he'd get hold of a car so he could drive the women to a local shelter and turn them over to the first social worker he came across.

Jared had never taken in strays or befriended people down

on their luck. He was a loner, only looking out for himself. For him to worry about Rachel's situation suggested a chink in his armor.

He thought of explaining to her that he was happier when he was alone.

Then he looked at her.

There was something in her eyes that tugged at him. They held a calm resignation, as if she'd read his mind and knew exactly what he was going to say to her. As if this was something that had happened to her before. Not that he could imagine anyone ever rejecting her.

But there was also something there he couldn't read as easily.

The lady had secrets. He'd bet she had a lot of them.

He didn't like secrets, even if he had more than a few of his own. He'd learned the hard way that he couldn't trust people with secrets.

He knew he should stick to his guns and get them out of his house, but there was something else bothering him. He didn't know why, but he had the sensation that he'd met her long before that night she'd tended to him.

Once Jared made a decision, he never backed down. It was one of his few hard-and-fast rules. The only other one he had was that he refused to talk about his father.

He looked at Rachel, who sat there quietly, as if she knew her future hinged on his next decision. He sighed heavily. He knew he wasn't going to borrow a car and drive them to a shelter, and he wasn't going to talk to a social worker about them. At least, not yet.

"This is still no place for you, but I'll help you clean up one of the rooms for you two to use until you can find a new place. It's still only temporary," he warned her.

"We will be no trouble," she assured him.

He never thought anything could warm his scarred soul—until Rachel smiled at him.

Chapter 3

Jared's shoulders burned, his legs ached and he was positive his back was broken in a multitude of areas. He wanted nothing more than to lie down somewhere and not get up for at least a year.

He kept himself physically fit by running most mornings and he made regular use of the weight room at the station, but he hadn't realized that lifting weights didn't make a difference when performing hard physical labor. He thought longingly of the spa at his former apartment building. What he wouldn't give to sink down in that hot bubbling water until the kinks left his body. He wouldn't mind having one out here. It would be nice to relax in, with only the night sky and stars for company.

He'd tied a bandanna around his forehead to keep the sweat from dripping into his eyes. His leather work gloves were good protection, but he still suffered a couple blisters on his palms.

Maya had studied his damaged hands that morning, muttered something under her breath and went off for a few minutes. She'd returned with a jar of some evil-smelling salve that she'd slathered on his hands, then had wrapped strips of cloth around each palm. Jared had fumbled his way through breakfast and gingerly put on his work gloves. He'd been surprised to discover the salve seemed to have taken some of the pain out of his hands, to the point he could comfortably use them.

When he asked her where the salve came from, she shrugged and said it was something she had made up from the plants outside. He didn't ask if she believed it would work. Knowing the woman, she wouldn't use anything that didn't work the way she intended it to.

"No one in their right mind would do this for a living," he muttered, after sinking a replacement post.

The anguished howl of an animal in pain snapped him to attention. He swiftly headed in the direction of the sound and stopped short at the sight before him. Because the three men had their backs to him, they hadn't noticed his approach. Jared frowned when he saw they were alternately teasing and poking at a young dog with sticks, while one of the men tugged on a rope tied tightly around the dog's neck. The puppy whimpered and strained at the rope, trying to get away, but his tormentors blocked any hope of escape.

"Dammit," Jared growled under his breath. Then he raised his voice. "Hey, guys! You're on private property."

The three men stopped their game and turned around. The fact that he was outnumbered three to one didn't bother Jared. Old habits died hard. Along with his work gloves, he didn't leave the house without making sure he had his weapon tucked in the back of his belt. For backup he carried a wickedly sharp knife secured in a sheath in his boot. He recognized the men as regulars at The Renegade. He'd even beaten one of them at pool one night. Not that that made them all friends; hell, for all he knew these guys could have been the ones who'd tried to turn him into a punching bag the other night. If that was the case, he was damn glad he was armed and ready for payback.

The man holding the rope tightened his grip. The young dog struggled and howled a canine protest as he dug his paws into the dirt and backed up on his haunches, attempting to free himself from his tormentor.

"We're not doin' anything," one man argued in the raspy voice of a heavy smoker.

"Yeah, you are. You're on my property and you're scaring the dog," Jared pointed out in a careless tone, although inside he seethed at the idea of anyone harming a defenseless animal. He didn't want the men to know how he truly felt, because he wouldn't put it past them to try something he wouldn't be able to stop in time. "Tell you what, set the dog free and the three of you can go off wherever you want."

The man holding the rope opened his mouth as if to argue, but one of his friends poked him in the ribs with an elbow.

"We didn't know anyone lived around here," he said, again tightening his hold on the rope until the puppy whimpered in distress once more. "But the dog comes with us. He's mine."

"Not anymore." Steel crept into Jared's voice. "Like I said, you can go, but the animal stays here."

He held his angry gaze until the man tossed the rope to one side.

Jared ignored their mutters as they took their time walking away. He waited until they were gone before he walked over to the puppy and took the rope off his neck. He chuckled when the pup jumped up on oversize paws and licked his face in gratitude.

"I know I said I should get a dog so I wouldn't be talking to myself all the time," he told the puppy. "That didn't mean I was actively looking for one." He lifted one paw and shook his head at the size. "Especially one who's going to grow up to be the size of a small horse." He noted the rough coat and jutting ribs and backbone that indicated the dog hadn't been properly fed for a while. "It looks like they forgot to feed you too. At least that's something I can handle. Let me give you some advice. Look pathetic and I just bet the wicked witch guarding my kitchen will put out some food for you."

It didn't take much persuading on Jared's part to get the pup to follow him. As if sensing he was now safe, the dog happily loped alongside as Jared headed back to the house.

"Damn, what did I get into? I have a house, two women living with me and now a dog," he muttered. "At this rate, I'll soon be driving one of those yuppie minivans and coaching Little League."

The puppy yipped excitedly as they reached the weedy front yard. Maya stood on the porch with a broom in her hand, furiously sweeping, as if pushing the devil himself off the porch. She looked up at the sound of the puppy's barks.

"Dios mío," she breathed. "What have you done now? Why did you bring this animal here?" She jumped backward as the young dog raced up the steps and bounced up on his hind legs, planting his muddy paws on her skirt.

"He's just a puppy," Jared explained.

She made a face as the dog dropped back down to all fours and pushed against her legs. "He is dirty and probably has fleas." She shot Jared a knowing look when the puppy sank back on his haunches and lifted his rear leg to scratch behind his ear.

Jared sighed. Maybe she was right—perhaps he should

take the puppy into town and drop him off at the local animal shelter. He was positive the young dog would be adopted right away. But a part of him couldn't do it. Maybe because there had been a time when he'd wanted a dog and wasn't allowed one. His dad had insisted he had enough trouble looking after a snot-nosed kid without the hassle of a dog, too.

"So we get him a flea collar for now and some of those pills to keep the fleas off him. Some soap and water will take care of the dirt."

The puppy suddenly nosed past Maya's skirts and ran into the house. They could hear him emitting high-pitched barks.

Maya muttered what could have been prayers, curses or both as she ran after him, with Jared following her.

The puppy stood in the middle of the living room, barking at thin air.

"He'll be a good watchdog," Jared said in a mild tone.

Maya shot him a dark look and shooed the puppy into the kitchen.

"I will not bathe him. You will do it outside and do something about his fleas so he will not bring them in here," she ordered over her shoulder.

Jared grinned. "Done."

"He will grow up to be as big as this house, perhaps even bigger," she predicted dourly. "It will cost you much money to feed him. More than to feed you."

"Since I'm paying the bills you don't need to worry." He watched the puppy fall over paws too big for his body and plop backward on his haunches. What surprised him was seeing the animal look toward a section of the room, as if staring at someone. His tongue lolling, he lifted a front paw to bat at the empty air as he yipped several times in greeting.

Maya stared at the puppy for a moment, then looked up at

Jared. Whatever she was thinking was masked behind stoic features.

"Yes, I see how well he will protect me from nothing." She kept her dark eyes fastened on Jared. "Puppies make messes unless they learn to go outside. I will not clean up after him."

Jared didn't miss the look on the puppy's face that warned of an impending accident. He quickly snatched up the dog and carried him out, praising him lavishly for waiting until he was outside in the dirt. The puppy jumped up against his legs and happily yipped.

"So what were you barking at in there, fella?" Jared asked, scratching the puppy's ears. "The house ghost?" he joked. He looked up to see Maya standing on the porch. "I'm going to take him into town to see a vet and get him his shots and such. I guess you need more cleaning supplies? Any groceries I need to pick up?"

She rattled off a list of items that still surprised him.

Maya's mouth turned up at one corner. "You will take him on your machine?"

Jared cursed under his breath. He hadn't thought about the dog having to ride on his bike.

"I've seen dogs on bikes before," he replied. "Plus he's small." *For now.*

"His feet are not. I will make stew for dinner." She turned around and walked into the house.

Jared looked down at the dog. "Maybe I need to take her in along with you for shots." He sighed and picked up the dog. "Trust me, you'll like the other one a hell of a lot better."

"It is not good that he is living here now," Maya proclaimed, waving a large spoon in the air as she stirred the stew. "No one has lived here for years. Why did he have to come here?"

This is his land. Rachel knew the older woman couldn't hear her, but it didn't stop her from answering.

"He does not appear to be dumb. If he stays here much longer he will find out the truth. What will happen then?" Maya knew she couldn't hear Rachel, either, but the scent of jasmine always told her when she was nearby.

Maybe he will not find out. What happened to him as a child turned him into a bitter and lonely man, even if he will never admit it. Maybe if we are here he will not turn out to be dark as Caleb was. Look how Jared is with the puppy.

As if Maya heard her, she mumbled her opinion of the young dog, then she muttered, "Señor Caleb treated his dogs better than he treated you." She paused in her work. "Oh, *niña*, what if he refuses to believe the truth?"

He will have to understand, especially when he sees I cannot leave the house. Besides, it is not as if he can hurt me.

A strange light appeared in Maya's eyes. "Then perhaps it is meant for him to be here now. He may be the one the gods have decreed will help you find the key that can free you."

If Rachel had been able to sigh, she would have. She wanted to tell Maya that she was convinced the story of the key was just that, a story. Either that or the legendary key had disappeared years ago and would never be found. Maya told her the gods did not lie. While Rachel wouldn't accuse them of lying, she believed that they might hold back parts of the truth when it suited them.

Maya looked up when she heard excited yips from outside. She also sensed the sun dropping down behind the mountains.

When Jared stepped into the kitchen with the puppy stumbling after him, Rachel stood near the stove, turning down the heat under a pot emitting mouthwatering smells.

"Hey, Rachel." He greeted her with a broad smile that she

found easy to return. Even tired and dirty from hours of physical labor, there was something about Jared that touched a part
of her deep inside. Sometimes, the intensity of the feeling almost frightened her. She'd never felt anything like it before.
"What have you been up to today?"

"Exploring," she replied, leaning over and holding out her
hand. The puppy immediately ran over and sniffed it. Her
smile hitched up a few notches when the puppy licked her
fingers.

Jared noticed the exchange. "He's not too happy with me
after having a bath and flea dip, plus getting all his shots,
along with an appointment for some special surgery." He confided the latter in a low voice.

"I always wanted to have a dog." She didn't take her gaze off
the puppy, who heaved a huge sigh and leaned against her legs.

"You couldn't have one?"

She shook her head. "I was always told that dogs were
meant to herd sheep and cattle. They were not meant to be pets
inside the house." It was clear she recited someone else's words.

Jared took a chair, turned it around and sat down, resting
his arms along the back. "My old man said I cost enough
money and was enough trouble without having any pets that
would just make more work for him. As if he bothered with
me all that much, anyway. When I thought about it later, I realized it was better we didn't have a dog. Who knows what
he would have done to one?" he muttered darkly.

"Where did this little one come from?" Rachel asked.

"I came across some jerks teasing him. I ordered them off
the property and told them there wouldn't be any trouble as long
as they left the dog. So now I guess I have a pet," he said wryly.

"You should give him a name, so he feels as if he belongs."
She buried her fingers in the dog's fur.

Jared nodded. "I'm thinking of calling him Harley. He sure didn't mind riding on one today when I took him into town."

She looked confused. "You are naming him after your vehicle?"

He pretended to be shocked. "Honey, we're talking about the motorcycle to end all motorcycles. Harley-Davidson, to be exact. The ultimate riding machine. I'll take you on it one day so you'll know just what I'm talking about."

She looked pensive. "I do not think I would be comfortable on something like that."

"Sure you would," he declared. "Believe me, once you ride a Harley you'll never want to ride in a car again."

"Maya calls it a devil's machine," she murmured.

Jared leaned toward Rachel. "If you want to talk about a devil…" he raised and lowered his eyebrows comically "…truthfully, the woman scares the hell out of me." He grinned at the sound of Rachel's giggle. He'd noticed that her laughter seemed rusty, as if she hadn't had much cause to laugh. He couldn't understand why, since he considered her laughter one of the most beautiful sounds he'd ever heard.

Domestic crimes weren't part of Jared's job, but his work as a homicide detective brought him in contact with victims of abuse. He knew all the signs of physical and emotional trauma. And as a homicide detective, he'd seen more than his share of what happened if an abuser wasn't stopped in time. Jared could see that Rachel displayed some of those signs. He hadn't missed the wariness she sometimes displayed around him or the time she'd flinched when his temper got out of hand when he'd hit his thumb with a hammer fixing a bedroom door one evening.

Jared was positive a man had mistreated her, and he'd bet everything that the abuse had been physical as well as verbal and emotional. He wouldn't be surprised if there weren't faded bruises hidden under those long sleeves and ankle-length skirts. She'd said her husband was dead, but she could be lying because she was hiding from him. At the same time, her abuser might not have been her husband. If she was hiding from someone, Jared knew he couldn't take her to a shelter. At least, not until he had a chance to learn her story and find a way to help her. He knew about abuse firsthand, but he also knew he could ask Detective Celeste Dante for help. She worked Domestic Crimes and would know what to do.

"No one is ever going to hurt you again, Rachel," he said quietly.

The small smile that flirted with her lips moved up to her eyes. He was relieved that she didn't pretend to not know what he was talking about. He worried that meant the abuse was more recent than he'd like to think.

"Thank you, Jared Stryker," she murmured in her honeyed drawl. "I have not felt safe in a long time. But I feel safe with you."

His smile was wry. "I'm not sure you should count on me. I'm not considered all that reliable."

"I think you are a very reliable man," she assured him. "You're a man who never goes back on his word. And you rescued the dog, who needed a home."

"Those men were trespassing. In fact, I can't guarantee they won't be back." His face darkened at the idea of sweet Rachel facing bastards like the ones he'd rescued Harley from. He knew that slime like that wouldn't think twice of preying on an innocent woman, though he doubted he'd have to worry about Maya. He figured she'd take them out with one whack of that cast-iron frying pan she loved so much.

As they ate their meal, Jared looked at Rachel.

"I've got someone coming out in the morning to install a satellite dish," he said. "I'm going to stick around the house, so I can make sure there won't be any problems, or that Maya doesn't scare the guy off."

Rachel looked bewildered. "Satellite dish?"

"I'm a guy. I can't go without my sports channels for too long. Football season will be here before we know it." Jared wondered where Maya had disappeared to. He noticed she always seemed to be gone by dinnertime, although a few evenings she'd been around when he got home, but was gone by the time he got out of the shower.

After they finished eating, Rachel insisted on washing the dishes, and shooed him out of the kitchen when he offered to help. He decided that the older woman must not be feeling well and had gone upstairs. Not that he could imagine her ever feeling under the weather.

He went upstairs to work on one of the bedrooms. He had dismissed the idea of using the master bedroom, after walking in and feeling as if he'd been encased in ice. Jared never thought of himself as someone attuned to psychic energy in a room—he was definitely a skeptic—but he knew something evil had happened in there. Instead, he chose a room at the other end of the house that was just as large and didn't make him feel as if he needed to cleanse himself.

The door to the room he knew Rachel and Maya shared was closed. It was *always* kept closed. He never opened it. He didn't want them to feel he would invade their privacy. It didn't stop him from wondering what they had in there. Considering the clothing they wore, he had to assume they didn't have much.

Jared had worked for a construction company during summers when he was in high school, so he had a good feel for what to do to the house. At the same time, he realized that what he'd learned then didn't cover everything he had to do now. So far, he'd been busy replacing old boards with new ones.

"Even if you are a lawman, you enjoy building," Rachel commented.

He looked over his shoulder, spotting her in the doorway. He'd been so busy with his project he hadn't heard her come up the stairs. Nor had he smelled the hint of jasmine that always seemed to precede her.

"Police work involves using your brain and sometimes just plain luck," he said. "Getting out and using my hands is a nice change. But after doing all this work I think I'll be glad to get back to the station when my vacation time is up."

She walked into the room and settled down in a corner with her skirts tucked neatly about her legs. She looked around with a faint smile.

"The floor up here is still pretty dirty," he warned her.

Rachel didn't look worried. "Dirt never hurt anyone."

They both turned their heads when they heard thumps on the stairs.

Jared grinned at the sound. "Harley really likes running up and down those stairs, doesn't he?"

She smiled back. "I don't think he likes to be alone. Do you notice how he always comes to whatever room we're in?"

"After what he's been through it makes sense." Jared nodded.

A moment later, the puppy skidded into the room, stumbling over his big feet as he attempted to make a quick stop. He ran up to Jared, received a scratch behind the ears, then made his way over to Rachel. He leaned against her side, then plopped down with a big doggy sigh of contentment. She stroked his fur as he yawned widely and rested his head in her lap.

"What kind of dog do you think he is?" she asked.

Jared grinned. "Spoiled."

She shot him a please-be-serious look.

He shrugged. "The vet thinks he's shepherd with some rottweiler in the mix. He's a perfect dog for the outdoors, and should grow up to be a pretty good guard dog."

Rachel ducked her head as she continued stroking the pup's head. "Yes, he loves the outdoors."

She continued running her hand along Harley's back. He immediately rolled over so she could rub his tummy. "You chose this room for yourself?"

Jared nodded as he looked around. "It seemed like a good idea."

"I thought the room in the back of the house was the master bedroom," she said casually, noting how he had arranged the furniture.

"It probably was, but I like this one better. It will catch the morning light and it has a better feel to it." He drilled holes in the wall and attached a curtain rod over the window, then carefully draped a sheet over the rod.

"Most of the rooms seem the same." She obliged Harley by scratching behind his ears.

Jared shook his head. "I'm not superstitious or anything, but that back bedroom is…" He paused.

"Is what?" she prompted, curious to hear his observation.

He set the drill on the floor and sat down with his legs stretched out in front of him. "My work involves a lot of unhappiness," he said finally. "A murder investigation usually means notifying the next of kin, getting a positive ID of the body and then finding out who murdered the victim. Sometimes I'll walk into the crime scene and just feel something there. Maybe it's anger still lingering in the air, maybe sorrow. It's as if what happened in the room has become a part of the space."

"And you felt something in that other bedroom," she guessed.

He nodded.

"Something not good."

He nodded again. "I'd say something very bad happened in there and it still lingers in the atmosphere." He looked around. "I'm surprised that feeling doesn't permeate the whole house."

Rachel knew exactly what had happened in that room, but she wasn't about to talk about it. Even after all these years, the memories were still strong within her. She kept trailing her fingers across Harley's back in long strokes that were meant to soothe her more than the young dog.

"And you do not feel it in here," she murmured.

"Nope." He got to his feet and moved over to the other window, where he efficiently drilled holes and hung the other curtain rod. "You and Maya don't have to share a room, you know. There are plenty here. I doubt I'll be doing anything with them all anytime soon."

"We like each other's company," she said, looking at the furniture. It was like the man—functional, with no fancy carving in the wood. The sheets on the bed were light blue, with a navy bedspread partially pulled back. The only sign of disarray was a faded gray T-shirt tossed on top of the bed. Two pillows were placed against the head of the bed. Even the throw rug by the bed was dark blue.

She couldn't recall ever seeing a bed as large as his. Her face burned at thoughts of what had happened in that bed in the past, and what, she was certain, would happen in the future. Jared was too male to remain celibate for long. She resisted pressing her hand against her stomach. Just thinking about it sent a strange feeling through her.

"Do you like being a police officer, Jared?" she asked, desperate to say something before her fanciful thoughts took her down a road she shouldn't travel.

"Funny thing is, I do. When I was a kid I was given the choice of going to jail or going into the army. The idea of sitting in jail didn't sit well with me, and I figured the army would be easy. I didn't expect to have a drill instructor who knew how to put fear into a smart-ass recruit like me. Tests showed I'd be good in law enforcement. I thought that was pretty funny, considering I was usually on the other side of the law. Maybe I was good at it because I could figure out what some guy would do before he did it. And it beats what could have happened to me if I hadn't made that choice." He returned to his spot on the floor.

She cocked her head to one side. "What do you think would have happened if you had not joined the army?"

Jared chuckled. "That's pretty easy. I would have spent a few years in prison."

Rachel's eyes grew large. "Why would you have spent time in jail? You are not a bad person."

"Back then I was considered a kid who was well on his way to hell," he said without apology.

He paused for a moment, his expression pensive as he thought back to early years that obviously didn't hold pleasant memories for him.

"You have to understand that my role model when I was growing up was a father who didn't see anything wrong with breaking into houses and stealing whatever small things he could carry and easily fence. He prided himself on not using a gun or a knife, so he could never be charged with armed robbery. But he was also a mean drunk with a hot temper, who liked to vent his rage on his only son," he said matter-of-factly.

"What about your mother?" she whispered, feeling a wealth of sympathy for the damaged little boy he'd been. "Couldn't she protect you?"

He shrugged and shook his head. "She couldn't take his beatings anymore, so she took off when I was six."

Rachel looked horrified. "She left you with such a horrible man?"

"I guess she was more worried about herself." He ignored the pangs of long-buried sorrow that his mother could leave him so easily. "Who knows? With the way his temper blew at times, she might have been right to get out when she could."

"Was there no one to help you?"

"Child Protective Services stepped in a few times and put me in foster care, but as long as my dad appeared sober, and was holding down a job, they'd hand me back to him," he said. "It got so when I knew he was out getting drunk, I just took off, so I wouldn't be there when he got home." He looked around the room. "Most of the time, I ended up out here. The apartment we rented was on the outskirts of town, so we didn't live all that far away. Plus I figured he wouldn't look for me here. There were lots of stories saying this place was haunted. Funny thing was, I was never afraid here." He looked a little embarrassed by his stark admission.

She understood more than he would ever know. "You needed a safe place and you found it here."

"Yeah, I guess I did. Anytime I was here I felt as if someone was watching over me. Sometimes I brought a friend with me. Her home life wasn't much better than mine," he said.

Rachel was content to sit there and just let him talk. She sensed Jared kept a lot of his past to himself. The fact that he was talking about it with her suggested he felt he could trust her. She knew he had no idea he was talking to someone who had watched over him when he was younger.

She remembered seeing and hearing a boy's anger at the mother who'd abandoned him, and the bitter hatred directed toward a father who believed violence was the answer. Rachel doubted he'd talked to anyone else back then. What boy wanted to admit his father beat him? Out here, he talked out loud, as if he thought someone was listening. Little did he know someone *did* listen to his anger and anguish. Rachel had heard every word and tucked them away in her heart. She'd ached for the boy, but now that emotion had changed into something entirely different for the man. She felt something for Jared she'd never experienced before. The dizzying feelings that invaded her body frightened her.

She knew Maya was right to worry. With Jared living here, both women's very existence, or lack thereof, was in danger. Rachel didn't regret that he had discovered her that night. Indeed, it was a relief to her that she didn't have to hide from him. And to be honest, she enjoyed his company. It had been a *very* long time since she had been able to have a conversation with someone. She had forgotten how good it felt.

Rachel looked at Jared. She studied his solemn expression and listened to the words spill from his mouth. She enjoyed listening to him talk. She found his deep voice pleasing to the ear. Sometimes he paused, as if he was mentally searching for just the right word. At other times he spoke quickly, caught up with enthusiasm. She wanted to chuckle when he joked about the ghosts haunting the ranch. She wondered what he would say if she told him he was talking to a ghost right now.

She also wondered what would happen if she told him the truth about herself. What would he say if she admitted she had been born in 1856 and died in 1880 at her husband's hands, when he discovered she was going to leave him? What would Jared say if she explained that, as her husband stabbed her to death, a *bruja,* a local witch, had leveled a curse at her? That from the moment of her death, Rachel was doomed to an elusive existence where she was nothing more than a gentle breeze during the daylight hours, and could take human form only at night? Maya had tried to intervene in an attempt to protect her mistress, appealing to her own ancient gods to save the young woman she saw as the daughter she'd never had. They listened to Maya's pleas and gave Rachel a second chance; Maya was allowed to remain with her. Except the older woman's human existence was limited only to daylight hours. Which meant Rachel was doomed to a lifetime of loneliness at night.

As she studied Jared's rugged features, she knew she couldn't say a word about her past to him. How could he understand what had happened to her when there were times she herself didn't understand? She knew she would have to make a concerted effort to find the key that would free her—before Jared learned the truth about her.

A part of her feared there was a darker side to Jared Stryker's nature. But as she watched Harley wake up and amble over to his owner, who started playing with the dog, his laughter rich and full, another part of her worried that it would be very easy to fall in love with him. She had always yearned for a man to ride in like a knight in shining armor and carry her off to his castle. Restore peace to her mind and spirit.

Falling in love was not an option for her.

After all, what good would it do for a ghost to fall in love with a mortal man?

Chapter 4

"I am sorry. I think I was wrong to have you put the cabinet there." Rachel pressed her fingertips against her lips. "It really does not look good against that wall."

Jared swallowed the curse that wanted so badly to creep up his throat. Even with the windows open, the warm spring air didn't offer a lot of relief inside the room, which he swore soaked up the day's heat. He knew he'd have to consider getting an air conditioner before summer fully settled in.

But then, spending the evening moving furniture around wasn't a good way to cool off, either. After dinner, he'd asked Rachel to make sure the cabinet was lined up against the wall correctly. He'd had no clue she would have other ideas for it. Or that she'd pretty much have him moving everything in the room except the TV.

"In case you haven't noticed, there are only four walls in this room, Rachel," he pointed out unnecessarily. "And there's a large window that takes up almost one whole wall, and a door in the other. It's not as if you have unlimited options for this thing."

"But that also means we have two walls where it can go. And now that I think about it the cabinet did look much better when it was over there." She pointed toward the opposite wall.

He silently vowed once the cabinet was settled in one place it was staying there. Forever. He'd nail it to the floor if he had to. "Are you sure?"

She swiveled her head to look at the large, heavy cabinet. "Yes. Yes, I am. It must go back." She nodded emphatically.

Stryker took a deep breath, then grunted as he laboriously pushed the piece of furniture across the room to the exact same spot Rachel had earlier deemed unsuitable. With his back against the side of the cabinet, he slid down the side until he sat on the floor with his legs sprawled out in front of him. He glared at Harley, who was snoozing on the couch. The pup knew he wasn't allowed on the cushions, but that didn't stop him from climbing up there every chance he got.

Lucky dog. He didn't have to move heavy furniture and worry that he might strain something in the process.

With her skirt rustling as it brushed the bare wood floor, Rachel walked over and held out a bottle of water she had retrieved from the kitchen. He mumbled, "Thanks," and drained half the contents without taking a breath.

"Please tell me you won't change your mind again," he begged once he'd finished.

The slightest of smiles curved her lips. "You did ask for my advice."

Jared winced. "Yep, I did."

"And you only had to move the couch and your chairs once," she pointed out.

Something he was very grateful for, since the couch weighed at least a ton.

He looked up at her face. The shadows he remembered from the first times he'd seen her were almost all gone. Even now, though, he still knew very little about her. To date, she hadn't even shared her last name with him, and he hadn't pushed for the information. He had no idea how her husband had died or why she'd come out to California. Or how she'd ended up with Maya. Or why she wore the same old-fashioned dress all the time. He hoped the time would come when she would feel comfortable enough with him to divulge more pieces of her past.

He noticed that Rachel preferred asking him questions, not answering his, but he couldn't complain, since he was usually the one who avoided revealing pieces of himself. He'd found from the beginning that questioning Maya didn't get him anything other than a headache. He swore the old woman just plain ignored him or pretended not to understand English.

Each morning Jared woke up and told himself that was the day he would rent a car and drive Rachel and Maya into town to a shelter. And every evening he looked into those luminous purple eyes and told himself he'd do it the next day, or the next. Or maybe he just didn't want to add any more sorrow to those eyes, which he sensed had seen a lot of grief in their time. It was easy enough for him to put off taking Rachel to the local shelter, since he didn't see her during the day. But then, for the past couple of weeks, he was always outside, working on the property, and only came in for lunch. He rarely stayed long after his noonday meal, since there was so much to do around the place. He never asked Rachel where she went during the day. He sensed she wouldn't give him a truthful answer, although he guessed she hadn't lied to him.

Yet. As a man who kept his own secrets close to his heart, he didn't feel it was right that he ask her to bare hers. And he'd bet everything the lady had a lot.

He usually found Rachel in the kitchen when he returned to the house for dinner, and Maya was gone. He never bothered asking about the older woman's whereabouts, either. To be honest, he was downright joyful when she wasn't around the house even if she could cook like a dream and cleaned his house so thoroughly he doubted any sane dust bunny would dare come within a mile of the place. He swore Maya wanted him to believe she'd been put on this earth to make his life miserable in between those great meals.

Jared knew his feelings about Rachel and Maya were at odds with his usual suspicious cop nature. In the past he would have immediately taken something with their fingerprints into the station and had them run through the database. Instead, he'd done nothing. He figured this odd lack of suspicion on his part was just one of the many changes he'd suddenly made in his life.

Or maybe Rachel had cast a spell on him with her beautiful violet eyes, he thought jokingly.

The biggest decision, of course, had been moving out of his tiny apartment into a house that needed a hell of a lot of work. And since he hadn't won the lottery lately, he had no choice but to do the work himself.

He walked over to the window and looked out. The full moon allowed him to easily see the wooden fence he'd labored long and hard to replace and strengthen, though it still tilted here and there. At least he didn't have to worry about any animals getting out.

Or people getting in.

"Better not quit your day job, bub," he muttered to himself.

Rachel came up to stand beside him. He couldn't read the expression on her face as she gazed out the window. If he didn't know any better, he would swear she looked wistful.

"Are you going to run cattle here?" she asked.

He chuckled. "Nope. The only thing running around here will be the dog and my Harley."

"That is probably a good thing. I know you worked on your fence to keep your Harley in, but I am afraid it would escape through it very easily." Her voice was grave, but he could see the faintest of twinkles in her eyes as she looked up at him.

Jared grinned at her dry humor. "It would be worse if there were cattle out there. It would only take one butt of their heads and they'd be down the road and on someone's barbecue." He looked around the room. Maya's preoccupation with dirt had the wooden floors clean and shiny, with cobwebs gone from all the corners. The locked cabinet he'd purchased for his weapons was finally, he hoped, in place. His prized possession, a plasma screen television, was on one wall, with his stereo system set up nearby. He'd told Rachel she could make use of any of the equipment, but so far she had kept a discreet distance from it—the same way Maya had cursed his microwave oven. He didn't understand what the woman said under her breath whenever she glanced at the oven and he wasn't sure he wanted a literal translation. He had a pretty good feeling some of those words were directed at him.

He turned toward Rachel, who still stood at the window. It was odd how what he'd thought was a wistful look seemed more like desolation.

"What do you see out there?" he asked curiously. The moon was now hidden by clouds, leaving the grounds in shadow. He moved to stand behind her, close enough to smell the faint hint of jasmine that seemed to drift around her. Now, whenever he smelled it during the day, he thought of her.

He was tempted to wrap his arms around her and pull her back against him, and he finally gave in to the temptation. At first she stiffened at his touch, but a tiny hitch in her breath alerted him that she wouldn't reject his gesture. He kept the embrace light and nonthreatening, and after a moment, she relaxed.

But Rachel continued to stare out the window as if something had caught her attention.

"The day is sunny and warm. It seems so perfect, and you know it is because spring is finally here. You can see a sky so blue and beautiful you would think it was a painting, with those white fluffy clouds overhead," she said softly. "You can feel a faint breeze on your face and you would swear you can smell the ocean, even though you know it's far away. Because of all the rain we've had this winter the grass is thick and a rich green. Everywhere you look you can see grazing horses out in the paddocks, enjoying the beautiful day. Some of the men are out there training the colts. One old man is in the barn repairing tackle, and another works at the forge fashioning shoes for the horses. The metallic ring of his hammer against the anvil is just another sound of the ranch. Behind the house, you hear the chatter of the maids as they hang the washing, and the cook demanding that someone go out to the kitchen garden and pick her some beans for dinner."

As Jared listened to her words, he felt an odd prickling sensation along the back of his neck. He stared out the window, caught up in the spell of her words.

"You make it sound real."

She stood as still as a statue for a moment, then seemed to shake off the magical moment.

"Maybe it is the spirits of the land that paint the word pictures for me," she said.

"I don't know if you'd find too many good spirits around here. Local historians say the man who originally owned this land was pretty much a cold-blooded bastard. Ole Caleb Bingham was the stuff of nightmares." Jared saw her mirrored reflection in the window glass and thought she flinched. "Probably why over the years a lot of kids thought the house was haunted."

Rachel took a deep breath. "Did you think it was haunted?"

He nodded. "I guess in a way I did. It's easy enough for stories to start up, since no one's sure exactly how Caleb died. Rumor has it his death wasn't a pleasant one and that his ghost would come after any innocent who entered the house. That's probably why I was always safe from him." He chuckled.

Rachel turned away and walked over to the couch. She ran her hands across the back.

"Perhaps he did leave something behind to haunt the house." Her head was bowed, as if she was fascinated with the couch's khaki-colored fabric.

"I didn't see or hear anything the times I was here. I always thought the stories were told to keep us kids out of here," he assured her. He was puzzled by her manner. "The trouble was, the stories only dared us to come out. There's nothing like a haunted house to tempt kids."

She lifted her head and studied him. "You're not afraid of anything, are you, Jared?"

"Maya. The woman scares the hell out of me," he said, in hopes of making Rachel smile. He was gratified to see it worked. But he also noticed that while her lips tipped upward in a smile, it wasn't echoed in her eyes. He was tempted to ask her what scared her, but feared if he voiced the question she would withdraw from him.

"Maya likes you."

"That's not the way she acts." He grinned, looking around the room. "I guess I'll need some kind of rug next. Want to go into town and help me find a rug for this room?"

Rachel again ducked her head. "This is your house. You must choose a rug you like."

What is she hiding from me?

Jared buried his instinctive need to discover all the answers. He sensed he'd have to go slowly with her. Even then he wasn't sure he'd learn everything he wanted to know.

"You know what? We need a big bowl of popcorn." He decided a change of subject was in order.

Rachel's face brightened. In the past couple of weeks, Jared had learned she was as big a popcorn addict as he was. He usually made up two bags of microwave popcorn, and between the two of them, with Harley's help, not one kernel was left.

"And a movie," he decided.

"Nothing frightening, such as the one you watched last night," she said, following him into the kitchen. She wrinkled her nose. "It was also very slimy."

"I'll have you know that movie is a classic," he stated as he dug the box holding the packets of microwave popcorn out of a cabinet. "You don't see quality horror movies like *The Blob* anymore." He could see she wasn't going to agree with him. He sighed heavily. "Okay, there's a great movie called *The Thing from Outer Space*. Another classic starring James Arness, later well known as Marshal Dillon of Dodge City." He placed a bag in the microwave and pushed buttons.

"When was he the marshal there?" she asked curiously. "I do not recall hearing the name before."

"I think the series was shown in the fifties and sixties, and it's still alive and well on cable." He found the large bowl he used for popcorn.

Rachel nodded. She realized Jared was talking about a fictional Dodge City on the television, while she meant the real town. She'd learned that he enjoyed watching programs about the Old West, along with those odd films he liked to share with her. If she could have slept she knew she would have had nightmares about vampires and werewolves and monsters that defied what she felt was a limited imagination. She enjoyed the western programs, though so much of what she saw had nothing to do with the Old West she was familiar with.

She found it easy to imagine Jared Stryker as a lawman living a hundred years ago, even if he was nothing like the sheriff in town when she'd been living here. At that time, the man sworn to uphold the law only upheld it for those who could afford to slip him extra funds. She knew Jared would have honored the law in regards to everyone.

She wished he had existed in the world she'd lived in one hundred and twenty years ago. That he'd been the one to enforce the law instead of Sheriff Mills. She doubted Jared could have prevented her death back then, but perhaps something could have been done so that she might have had a chance at life.

Not that she remembered all the details of the night of her death. Maya had explained long ago that the gods felt her suffering through it once was enough. They'd decreed she shouldn't have to relive the pain she'd suffered during her life. She was grateful for that small measure of mercy. She wished she could also forget the time she'd spent with Caleb. She told herself that she shouldn't expect that much compassion from beings that had the power over life and death. Even hers.

"Rachel?"

She jerked herself back to the present. "I am sorry. I must have been daydreaming."

Jared held up the large bowl filled with popcorn. Butter glistened on the fluffy white kernels. "I promise you the movie isn't real scary." He led the way back to the front of the house.

"How can you enjoy such things?" She watched the movies with him more for the company and popcorn than the film. She tended to close her eyes through the frightening parts.

"They're relaxing for me. Some men drink when they're off duty, others gamble or party. There's even some who go hunting or fishing. I'm not interested in the former and sitting there with a fishing pole in my hand waiting for a fish to bite seems a lot like watching grass grow. So I watch old movies." He inserted the DVD into the player and walked back to the couch, where Harley still dozed.

Jared picked up the young dog and deposited him on the floor. Harley uttered a few puppy grumbles as he curled up in a tight ball and went back to sleep. Rachel smiled at the affection Jared showed the dog. He grumbled about Harley costing more money than he was worth, but Rachel saw the fondness he held for the pup, who was only too happy to follow him around during the day. She was surprised that the dog sensed her presence during the daylight hours. More than once Harley would sit in a room and stare at what others would call empty space, but was actually the tiny area she occupied.

Rachel cherished her evenings with Jared. She had no idea what she would do in years to come. She knew the time would arrive when he would sense she wasn't a normal human woman, and would ask her for the truth. She didn't know what she would tell him, or if he would believe her.

But for now, she would sit here and eat popcorn and

watch…she wasn't sure exactly what she was watching. After a while she knew that this action movie had to be the kind of film men enjoyed. Oh yes, she was very glad she didn't have to worry about nightmares.

Hours later Rachel stood at her bedroom window and looked out at the black expanse of land. Jared had gone to bed and thought she had done the same. Even when in human form, though, Rachel could no longer sleep. In the past weeks she hadn't wanted that luxury. She wanted the hours she spent with Jared to last forever. She had forgotten what it was like to talk to another human being. And she had never been treated with such courtesy by a member of the opposite sex.

She knew this time with him couldn't last long. This was his land. His house. She shouldn't even be here.

Rachel had never had a place she could truly call her own. Growing up, she'd been told to be grateful for what little she'd been given, since she could have been placed in an orphanage, where she would have had nothing. Along with the gratitude, she was expected to reimburse the minister and his wife for her care from the time they took her in. When she first came to the ranch she'd thought it would be the place she could call her own, but instead she was treated as another piece of property that could be disposed of when she was no longer considered of use.

She wondered what would happen now. Would the day come when she would no longer exist, even in this half-life? For decades she'd prayed for that to happen. But now she wanted more. She wanted the life she had been cheated out of. She wanted a chance to go outside again and feel the sun on her face. She wanted to breathe in the magical fragrance of fresh flowers. She wanted the chance to have a real home. Perhaps even have a family she could call her own.

She tamped down the tight knot of sorrow that suddenly rose deep inside her. She knew it was best not to think about things she would never have, but being around Jared had her dreaming of them again.

Her attention was diverted by the sight of the flickering lights high up in the hills, even though some looked as if they were much closer. There were many nights she'd stood here and seen them, but she never gave them a second thought. Now she felt a frisson of unease.

Normally she found them comforting, evidence of other people in the world. The lights gave her hope and confirmed that she wasn't alone.

Now, however, she saw them as ominous. She felt as if they were watching the place. She hadn't forgotten the men who'd dumped Jared in the house as if he were nothing more than a bundle of old rags. He had once told her that many of the homes in the surrounding mountains were vacation homes, used only a few times a year, while other, smaller places were used by people who couldn't afford such luxury. She suspected those men lived up in the hills, and that she was looking at *their* lights. She was convinced they meant danger to Jared.

Rachel recalled Caleb often accusing her of having an overactive imagination. More than once she had been told she saw things where they didn't exist. He'd blamed her "female hysteria" on too much reading, and had destroyed her own small cache of books.

This time she didn't believe it was her imagination that made her feel uneasy. She looked up and saw dark, shadowy clouds cross the moon, and suppressed a shiver. A shiver that had no meaning for her, since she had no ability to feel any change in temperature. But right now, she suddenly felt as if a core of ice had settled deep inside of her and no fire could warm her.

* * *

Jared's furious gaze could have caused the damaged fence to burst into flames. He didn't want to think how long it had taken him to replace the rotted rails and posts. All the new rails now lay scattered on the ground, many of them splintered as if someone had used them as makeshift baseball bats. Obscenities were spray-painted on the wood.

"Bastards can't even spell," he muttered, kicking at a fallen post. "Maybe if you'd stayed in school instead of ditching class to raise hell, you'd at least have learned to spell the words right," he shouted, as if his tormentors were nearby.

His gut instinct told him the damage in front of him had nothing to do with a gang of kids having fun at his expense. He was convinced it had been inflicted with malice. He lifted his head when he heard a faint rumbling sound off in the distance.

If there was one thing Jared Stryker was familiar with, it was the sound of a Harley-Davidson engine. He estimated it was two or three bikes. Maybe even four. And the bikes he heard weren't heading for The Renegade. The rumbling sounded closer, in the hills. The riders were probably climbing the winding road that led to the hodgepodge of vacation homes intermingled with beat-up mobile homes parked on small pieces of property. Because of his old man's penchant for violence, and his own need to keep a low profile to stay away from abuse, as a boy, Jared was quite familiar with the hills, and in particular, a battered old mobile home partially hidden behind a stand of trees so it wasn't easy to find. That was likely where the Harleys were heading. And he was positive the riders of those motorcycles had been on his property sometime before dawn, turning his fence into firewood.

Harley trotted over to Jared and sat back awkwardly on his haunches. The gangly puppy cocked his head to one side as he watched his human stomp around and mutter until he once more exploded with anger. Since he wasn't the focus of the man's temper, Harley settled for lifting a hind leg and lazily scratching a spot behind his ear before he dipped his head and investigated his tummy.

"You better grow up to be a badass dog that can do some serious damage to trespassers," Jared snarled, as he started tossing broken rails to one side.

He dragged the ruined wood into a pile. Now it was fit for nothing more than a bonfire. As he worked, his gaze swept the area for visible signs of the trespassers, but he saw none. Whoever wrecked the fence had been pretty good at covering their tracks.

"Or maybe you're the one behind this, Caleb, you old son of a bitch," Jared muttered, once he'd finished stacking the damaged wood. "What did you do, climb your way out of hell to make my life miserable for trying to make this place livable again?" He kicked one of the wooden rails, then cursed as painful vibrations ran up his leg. "Serves me right for inheriting a haunted house."

He looked up at the aging structure, noting that it and the nearby barn still needed a paint job. And he should probably plant something around the house to make it look more like a place someone was living in.

"Damn, before I know it I'll be trading in the Harley for a minivan and drinking lattes," Jared muttered as he pulled off his T-shirt and tossed it to one side. Then he returned to work, stacking rails and fence posts, with no idea he was under observation.

She made her way to Jared's bedroom. She'd learned that the window there had the best view watching him while he worked. Not that she could see him with conventional eye-

sight. *His image came to her the same way a dream might visit her in the middle of the night, if she could still dream. She hovered at the window, which was now kept shiny clean, thanks to Maya's regular applications of vinegar and water. From there, she "saw" him working on the fence.*

Was there a chance that while Jared worked to clean up the property he might come across the key that would release her from this maddening existence?

She also wondered about the location of the treasure. Was it hidden separately, or in the same place as the key? Maya's gods had never made that clear. It was as if they had enjoyed weaving puzzles for Rachel to solve.

Thoughts tumbled around her like skeins of tangled yarn. So many days she'd drifted along the windows of this house in vain hopes of seeing a human being. More often than not she'd viewed little outside, other than field mice or wild rabbits scampering across the weedy fields. No human had lived on the property since 1956, when the owner at the time arrived with the idea of turning the property into a dude ranch. Except he'd stumbled upon her one night, screamed "Ghost!", run out of the building and never come back. If he ever told anyone what he saw, they must not have believed his story. Or they chose to stay away.

She wondered what Jared's reaction would be if he knew the truth about her. She had been spending all her evenings with him. She knew the more time she spent with Jared gave her a larger risk of discovery.

"I know you are in here, *chica*. I sense your presence." Maya walked into the bedroom. She crossed the room and threw open the window, allowing the morning breeze to flow in. "It is not good for you to be in here."

Why not? He can't see me. She was always surprised that her sense of humor had remained intact through the decades.

Rachel watched Maya turn to Jared's bed. The older woman shook her head in disgust at the sight of its sheets and lightweight blanket pulled haphazardly up to the pillows, which were stacked against the wall. She muttered under her breath as she pulled the covers back to the end of the bed so she could straighten and tuck them in, so tightly a marine drill instructor would be impressed. Once bedding was adjusted to her satisfaction, she fluffed the pillows and placed them neatly side by side. From there, she moved to the chest of drawers, pulling a rag out of her skirt pocket and dusting the surface, which hadn't been allowed to gather a speck of dust since she had taken over the household duties.

"With all that he is doing with the land, he may find the key that will free you," she continued, voicing Rachel's own thoughts. "I know there are times when you have felt like a prisoner because of the curse that *bruja*—" she spat out the word "—placed on you, but my gods were also able to save you by offering you a safe place. I feel it in my heart that the key will be found soon, *chica*. And once we are free, we will go to all the places you read to me in your books." Her dark face was wreathed in a broad smile as she worked. "You will see all the places that you have only seen in that box Señor Stryker watches. We will be happy again. We will be free and we will be safe. I feel it in my heart."

I thought I would be happy here before. I wanted to be a wife and mother and have a full life. Rachel drifted back to the window. Harley was running in circles around Jared. Faint sounds of his barking drifted through the open window.

"That dog is noisy and he leaves fur everywhere. He sometimes smells bad and he scatters his food around the kitchen." Maya sniffed. "Dogs are meant to live outside and guard a house. They are not meant to live indoors. And I find him sometimes sleeping on the couch." She bent down and plucked a tuft of fur off the small rug by the bed. She sighed as she held the clump in the air. "He will be the death of me yet."

Sorrow filled Rachel. *But we're already dead.*

Jared didn't need any training to tell him something was bothering Rachel. Plus, things still didn't add up where she and Maya were concerned. Why did Rachel wear the same old-fashioned dress every day, but always manage to look clean and neat? Why wasn't she willing to tell him anything about herself? Maya was extremely protective of Rachel, yet so far he'd never seen the two women together. It seemed all he did was come up with more questions.

"She's a vampire, that's what she is," he muttered to himself as he trudged back to the house. "She sleeps in a coffin under the house all day and only comes out at night. She just pretends to eat dinner. And Maya's her Renfield." Grinning at his fanciful notion of the old woman being vampiress Rachel's human servant, he paused by the back door to pull off his boots, and walked inside in his stockinged feet. It only took one time walking through the house with muddy boots to learn never to do it again.

The rich aroma of chicken and dumplings teased his nostrils, making his mouth water in anticipation of the meal. His hunger pangs dimmed when he noticed strain etched on Rachel's face.

"Are you okay?" he asked.

She attempted a faint smile. "I am all right," she assured him.

What if she was sick? In the short time Jared knew her, he'd never seen her look this wan.

"Maybe you need to see a doctor." *Or blood,* a tiny mocking voice in his mind added.

Rachel didn't look at him. "I don't think a doctor could help me. Besides, the stew is ready."

He looked down at his filthy clothing. "Give me about ten minutes to get cleaned up." As he walked out of the kitchen he didn't see the pained look on Rachel's face, one that had nothing to do with physical hurts.

When Jared returned to the kitchen, Rachel spooned out the chicken into two bowls, adding fluffy dumplings to both.

Throughout the meal he watched her pick at her food. For once there was no attempt at conversation, and when they were finished, she was a bit abrupt when she pushed him out of the kitchen so she could clean up.

"Hey, Rach!" Jared called out ten minutes later. "There's an all-night *Avengers* marathon coming on. Feel like staying up and watching it with me?"

She found him sprawled on the floor with his back resting against the couch. He looked up and grinned.

"I always thought Mrs. Peel was kinda sexy in all that black leather." He raised his eyebrows up and down in a comical fashion.

"And you expect to stay awake all night for this marathon?" Rachel sat primly on the couch.

"Sure, why not? All I'm going to do tomorrow is head into Sierra Vista to pick up some supplies. The way I see it, I'm giving you an education in classic television."

She looked down at him. The ends of his hair were still damp from his shower and lay against his collar. Her fingers itched to touch the strands to see if they felt as silky as they looked. She settled for breathing in the clean crisp scent of his skin. She noticed he never wore any kind of cologne. Caleb had worn so much bay rum it had seemed to seep out of his pores.

Every time she looked at Jared she felt an odd sensation, as if she was looking down from a high precipice, or tumbling down a mountain. What surprised her was that it was a good feeling.

Jared was a very masculine man who should have made her uneasy. His job was violent, but while she'd seen him lose his temper, she'd never seen him take it out on anyone. A tiny part of her whispered that there was still the chance something could happen that would turn him brutal. Caleb had first given her the impression that he was a kind and gentle man. It wasn't until they were married that his true nature asserted itself. Her wedding night had given her her first glimpse of an angry man who insisted everything be done his way. Or else there was Hades to pay.

She tore her eyes away from Jared and focused on the television screen. "Jared, this woman is fighting the men and winning," she said in surprise.

He nodded. "Yeah, she kicks butt, all right."

As the night progressed, Rachel curled up on the couch with her legs tucked up under her heavy skirt, her cheek resting on her arm. Harley used great stealth to creep up onto the other end of the couch and curl up on the cushions without her noticing, she was so absorbed in the show. Rachel didn't understand half of what the people said or did, but she enjoyed it much more than Jared's usual choices.

All day her invisible self thought of Jared Stryker and what she knew she had to do before her secret was revealed. Anticipating the day, or night, would come when Rachel would need to hide from Jared, Maya had fixed up a small room in the attic that wasn't easily discovered. No one had gone up there for years, and she doubted Jared would have a reason to do so. It wouldn't be easy for her to remain hidden at night when Jared was downstairs, but she knew it would be for the best. She could venture through the house while he slept or when he worked night shifts at his job, and she could still hover during the day. She had to remind herself that her first priority was finding the key so she could obtain her freedom.

Rachel told herself it would be best if this was her last night spent with Jared. She could count on Maya manufacturing a story to explain away her disappearance. Rachel dreaded the thought of never talking to him again. The idea of no longer spending time with him was painful. She knew she would treasure the memories she had stored up, and keep them close to her heart.

"Aren't you sleepy?" she asked him a few hours later. "You were up early this morning and now it is so late."

Jared shook his head. "Working nights all these years changed my body clock. It's probably why I find it hard to get up in the morning. I'm used to sleeping through half the day." He turned his head and glanced at her. "Are you tired?"

"No," Rachel said softly. "I like this program more than those scary movies you enjoy so much."

He continued looking at her. "Why don't I get a pillow for you? There's no reason why you shouldn't be more comfortable."

She shook her head. "I am fine the way I am." But she couldn't help giving in to temptation by placing her fingers on top of his head and turning it so he was again looking at the television. She was right that his hair felt like heavy silk. She ignored further temptation to let her fingers linger there.

Rachel wasn't the only one resisting temptation. Jared's senses were more tuned to Rachel than to the classic British television series he was pretending to be interested in. All evening he'd been breathing the fragrant jasmine scent he now associated with her, and he heard the silky rustle of petticoats each time she shifted her position on the couch.

He wanted to climb up beside her and gather her in his arms. He had it all planned in his head. He'd settle her on his lap and wrap his arms around her. Then he'd find out if her lips were as soft and kissable as they looked. He'd make sure to tease her into saying his name in that slow drawl that sounded as if she'd just walked off the set of *Gone with the Wind*. He was also curious to find out what was under that old-fashioned dress that covered her so thoroughly from her throat to her ankles.

But he held back because he knew touching her so intimately wouldn't be right. Not when he still knew so little about her.

Both were lost in their own thoughts and unaware of the minutes, then hours, passing. When the marathon finished, Jared stood up and stretched his arms over his head.

"Look at this! You stayed awake all night," he teased, gazing down at Rachel, who was still curled up on the couch. "I bet you'll want a nap right after breakfast."

"I just might." She smiled back at him. Then her eyes widened with shock as she realized the implication of his words.

All Jared saw was a woman who invited kissing. He took a chance and leaned down to kiss her.

But before his mouth could settle on hers, Rachel was gone.

Jared was so stunned by her sudden disappearance that he stumbled forward and almost fell onto the couch. Righting himself, he stared at the sofa as if it unexpectedly contained a wormhole leading to another dimension. If he didn't know it was impossible, he'd swear she'd disappeared right before his eyes.

Awakened by the commotion, Harley sat up and batted a paw at the empty space that Rachel had occupied.

"Whoa!"

Jared staggered a bit as he fought to come to grips with what he'd just seen. Or not seen. He felt light-headed, as if he'd been punched in the stomach. He continued fighting for breath. Logic told him that people didn't disappear into thin air, even if it had just happened in front of him. "What happened here, Harley?"

The puppy's whine wasn't the answer Jared was looking for. He felt the need to sit down, but settling on a couch Rachel had just disappeared from didn't seem like a good idea. For all he knew a black hole resided there and he'd be sucked down next.

At that moment, Jared heard sounds of Maya walking around in the kitchen. He wondered if Rachel might be in there, except Maya wasn't speaking, which was unusual in itself. Not to mention he didn't know how Maya could have gotten into the kitchen without him seeing her, since he knew full well the back door was locked. She couldn't have gotten there any other way unless she'd somehow slipped past him at the same moment Rachel disappeared.

"Why is that demon box on now?" a scowling Maya muttered, walking into the room.

She stopped short when she saw Jared's rigid body and stunned expression. He slowly turned to face her, opening his mouth as if to say something, but seeming to have trouble forcing words out.

She immediately sensed what was going through his mind, and knew none of it was good.

Chapter 5

"*Maya, what the hell is going on?*" Jared broke free from his frozen stance and marched into the kitchen with the force of a vengeful tornado.

She ignored him as she filled the carafe with water and poured it into the coffeemaker. She used the amount of coffee grounds Jared preferred to make a heavy-duty brew, and switched it on. She then moved to the refrigerator and pulled out eggs and bacon.

Jared moved swiftly to block her way. When she started to go around him, he shifted in the same direction. His harsh expression boded ill for the old woman. That same look had put fear into more than one killer, but Maya didn't reveal any apprehension. Instead, she faced him squarely, her dark eyes snapping with irritation as he prevented her from performing her duties.

"Where is Rachel?" he demanded with a deadly inflection in his voice. "And what the hell just happened in there?"

Maya arched an eyebrow, not bothering to pretend she didn't know what he was talking about. "What do you think happened?"

He took a deep breath to keep his temper in check. He was still in shock that a scant second before his lips would have touched hers she'd suddenly disappeared into thin air.

"I think I imagined that Rachel disappeared in front of me." He remained on the housekeeper's heels. "And it seems that just as she vanished, you somehow popped into a room I know for a fact was unoccupied a few minutes ago. Just don't tell me you two are the same person or I might have to shoot someone. And it won't be me!" He managed to keep his voice down to a dull roar.

The woman displayed no fear of his threat.

"If you wish answers, you will have to ask *la niña,* Rachel." Maya cracked three eggs and dropped the contents into a sizzling frying pan.

"What a great idea," he said with a sarcastic bite. "And I'd do it except *she doesn't happen to be here, does she?*"

The woman didn't turn a hair at the sound of his increasing roar. "Do you think you can frighten me?" she asked. "You may make a lot of noise and you have guns you could threaten me with if you wished, Señor Stryker, but nothing you say or do will make me afraid of you. Many years ago cruel, evil men with black hearts tried to frighten me. Once they almost beat me to death, but I never begged for mercy or allowed fear to enter my heart. I refused to show them fear and I will not fear you, either, *señor.*"

He felt anger that anyone would hurt this proud woman. Maya had a habit of irritating him no end, but he would never dream of hurting her physically. He drew in a deep breath. "Crazy things have gone on here that I don't understand. I haven't asked questions before because I wanted to respect Rachel's and your privacy, even if you were trespassing. Hey, it was obvious you'd both been through something bad. But I can't ignore all this weirdness anymore. Why do the two of you look as if you walked out of a history book? Why do you stare at my microwave oven and call it the work of the devil? Why did you scream with horror the first time I turned on the TV?"

Maya's nostrils flared, as if the idea of her screaming in horror was impossible, but Jared wasn't finished.

"Then let's discuss why I only see you during the day and Rachel at night. Just tell me one thing. What exactly are you two?" He felt his patience unraveling with every passing second, and his sanity trailing not far behind.

Maya's never-idle hands stilled ominously over the frying pan.

"We are a part of your past," she said softly.

He wondered if there was something wrong with his hearing. "The past *what?*"

She shook her head. "For you to truly understand what is going on you will need to talk to the *niña,* Rachel. Much of it is her story to tell, not mine."

Jared felt his blood pressure rising. He threw up his hands. "Fine, then why don't you tell me *your* story."

"You must know hers before you can understand mine." Maya filled his plate with eggs and bacon. "It will be very warm today. You should do your hard work early, before it gets too hot outside."

If she could ignore his questions, he could ignore her orders, even if they made perfect sense. The last thing he'd want was a bad case of heat stroke. But he had to figure this out. The trouble was, his tangled thoughts were making him more than a little crazy. At the moment, he felt a strong need for some distance.

"I'm going into town to pick up supplies. Let me know what you need." He fixed a skeptical gaze on her as he ate. "Should I find some silver bullets or wooden stakes? Or maybe a few gallons of holy water?"

Maya's upper lip curled as if she knew he was making fun at her expense, even if she didn't entirely understand what he meant. She set his refilled coffee mug down next to his elbow with great care. He got the feeling the hot coffee could have just as easily landed in his lap.

Jared deliberately took his time eating breakfast, and ignored Maya's gloomy mutterings that the day was already half-gone. Since dawn was a little over an hour old, he disagreed with her. Not that he'd say so aloud. The coffeepot was still half-full.

As he ate, he thought about Rachel's apparent disappearance. He told himself it was nothing more than some kind of trick. For all he knew he'd fallen asleep and just thought she'd disappeared in front of him. Maybe he hadn't tried to kiss her, after all. Maybe he only dreamed that he did.

But people didn't just disappear unless David Copperfield was in town. There had to be another explanation.

He only saw her at night, and she didn't seem to have anything that resembled a magic wand.

Then there was her refusing to talk about her past.

He recalled the night she'd talked about life on the ranch. Her description of a working ranch from more than a hundred years ago sounded pretty real to him. Was there a chance she was describing the ranch as it once was? Maybe she'd seen pictures of it at the historical society. Or in one of the few books that talked about the town's history. Maybe she just had an incredible imagination.

And Maya. Sadly, there were still people who couldn't read or write, but there was something about her that spoke of a culture that hadn't existed for more than a century.

He could have been eating sawdust for all the attention he gave his food.

As a homicide detective, Jared was used to dealing with puzzles. He didn't like puzzles that made no sense. What had happened with Rachel that morning didn't make sense. And it was apparent that Maya wasn't going to explain things to him.

Once he'd finished his meal, he refilled his coffee mug and carried it into the other room. He sat down with his laptop computer and logged on to the Internet. He wasted no time tracking down the Web site of the local historical society. He didn't know what he was looking for, but it was the only place he thought might have some answers for him. He clicked on the link taking him to the section displaying historical photographs from the county's past.

He felt another punch to the gut when he spotted an old photograph showing a local rancher and his wife. Jared stared long and hard, as if he couldn't believe his eyes.

The black-and-white image was faded by time, the couple in the stiff pose of that era as they faced the camera. The woman was seated primly in a chair, with her hands folded in her lap, while the man stood behind her, a hand resting on her shoulder. As had been the norm with photographs in the 1800s, neither person wore a smile. Jared didn't bother looking at the man; it was the woman who caught his attention. The stark photo depicted her delicate features, large eyes and hair pulled back in a neat coil. Her lush mouth looked ready to smile if given the chance, but her eyes told a different story. They told him of a woman who was unhappy, frightened even.

The man's conservative suit did little to disguise the bulky build of someone who enjoyed his food and drink. His fingers were large and blunt. The hand lying heavily on her shoulder looked accustomed to hard labor, and had probably engaged in a good share of physical battles during its time. Jared was positive this man was possessive of anything he considered his. There was no doubt he considered the woman seated in front of him as one of his possessions.

With a sense of doom, Jared read the caption under the photograph.

Caleb Bingham, one of the founding fathers of Sierra Vista, then a dying mining camp dubbed No Name Camp, and his wife, Rachel. Mr. Bingham was known for his drive in building the camp into a thriving town.

Jared felt a strange chill invade his body as he stared at the picture.

Rachel Bingham.

The Rachel Bingham shown here was married to Caleb Bingham in the 1800s. *That* Rachel Bingham could be *his* Rachel's twin sister. While the photograph wasn't in color, he didn't miss the style of dress the woman wore. He'd swear it was the same gown he saw on Rachel every night.

He felt as if the air had been sucked out of the room. Jared worked with logic, not fantasy. He didn't believe in the supernatural crap so popular these days.

As he stared woodenly at the photograph, the barest hint of jasmine teased his nostrils.

"Maybe I'm imagining that, too," he muttered, without looking up from the computer monitor. "For all I know, Maya could be putting something funny in my food." He clicked on another page, which gave an abbreviated history of Caleb and Rachel Bingham. He skimmed most of it until he came to the section that mentioned Rachel's death as one of the most heinous crimes in the area.

He read the chilling story—that she'd been killed by one of the ranch hands, who was immediately caught and hanged for the murder. Barely twenty-four hours later, Caleb Bingham had been brutally murdered. His killer had never been found and the murder remained unsolved to this day.

The coffee Jared had been drinking suddenly tasted like acid in his stomach. He set the mug down and closed the Web page. He noticed the scent of jasmine was now absent.

"Terrific. All I got were more questions and not enough answers," he muttered, shutting off his computer. He got up and walked back to the kitchen.

Maya was strangely reticent as she recited her list of items needed. Jared didn't look at her once as he wrote them down.

"I'll be back later this morning." He whistled for Harley.

She followed him out onto the back porch. "If you wish, the dog can stay here," she said grudgingly. "You say dogs cannot go into your general stores now. If you leave him by your smelly machine, someone might think he is a useful dog and try to take him. Not that I would miss him. He is a great deal of trouble."

Jared was stunned—not just by Maya's offer, but that she had spoken more directly to him than she usually did.

"Tell me something, Maya. If I brought back something fancy for you would you throw it at me or thank me?"

She sniffed loudly as if she encountered a bad smell. "Men think they can tempt a woman with a few pieces of ribbon or a new hat, but we know better."

"Then I'll make it easy on both of us and just bring you a

new broom to fly on." He walked over to his Harley. When the dog started to follow, he gestured for him to return to the house. The young pup whined in disappointment at not being able to go along, but made his way slowly back to the steps.

"Do you think I do not know what you mean when you speak of flying brooms?" Maya called after him. "Do not talk lightly of such things, Señor Stryker. There are powers in this world you cannot even imagine. Just because you die does not mean you leave the land. Some spirits remain and continue to be aware of what goes on around them."

About to swing his leg over the bike, Jared paused. He turned around and walked back to the bottom step, looking up at Maya. He guessed he had just been given an important clue, or else she was messing with his mind big time.

He shook his head, refusing to accept what he'd just heard.

"No way. *No way,*" he declared, more strongly the second time.

She crossed her arms in front of her and stared down at him. Her silence told him that she believed every word she spoke was the truth.

"You're saying Rachel and you are…?" He couldn't use the word. "That you're…" He shook his head again, still refusing to accept what she implied. "No way. That is not possible in this world."

The older woman's black eyes betrayed no emotion as she gazed down at him with the haughty manner of a queen born in an ancient land. A sensation skittering along his spine told him this woman was more than a mere housekeeper. Logic would never be able to explain her existence.

"History says that Caleb was a cold son of a bitch who ruled his land with an iron fist," Jared murmured. "But you never let him rule you, did you? You always looked him in the eye like you're looking at me right now." He didn't believe one word he said. There was no way she could have been alive back then. He just threw out the bait to see her reaction.

She crossed her arms in front of her. Normally this would be a defensive gesture, but with Maya it was the opposite. "History depends on who tells the story."

"Then why don't you tell me your history?" he invited.

Maya's smile was a bare twist of the lips. "Go ride your machine of noise and do what you must do. You will learn the truth when it is time." With a swirl of her ankle-length skirts she turned around and walked back into the house, slamming the door behind her.

He stared after her for a moment, then mounted his bike and headed for town.

Jared did a lot of hard thinking during his ride into Sierra Vista.

What flashed into his mind was the look of faint resignation on Rachel's face just before she'd faded into nothing.

For all he knew, he'd been having a pretty incredible dream these past weeks since he'd moved into the house.

But if he wasn't dreaming, the Rachel he knew was the same Rachel who'd been murdered more than a hundred years ago.

Jared might enjoy watching science fiction and horror movies, but that didn't mean he believed little green men lived on Mars. He liked the escapism the films offered, so he could briefly forget the nights he spent visiting crime scenes that always involved at least one dead body.

In his world, the dead *stayed* dead.

Jared parked his Harley in front of the Sierra Vista Historical Society, set on a side street only a few blocks from the police station. The elegant Victorian-style house was painted a pearl-gray with white trim. A white wicker settee, chair and small table sat on the porch, and a basket of colorful flowers had been placed on the table, as if the lady of the house had just selected them from her garden. On one side of the front door was a small bronze plaque posting the society's hours. A plaque on the other side announced that the house was listed in the state's historical register. He noted that it had been built the year Rachel Bingham died.

When he stepped inside the foyer he looked to one side and noticed the parlor, where he found two elderly women seated on a dark red velvet antique love seat that, to him, looked very uncomfortable, but appropriate for the room. A china tea set sat on a small table in front of them, as if they were two old friends enjoying a morning visit. Jared's first thought was that Rachel would look right at home in this room.

The women looked at him warily when he stepped inside. He hid a grin, doubting that someone dressed in a much faded green T-shirt, tan jeans and scuffed boots was a typical visitor. Jared told himself it was a good thing he'd left Harley home. He doubted the wicker furniture on the porch would have survived the dog's chewing skills.

He brought out the smile he used when he needed to reassure panicked witnesses, along with his detective shield, to assure them he was one of the good guys. He noticed both women wore dresses that looked very similar in style to the gown Rachel wore. One of them had an old-fashioned cameo pinned to her lace collar. The smell of something floral emanated from a crystal dish on a table near the love seat. He struggled not to sneeze.

"Good morning, ladies." He nodded at each one. "I am hoping you can help me with something."

"Yes, young man?" The one whose tiny badge pinned to

her breast declared her to be Daisy spoke first. Her silver hair was piled on top of her head in a series of curls.

Luckily, he'd prepared his story during the ride in case there was a chance someone was here to help him. "My name is Jared Stryker. I own the Diamond B property just outside town."

The other woman, named Clara, nodded. "You're Winnie Davis's grandson." Her gray hair was pulled back in a sedate coil on the back of her head.

"My grandmother died before I was born, ma'am." He realized this was going to take more socializing than he'd planned on. Not to mention had the patience for. Evenings spent at The Renegade hadn't given him the right kind of education for dealing with sweet little old ladies who'd known his mother's mother.

"Your father was a nasty little boy," Clara said bluntly. "I wasn't surprised he ended up in prison. If you follow a life of crime, you must expect to pay the price. At least you had the good sense to make a better life for yourself."

"You're embarrassing the boy, Clara," Daisy chided, before turning back to Jared. "When you get to be our age, you tend to speak more openly."

"It's nice to know that someone doesn't try to lump me with him," he admitted. "Actually, I'm here to find out more about the ranch. I'm curious about the original owner. I've heard some pretty fantastic stories, but I thought I'd come here to see if there's more known about him."

Daisy's nose twitched as if she smelled something foul. "Caleb Bingham!" She said the name with contempt. "Some say he gave life to the town when it was nothing more than a camp, but that's not true. He took advantage of gaining a great deal of land by cheating people. He was a very evil man."

"But as you said, he was one of the town founders and

helped make it a thriving area," Jared stated, recalling what he'd read on the Web site. "It's even been said Sierra Vista wouldn't have existed without him and the horse ranch he built. That without his influence, the town would have been nothing more than a dead-end mining town. He even built a racetrack, thinking it would generate additional business, but that didn't work out."

Daisy nodded. "I'm sure he preferred history say he was a wonderful man only thinking of the community, but that is not true. The trouble is, no one likes to air a town's dirty linen. Especially any as nasty as Caleb Bingham's."

"What is it you wish to learn, dear?" Clara asked.

"Whatever you might know about the ranch's beginnings. About the people living there." He didn't know why, but he didn't want to voice Rachel's name out loud.

Clara stood up and crooked her finger. "Come with me and we'll set you up. Would you like some tea? No, I suppose you don't drink tea." She looked him up and down. "But we do have some nice iced raspberry tea."

"No, thank you, ma'am, I'm fine." Jared realized he was using up all of his limited social skills in a very short period of time.

Clara led him down a narrow hallway to a rear room she described as the former butler's pantry, although the owners of the house at that time didn't have a butler. Now the room held several tables with computer monitors on them, hooked up to a computer network. She soon had him seated in front of a monitor. "We were able to scan many of the old records. All you have to do is type in the name you're looking for," she explained as she carried out two large books and set them on a nearby table. "You will also find newspaper articles from that time period in here." She studied him. "So you're currently living in the house?"

He nodded. "Yes, ma'am, for about six weeks now. I inherited it when my mother died, but it was held in trust until
my thirtieth birthday."

"At least she had the good sense to insure the property
would be saved for you. That way your father couldn't try
to sell it," she said bluntly upon seeing his shocked expression. "It's a small town, young man. There are no secrets here."

I can think of one. He composed his expression so he
wouldn't laugh.

"Thank you for your help," he murmured, hoping she
would leave him alone with his research.

She smiled. "We're here to help. Just call out if you have
any questions."

Left alone, Jared turned back to the monitor. He spent the
next two hours reading newspaper stories about Caleb Bingham obtaining land with the intention of building a ranch and
stocking it with prime horseflesh. Bingham vowed that, once
his ranch was successful, he would find himself the right
wife, so he could start his own personal dynasty. Jared fast-
forwarded until he found the story of Bingham's marriage to
Rachel Weatherly of Atlanta, Georgia. The story added that
her family owned one of the few remaining plantations to sur-
vive the Civil War, but her parents had died of fever when she
was a small girl and that she had been cared for by distant rel-
atives. He noticed the picture in the newspaper was the same
one he'd seen on the historical society's Web site.

Jared felt acid eating away at his stomach. "He wanted a
wife with a pedigree as good as his horses," he muttered.

But after that article there was nothing else on Rachel until
he found a story dated almost eighteen months later, where a
headline announced that Caleb Bingham's wife had been

murdered. He noticed that Rachel's name wasn't mentioned once in the article.

Jared scanned the article.

"No worrying about readers' sensibilities here," he muttered, wincing at the lurid descriptions of stab wounds and the blood-covered body found in the Bingham house. He would have sworn he was reading a crime scene report.

A distraught Caleb Bingham was quoted as saying he didn't know how he could go on without the woman who'd had given him so much. He claimed she had been his whole life. Below the story was a small picture of a man's body hanging from a tree, and two lines stating that Rachel Bingham's killer had been found and executed.

The article following the gruesome account of Rachel's murder stopped him short. This one declared that Caleb Bingham had been brutally murdered.

If Jared thought the story about Rachel's murder was macabre, he found the account of Bingham's death well beyond that. According to the story, one of the ranch hands found what was left of Caleb's body in the barn the night after Rachel's death. The shaken man was quoted saying his boss had been torn apart by devils.

"Something tells me it couldn't have happened to a nicer guy," Jared mumbled aloud. "That was one crime scene I would have happily ignored." He amended that thought. No, he would have investigated the case if only to learn who, or what, had committed the crime.

He stood up and stretched his arms over his head to relax the kinks in his shoulders before he walked to the front of the house.

"Where would you like me to put those books?" he asked Clara.

"I'll take care of them, dear," she assured him with a warm smile. "Were you able to find what you were looking for?"

More questions. "I think so. Thank you."

"Come again, anytime." Daisy smiled at him.

Jared started to open the door, then paused and turned around. "Do you have any idea why there weren't more newspaper stories about Caleb Bingham's wife? I saw stories about ladies' meetings and parties, with a listing of who attended, but her name was never mentioned. There wasn't even anything said about parties given at the ranch. Anything written about Bingham was only about him or the property."

"I'm afraid we only have other people's accounts to go on when it comes to information about the residents' social lives," Daisy explained. "We were lucky to obtain quite a few ladies' diaries that had been written back then. They are a wonderful source of information about life in the area. I recall that one woman wrote she felt Caleb Bingham kept his wife a virtual prisoner out at that ranch," Daisy confided. "She wasn't even allowed to come into town for church, to attend any of the church socials or even to do any shopping." She tsked and shook her head. "Everything she required was ordered through catalogs. He did bring her into town for the annual Christmas pageant, but that was more to show her off to the townspeople. Nowadays, she would be considered a trophy wife. I don't think the poor dear had a good life out there. Then to die so young…" She shook her head, a sad expression on her face.

Jared felt as if a block of ice was planted right smack in his middle.

"Murder is never good," he murmured.

"I don't think she had an easy life with that man," Clara said. She leaned forward as if confiding a huge secret. "I wouldn't be surprised if he wasn't the one who killed her."

"That is nothing more than a vague rumor," Daisy pointed out. "Some pieces of history about the town aren't as well known because many would prefer they be forgotten. Leading citizens in this town don't want people to know about the skeletons in their closets, or their less than favorable background. I'm sure you understand."

His attention was well and truly caught. He walked back to where they were sitting on the love seat. "What about Caleb's skeletons?"

"As I said before, it was widely known that Caleb cheated and murdered for his land," she said in her gentle voice. "And that he used less than admirable means to keep what he had. It was even said that he dabbled in some sort of witchcraft or old magic. Perhaps that's why there have been rumors that it's haunted out there. But that doesn't mean the land is tainted. With you living out there now, the rumors of the house being haunted and a treasure buried out there can finally be laid to rest."

Jared grinned. "You make it sound as if I need to have the house and land blessed or something."

"Are you married?" Clara asked.

"No, ma'am." He feared where this conversation could be heading. Didn't he have enough problems as it was?

"I think the best thing you can do for that house is give it what it truly needs," she said.

"And what is that?" The words left his mouth before he could call them back. The gleam in the woman's eye was very dangerous.

"Simple, my dear. What you need to do is fill that house with love and children," Clara said.

"I'm not exactly marriage material." He held his hands out from his sides. "Crazy job. Even crazier hours."

"Everyone is marriage material," Daisy told him. "All they

need to do is find their soul mate. I found mine more than seventy years ago, when we were in school. We've now been married sixty-three years."

"I have a lovely granddaughter. She's a stockbroker in Chicago and she's coming out to visit me in a few weeks," Clara stated, with a matchmaker's glint in her eye.

"I'm afraid I'll be back to work then, and with my hours, well, I can't commit myself to anything. Thank you again for all your help," he said hastily, making a quick exit before Clara was ready to announce an engagement.

He returned to his bike and climbed on. There was no reason to hurry back to the ranch. Since he'd never seen Rachel in the light of day before, he doubted he would today.

He looked down at his bike, thinking of what he had to do in town today and all the chores he still had to tackle back at the ranch. He started up the engine and drove off.

As always, before long his thoughts returned to the woman who occupied his house. "What's the real story, Rachel?" he muttered. "Maya's is that you two are ghosts, which I find pretty hard to believe. But if she's speaking the truth, why are you haunting my house?"

She had no idea what time it was. Time had no meaning for her when she was on this plane of existence. She "saw" Jared talk to Maya and watched him ride away on his motorcycle. She couldn't hover close enough to listen in on their conversation, but she sensed they were talking about her. The tense expression on Jared's face worried her.

She sensed he didn't want to believe what he'd seen when she'd disappeared at dawn. She hated it happening in front of him, but she had no control over it. She never had.

She was aware of Harley following her from room to room.

She wasn't used to anyone or anything having the ability to sense her during the day. Maya might talk to her as she moved through the house and did her work, but there were times when she would be in one room talking and Rachel would be in another.

Right now, the oversize puppy was staring intently at her. His head was cocked to one side and occasionally a soft whine would escape his throat, as if he was trying to catch her attention. He turned when he heard a rumbling sound approach the house. He spun around and ran toward the front door, which had been left open as Maya stood outside, sweeping the front porch.

"*Dios mío!* What is that?" Maya's voice sounded shocked.

Rachel drifted closer to the door. She knew she could go no farther. Too many times she'd tried to escape the house's boundaries, only to be pushed back inside. It was as if there was an invisible shield covering the place, keeping her a prisoner inside. She gazed out the doorway.

Instead of his motorcycle, Jared was climbing out of a large, shiny black vehicle that had four tires instead of two. She could see that the motorcycle was secured in the back of the truck.

"With all the stuff you have me pick up, I realized it was more than the Harley can handle," he said, walking up to Maya. Sunglasses covered his eyes. He pulled them off and tucked them into his T-shirt. "Having the pickup will save me truck rental fees. Plus I'll need something sturdier when winter comes. I've gotta say, for someone who's working for me for free, you're sure costing me a lot of money." He grinned to take the sting out of his words.

Jared wasn't angry that he'd had to spend a great deal of money. Not the way Caleb would have been. Caleb complained so many times that too much money was spent on food for the workers, or that Rachel needed to learn her proper role in his household was, one of them being finding ways to save money. He'd wanted her to understand that his money was meant to expand the ranch. No one, and nothing else, mattered. She was expected to look the part of a prosperous rancher's wife, but only when important people came to call.

She noticed that Jared's expression was affectionate even when he looked at Maya, as if he was looking at a cranky aunt. Rachel knew he would never admit it, but he liked Maya. And by the look on the old woman's face, she enjoyed his teasing and liked him, too, even if she wouldn't admit it under the threat of death.

Rachel wished she could communicate with them. She worried how Jared would act toward her when night fell and she reverted to her mortal form. She knew he would have many questions for her. But would she have the answers? She'd never had to explain herself to anyone before. And she knew Jared wouldn't accept anything less than the full truth. Except she knew she couldn't reveal some of that truth. How could she explain about the key in relation to her curse, when she didn't fully understand it herself?

The minute Jared entered the house he caught the scent of jasmine in the air. He glanced at Maya.

"Not exactly your fragrance," he said.

"Someone gave her a bottle of jasmine perfume," Maya explained, detecting his unspoken question. "She always wore it." A strange smile touched her lips. "He didn't like it. He said it was too exotic. He only wanted her to wear expensive perfume that came from France, so she would smell like a successful rancher's wife. He always wanted her to look beautiful so men would envy him for having her."

Jared's stomach twisted at the idea of the delicate Rachel

having anything to do with the harsh-featured man he'd seen in the photograph. Jared tamped down the idea immediately. He rejected the possibility that she was a ghost. Yet he couldn't think of one logical explanation to support the theory that she'd lived over a hundred years ago.

"Maybe you spray jasmine air freshener everywhere," he muttered.

Maya scowled at him for daring to doubt her words. "One day I heard something on your radio that would describe Señor Caleb. It was his way or the road."

Jared nodded at her mangled phrasing. "You mean 'or the highway,'" he murmured. "I would think you could sense her all the time because…"

"Because I am like her?" Maya shook her head. "We are very different. Niña Rachel has her place and I have mine." She looked past him to the truck. "Did you bring what I asked for?"

He groaned at the idea of unloading the pickup. "Every single thing." He whistled for Harley. The dog immediately ambled after him.

Maya smiled as she watched them through the open door. "He has trouble believing what he saw, but deep down, he knows it is the truth. He is a good man, *hija.*"

Yes, he is a good man. And he didn't run away when I disappeared. I only hope he won't run away when I reappear after dark.

Jared deliberately stayed outside until it was completely dark. He thought about how he only saw Rachel after sunset. Would she be there when he walked into the house? Or was she now gone for good?

Harley looked toward the house just as twilight faded into night, and uttered a soft whine.

She's back.

Jared dismissed the thought the moment the words sounded inside his head. He wasn't waiting until evening fell to see if Rachel would be there. He looked down at the dog, who was straining to reach the house. His tail wagged so hard Jared thought it would fall off.

How had he missed it before? Come to think of it, every evening Harley acted the very same way. Jared had put it down to the pup being hungry for his dinner. But he also knew that Harley was slavishly devoted to Rachel, and not just because she sneaked him treats under the dinner table when she thought Jared wasn't looking.

Could that have something to do with the times Jared had seen the dog sitting and staring at one spot in an empty room during the day? Did he sense something there that Jared couldn't see?

"Are you telling me you know where she is all the time, fella?" he murmured, scratching him behind the ears. "They say dogs sense things humans can't. For all I know, you might even see her." He started slowly back to the house, then stopped, stunned at his own words. "Now I know I've *really* lost my mind. I'm talking to the dog as if he understands every word I say, and I supposedly have two ghosts in my house. But I swear, Harley, if you start talking back to me, I'll be in real trouble."

Chapter 6

Jared entered the kitchen and found Rachel standing by the stove with her hands clasped loosely in front of her. He didn't miss the tension radiating from her body as she stared at him with wary eyes.

He knew his own expression wasn't much better. He considered himself grateful she hadn't just popped up in front of him the way she'd disappeared.

"I never had a woman go to the lengths of literally disappearing in front of me just because I tried to kiss her. You could have just said no and I would have backed off," he drawled by way of greeting. He walked over to the sink and turned on the faucet, taking longer than usual to wash his hands. "You know, you look pretty good for a ghost. Here I thought you all were transparent and walked shrieking and moaning through the house in the middle of the night, maybe rattle a few chains to scare people off. Or is that what you did in the past to keep people out of here? When I was a kid, we all talked about the house being haunted. I wonder what people would think if they knew they were right. I bet I could even make a few bucks renting the place out at Halloween. Do you think Maya would be willing to help spook people? Not that it would take much on her part. She wouldn't even have to wear a costume."

"I do not understand," Rachel said, clearly uneasy around his dark mood. She hadn't moved from her spot, as if afraid to draw too much attention to herself.

He kept his back to her, even though he'd finished washing his hands, and now stood staring at the water flowing from the faucet.

"It doesn't make sense, you know. There's all sorts of explanations for what happened. Maybe I was just tired this morning after being up all night. Or maybe I closed my eyes for more than a few seconds and you went upstairs to your room. I could have even just fallen asleep and dreamed the whole thing. People just *don't* disappear into thin air. Not unless there's a magician or an alien ship nearby," he said sardonically. He turned off the faucet and braced his hands on the counter's edge. "Of course, that would only make sense to me if I'd spent half the night drinking at The Renegade. Maybe it's something else—chemicals leaching into the well water, perhaps—and you're nothing more than a figment of my imagination. Now *that* makes sense."

Rachel moved forward with her hand outstretched as if she meant to touch his shoulder, but drew it back to her side before she made contact. "That very first time you saw me, would you have believed me if I told you I died in 1888?"

The muscles in his arms stood out starkly as he pushed himself away from the sink. He still hadn't turned around, as if he didn't want to look at her. "No, I wouldn't. I would have figured you for a loony tune and found you a nice quiet room with padded walls."

"I—I do not understand."

Jared thought for a moment, so he could come up with a term she would better understand. If she wanted to believe she had lived in the 1800s, so be it. "A shrink. A psych ward. Mental case. What did you call it back then?" he muttered to himself. He snapped his fingers. "An asylum."

She gasped with true horror. "No! They are horrible filthy places where poor demented people are treated no better than animals!"

"Trust me, we've come a ways since then." He took a deep breath and turned around, crossing his arms. "Just so we have things straight, why don't you tell me who you are exactly." He was curious to hear her story and how it compared with what he had learned at the historical society.

"I am Rachel Weatherly Bingham of Atlanta, Georgia," she said in a formal voice. "I was born in 1865."

He did some mental arithmetic and came up with the realization she'd been born long before his great-grandfather had been a twinkle in his own ancestor's eye.

"How?" Jared drew in a deep breath. "What I mean is, how did you end up still being here? When people die they're supposed to…well, die. Be gone. If you're really dead, why didn't you move on?"

"I don't know." She gestured toward the table. "Maya left dinner. I do not think you want to eat cold food."

"Where is she?" He looked around.

"I do not know how to explain," Rachel said softly. "It's very complicated."

"I may not have all the college smarts like some of the

other detectives, but I can understand complicated," Jared said sarcastically.

Rachel's cheeks flushed a becoming dark pink. "I was not trying to insult you. I meant I do not understand it all myself. Would you please eat your dinner before it gets cold?" she pleaded, striving for a hint of normalcy. At least, considering the circumstances, as normal as possible.

Jared wanted to tell her the last thing he felt like doing was eat anything cooked by an alleged ghost, even if he'd been doing just that for days, but he stopped before one word escaped. Maybe it was the stark look on Rachel's face or the hint of tears in her eyes. It didn't matter. If he lashed out at her now it would be the same as harming a kitten. He knew he couldn't do that.

Rachel filled a plate and brought it to the table. She set it in front of Jared. He looked at the two grilled lamb chops, herbed potatoes and green beans. He looked at the much smaller helpings Rachel took.

"I didn't think ghosts ate food," he said, telling himself this was proof she wasn't what she claimed to be.

She nodded, but kept her head downcast. "I cannot actually taste the food since it is not necessary for my survival. But I enjoy the different textures."

"Because I would have wondered why you didn't eat," he muttered.

"Yes," she whispered.

"Yet Maya still has her sense of taste," Jared said.

She nodded. "It is another thing we do not understand."

Rachel hadn't felt fear in over one hundred years, but she felt it now. What if there was a way that Jared could banish her from the house? Long ago she'd prayed for a way to leave here because she didn't have a reason to stay. Since Jared had come here she hadn't wanted to leave—unless she found the key that would release her from her half existence.

Under lowered lashes she watched Jared eat. More than once he'd spoken of his lack of education and his common manners. Yet she noticed he wiped his boots on the mat outside the door before coming in, he washed up without any prompting and he never sat down at the table until she did. And not once had his eyes slid over her with the hungry leering look Caleb used to give her. Many times after Caleb stared at her with a dark fire in his eyes that led to his possessing her body, she'd felt the need to bathe in the hottest water possible to cleanse herself. Not once during her marriage had she felt clean in spirit. Before they were married, Caleb had told her he would worship her and give her the world. Instead, he threw her into a hell she felt she would still be in after death. And for decades, that was exactly what had happened to her.

She licked her lips. "Are there still other ranches here?" she asked, now feeling a little confident that she could ask the questions that had plagued her for a long time. "I remember there was a family about fifteen miles from here."

Jared shook his head. "There hasn't been a working ranch in this area for the last sixty years."

"Yet this one remained even if it wasn't occupied." She took a tiny bite of her meat.

"The way I understood it, Caleb's brother back East inherited the ranch, but he never bothered doing anything with it. Even after his death, it still sat empty for a number of years until a descendent moved in briefly." He slanted her a look. "But I guess you know about the empty part better than I do."

"Yet you chose to come here."

"I inherited this place from my mother and decided to move in. From what I was told, a trust account had been set up years ago to cover the property taxes, so I don't have to sell off any body parts to pay them."

Rachel scrunched up her face. "Sell body parts?"

He chuckled. "Another term from the modern world you claim not to know about." He shook his head and pushed his plate away, resting his elbows on the table with his fingers laced together. "I have lots of questions."

She looked apprehensive. "Would you like more coffee?" She jumped up from her chair and almost ran to the coffeemaker.

"Rachel!"

She froze as if he'd commanded her to halt. Jared sighed as he realized his harsh voice had frightened her.

"Rachel…" He said her name in a softer voice this time. "Let's go outside on the porch."

"I can't," she said in a strangled voice, refusing to look at him.

"Can't go outside? Why not?" he asked.

Rachel looked toward the back door as if she wished she could escape but knew it wasn't possible.

"I do not entirely understand how or why, just that I cannot leave the house," she whispered. "It is as if some sort of barrier exists at the doors and windows that will not allow me to leave."

Jared couldn't miss the fear in her eyes. "What are you remembering, Rachel?" He continued to use the quiet voice that worked with more than one traumatized witness.

Her brow furrowed in thought. "She's chanting."

"Who?"

She shook her head. "I never knew her name. She was Caleb's…" She suddenly blushed. "They were very close."

"You mean Caleb's mistress." He said the word for her, easily guessing why she blushed, while wondering why any man would want another woman if he had someone as special as Rachel.

She nodded. She still couldn't meet his eyes. "She hated me so much and I did not understand why," she whispered. "I never knew her and only saw her from a distance."

Jared felt uncomfortable with her distress. He didn't want to believe she was a ghost. He preferred thinking she was a harmless woman who had a problem with reality.

"Then if you can't go outside, let's go into the other room." He thought it might be easier for her if she was more comfortable.

Rachel moved toward the table instead. "The dishes need to be washed."

"They can wait." Without touching her, he guided her back into the den.

Rachel went in ahead of him and perched on the edge of a chair. She didn't take her eyes off him as he followed her, then took a seat opposite her, turning his chair around and resting his arms across the back. He racked his brain for questions that wouldn't bring back dark memories, but he couldn't think of one that didn't have to do with what was upsetting her.

Damn! It was easier for him to question a cold-blooded murder suspect than to interrogate this fragile beauty. He noted the tension in her mouth and the wary look in her violet eyes. He *refused* to believe she was a ghost. It flew in the face of all his beliefs.

"What do you do during the day? Where do you go?"

She appeared relieved by his question. "I remain here."

Jared looked around. "Here where?"

Rachel nodded. "In the house. I do not know how to explain it. It is as if I am inside a cloud."

"A cloud in the house," he mused, having trouble believing her, but doubting she was lying to him. "How come I don't see this cloud you're in?"

"Because it's not the kind of cloud you can see. It is just…there. I am afraid it is not easy for me to explain." She thought for a moment. "Do you know how it feels when a breeze touches your face?"

Jared knew that feeling only too well. There had been many times inside the house he'd felt something brush against his face. Was Rachel trying to say that sensation was her? He nodded.

"That is what I become. I cannot feel anything, but I do hear voices and understand what people are saying. And I am aware of everything around me. You might say I am an observer standing at a distance. I can travel to any of the rooms inside the house. I just cannot leave it."

"So you haven't been outside this house since 1888?" he asked slowly. He winced when she nodded. "What do you do after I go to bed?"

"I read, I watch programs on your television," she admitted. "And I stand at the windows and look outside."

A part of this world, yet not a part.

Jared still had trouble believing her, but the barriers were lowering bit by bit, and they were blowing his mind. She explained everything so logically. The idea of not having the freedom to just walk outside to enjoy a sunny day or moonlit night would have had him clawing at the walls. He couldn't comprehend someone handling such stark isolation for so many years, even if, in a sense, that being had company. But why, then, could Maya leave the house? She'd even been nagging Jared to find her seeds and plants so she could start a kitchen garden.

"Then why can Maya…?" he asked.

Rachel shrugged. "I do not know. It is the way it has always been."

"What about when the weather changes? Do you feel the cold night air or the heat of the sun? Do you feel the wind on your face? Smell the rain?"

Rachel shook her head. Her hands lay neatly folded in her lap, her ankles crossed in a ladylike pose.

"I feel nothing during daylight hours," she softly admitted. "I can enjoy looking at a fresh flower, but I cannot smell its fragrance. I can look out the window and watch the rain falling outside, but I cannot feel the dampness. I feel neither warmth nor cold. And I cannot leave this house to discover what lies outside the boundaries that hold me." Her shoulders lifted and fell in a shrug of resignation. "That is what my world has been for me for the past hundred odd years."

An existence with no meaning. A prison that didn't require jailers because there was no chance of escape.

Jared was still having trouble assimilating all the information she had given him. As it was, he had an idea Rachel had only related a fraction of the story. She hadn't said one word about what her life had been like before her death.

Her death. Another thing he couldn't understand. The woman seated before him looked vital and alive.

What if she *was* telling the truth? What had her life been like before she married Bingham and moved to California? What had happened the day she died? Why had that man killed her?

Jared mentally shook his head. No matter how he looked at it, it seemed more like a movie he'd see on TV.

"None of it makes any sense," he muttered to himself. He kept shaking his head in disbelief as he pushed himself upward. "No sense at all."

Her dark violet eyes tracked his movements. "That is why I never said anything to you before. I knew you would have trouble believing me. I do not lie, Jared."

He didn't acknowledge her words as he walked out of the house, with Harley on his heels.

Rachel remained seated in her chair. She thought of the warning signs of Jared's temper earlier that evening. Even in the face of his evident anger, she noticed he didn't allow his ire to get out of hand. Not once had he come right out and accused her of lying. She understood he had trouble understanding her story. After all these decades even she had difficulty comprehending what had happened to her after that horror-filled moment when she'd looked into her husband's crazed eyes and known she was about to die at his hands.

A moment later she heard the throaty rumble of his motorcycle as it raced down the road.

Rachel had told Jared she couldn't feel anything any longer. She'd lied.

At that moment, she felt a great sorrow tearing her apart inside at the idea that he might now have the power to banish her just because he didn't believe in her.

Emotions shot through Jared like poisoned darts, all with the intention of creating damage.

It had been a long time since he'd felt this unsure about the world around him. He was used to a lifestyle that followed a rigid set of rules he'd laid out for himself.

He worked the graveyard shift because he preferred it. His willingness to cover that shift made the other homicide detectives, those with actual lives, happy. He also preferred working alone. Something else they didn't mind, since it was known that Jared Stryker didn't always play well with others. But he was persistent when investigating a crime and he didn't quit until he got the job done.

Then he thought of the person who was turning his concept of reality upside down. Rachel. She was so beautiful she made his teeth ache and his body ache even more.

From that very first moment, she hadn't seen him as a thug with a badge. She didn't see him as a man with a less than perfect family tree. Someone she should avoid. In fact, she always sought out his company. He ignored the whispered thought that naturally she sought him out. She hadn't talked to anyone in more than a hundred years, so for all he knew she would have sought out the devil himself just to have a civilized conversation. For all intents and purposes, she was a literal prisoner in the house, with no hope of parole.

When Jared felt this way there was only one destination he could go where he knew he wouldn't feel out of place. A spot that had everything he needed: loud rowdy music, cigarette smoke guaranteed to burn the lungs, and an average of one fight a night.

"You look like hell," Lea said, setting a frosty beer bottle in front of him. She remained where she was, looking him over much too thoroughly.

He grimaced. "I've been better."

"How's the house coming along?"

The innocuous question sent a stab through his body. He should have known she would ask. And if he didn't put on a good front she'd suspect something was wrong. Lea was tenacious when it came to ferreting out information. She wouldn't let him alone until she got the whole story. Right now, he wasn't sure just what that story was.

"I'm learning I'm a hell of a lot better cop than I am a carpenter." He grinned when two leather-and-denim-clad men flashed him furtive looks and moved farther down the bar.

"We've discussed this before," Lea pointed out in her I-need-to-be-reasonable-with-my-favorite-idiot voice. "You don't mention your occupation while you're in here and I don't throw your cute ass out the door for scaring off my customers."

"Come on, Lea, most of them already know what I am. And they know this isn't even my jurisdiction," he pointed out, recognizing a few faces he'd arrested in the past. "Have you seen anyone try to pick on me?"

"Only because they're not that stupid." She rested her arms on the bar and leaned forward. "But they don't need to be reminded, do they?" she said in a soft voice, barely audible courtesy of Bob Seger's rough voice singing in the background. "Just because you're in a pissy mood doesn't mean you can take it out on my customers."

"You're a hard woman, Lea Raines." Jared flashed a grin that had seduced more than one woman into his bed.

Except this woman was immune to his charm. She preferred being a friend to being a lover. She'd once stated that friends were more important. She also sensed something was very wrong with him. "What is going on here, darlin'?"

He picked up his beer bottle and drank thirstily. "Not much. I'm just having a beer and enjoying an evening with an old friend."

Lea gave him a dirty look.

"I needed some time away from the homestead and didn't want to ride all the way into Sierra Vista," he explained, looking around. Even though his gaze wandered over most of the men and women in the bar, his mind's eye focused on two men in particular. "At least now it doesn't take me as long to come out here, since I'm practically a neighbor."

Jared looked at the woman who had been his best friend ever since he could remember. The shy girl who rarely looked anyone in the eye had grown up into a lovely woman with a self-assurance that couldn't be ignored.

He and Lea had survived abusive parents, indifferent educators and a world that looked down on them. Jared had ended up in the army, where his anger was channeled in a more positive way and he discovered what it was like to live on the right side of the law. In turn, Lea was determined not to turn out like her alcoholic mother and petty-criminal father. A college degree in business would have allowed her to work anywhere, but she chose to return home and run the bar her grandfather had left her after his death.

It was on the tip of Jared's tongue to tell her everything about Rachel. He wanted to ask Lea what she thought about such a fantastic tale. Maybe she could make sense out of what he couldn't.

He figured she'd listen politely, then either inform him there'd be no more beer for him, even though this was his first, or she'd call those men in the white coats who would offer him a jacket with lots of straps and buckles, and then escort him to a nice quiet room with incredibly soft walls.

Plus, right now, he felt like keeping Rachel's existence to himself. His very own secret. How many men had a real ghost in their house?

He froze. He couldn't be admitting he believed Rachel's incredible story, could he? Maybe he was losing his mind, after all.

Lea, standing a short distance away dispensing beers to several customers, looked in Jared's direction when she heard his chuckle. She arched an eyebrow. He shrugged.

"If you can't behave, you're outta here," she warned as she passed him to reach the other side of the bar.

"Yeah, yeah, yeah." He turned around and leaned against the bar as he idly scanned the room. He deliberately allowed his gaze to slide past the one man that interested him most,

but he retained the image. He raised his beer to his lips to en-
hance the idea that he was more interested in his drink than
the tavern's clientele.

His mind's eye pictured the man. He thought of the worn
leather chaps wrapped over equally worn jeans. Jared already
knew the wicked looking steel tips on the man's boots weren't
for decoration, nor was the obviously empty knife sheath on
his belt. Lea's rules were irrevocable. *Leave your weapons
outside, boys, or don't bother coming in.*

Greasy, shoulder-length blond hair was pulled back in a
ponytail, with a scrubby beard partially covering acne-scarred
cheeks. The man looked as if he hadn't showered in the past
week or so.

Something tightened in Jared's gut. He was used to the
feeling. It always meant something bad.

He thought back to the night he was beaten. His ribs still
ached a little at the memory. It seemed likely the man was one
of his attackers.

Before the character realized he was under scrutiny, Jared
turned back to face the bar with an unhurried motion. He offered Lea a hopeful smile. She rolled her eyes and replaced
his now empty beer bottle with a fresh one.

"Who's the butt-ugly blond guy with the scar across the
eyebrow?" he murmured. "He's playing pool with Crank."

She didn't look in the direction of the pool tables. "I don't
know his name. He comes in maybe two or three times a
week. Sometimes alone, sometimes with a couple of friends.
Drinks no more than two beers when he's in here, sometimes
plays a little pool, but nothing that could be considered high
stakes. He hasn't given me any trouble yet." Her gaze sharpened. "Or has he?"

"Those steel tips on his boots seem familiar." Jared lifted

the bottle to his lips and allowed the cold yeasty brew to slide down his throat. "Seems I've encountered them not long ago."

Lea's expression didn't betray her thoughts. "He was here that night, but I didn't notice what time he left."

Jared didn't bother asking her if she was sure. Lea's memory was better than any security camera.

"So when are you going to tell me what's bothering you?"

He paused. "When I've got it figured out for myself." He picked up the bottle and drained it dry. He pushed it across the bar toward her.

She arched an eyebrow but didn't remind him he'd already reached his personal limit. In the twinkling of an eye, the empty bottle was gone and a new one stood in front of him.

"When we hid out at the ranch I never thought I'd end up living there," he said. "I didn't even know it belonged to my mother. When you think about it, it's surprising my old man didn't find a way to get hold of it before she left him. Who knows, maybe she never told him about it." He thought of the woman who'd abandoned him so easily. Though she'd left him behind, she'd still left him a legacy. He wished he'd known exactly why she left. Maybe she hadn't wanted to leave him behind. God knows he'd hoped that enough times. She could have tried to get him later on. But she never did.

"Yeah, who knew you'd turn out to be a land baron?" Lea teased. "It's probably a good thing we didn't know it then. We could have moved in permanently and turned it into a happy place. Our very own refuge."

He picked up on her choice of words. "A happy place?"

She nodded. "Sure, it needed to feel happy. Didn't you ever feel the sadness in there?"

"I would have called it anger and despair that was coming from us, not the house," he said carefully.

Lea shook her head. "Maybe, but I think part of it was the house, too. We were young. True, anger and despair were the only emotions we knew back then," she said. "But maybe if we'd lived there, we would have lost all that anger and the house would have lost it, too. Instead, we grew up and went on with our lives. Still, I think we turned out pretty good."

"But why did you say the house felt sad?" he asked.

"Because that's what I felt anytime we were there. It was as if there was something there that understood what we felt." She looked off into the distance as she spoke. "Who knows, maybe that's why you and I went out there. The house understood us."

He shifted uncomfortably, all too aware how close she was to the truth. "That sounds like something out of a horror movie. All we'd need is a crazed killer stalking us to make it complete."

Lea grinned. "We had the ghost instead. Remember how the kids always expected Caleb's ghost to appear and slaughter them? You and I never worried about that."

"Yeah, we didn't," he reflected.

"Maybe you could rent the house out to a movie crew. Caleb's legend would be perfect horror movie material."

He made a face. "I'd rather change the image. Make it that happy place you talked about."

Lea chuckled. "Next thing I know you'll be planting flowers and putting up a white picket fence." She nodded when someone called her name. "Don't become too domestic, sweetheart. I love you just the way you are." She patted his hand before moving down the bar to a customer.

Jared divided his time between coming to terms with the possibility that two ghosts haunted his house and covertly watching the man he was positive had helped beat him up.

Jared left the bar not long before closing. He noticed the blond man remained by the pool table and left only about ten minutes before he did.

"Maybe you'd better bunk on my couch tonight," Lea said, when Jared announced he was leaving. A worried frown creased her forehead.

He shook his head. "I'm fine. I don't even feel a buzz. Besides, I have to get back to the house and make sure everything's still in one piece."

Jared found the chilly late-night air on his face better than strong coffee as he rode toward his ranch. But he wasn't so preoccupied that he didn't notice the faint rumble of another motorcycle engine sounding from not too far behind him, and no hint of a headlight. He slowed down and waited for the other rider to approach. Not that he expected it to happen. If someone on the road had his headlights off, it usually meant the rider didn't want to be detected.

Jared could tell the other rider was pacing him, deliberately speeding up when he did, slowing down the same way.

He swore under his breath at the idea he'd encounter someone he didn't want to. He was glad he had his Glock snug against his back. He hadn't told Lea he was armed when he was in the bar because she would want him to adhere to her iron-clad rules. But he wasn't about to end up someone's punching bag again.

He cut his headlight when he turned off onto the road leading to the house then cut the engine. He heard the roar of the other bike slowly fade away, as it took off in another direction.

"Good thing you changed your mind about stopping by for a visit. I'm not ready to entertain yet." Jared started up and rode the rest of the way up the drive.

Rachel hadn't moved from her chair while Jared was gone. It had been a long time since she'd felt such a crushing silence in the house, which had recently begun to show renewed life. But these past hours were a repeat of the overwhelming quiet she had grown to hate.

She listened to the sounds of Harley barking a welcome to his master and Jared putting his motorcycle away in the barn.

Her breathing caught in her throat as she heard the now familiar thump of his boots on the back steps as he climbed them toward the kitchen door.

"You been guarding the house, boy?" he was saying as he entered the house. "I guess there's not much for you to chase around here at night, is there?"

Her stomach tightened until it almost hurt. Even though there was no light in the room she could see him as clearly as if it were the middle of the day. His stride wasn't the least bit hampered, yet she sensed he had been drinking. She knew that just as she'd known every time Caleb had gone into town to visit the Golden Slipper, where he would proceed to get drunk and come home reeking of whiskey and women's cheap perfume. Then he would loudly proclaim she'd lied to him. He would accuse her of not being the lady he'd been brought to believe she was. And to make matters worse, she couldn't provide him with the heir he wanted. In his eyes, she was useless.

Was that what Jared would say to her? Would he tell her she was useless, the way Caleb had as he'd continually stabbed her? She'd welcomed her death.

Her breath hitched in her chest as a familiar tall figure loomed dark and dangerous in the lit kitchen doorway.

"Hi, honey. I'm home," Jared announced in a loud voice.

Chapter 7

Rachel's gaze was wary, her posture that of a trapped rabbit looking for a way to flee as she watched Jared enter the room.

He kept his catlike eyes focused squarely on her, walking over until he stood in front of her.

"Don't tell me you just sat in that chair the whole time I was gone?" He held his watch up to his face. "I've been gone a good four hours, Rachel. What was the problem? It's not as if Harley takes up the entire couch. Nobody expected you to stay there until I came home." His cocky smile wavered as he stared down at her face, which looked paler than usual.

"It was best I stay put." She recited words once said to her.

"So you're saying Caleb used to order you to sit in some damn chair until he returned?" Jared demanded.

She winced at his profanity, even as she recalled much worse from Caleb. "I try not to talk about that time of my life," she murmured.

"No, you just talk about turning into a damn ghost that can only be seen at night." He reached down to grasp her hands and tug her to her feet.

She tried to pull away, but he kept a firm grip on her hands. Her head remained downcast.

"Look at me, Rachel," he ordered.

Her hair, tied in its loose braid, swung over one shoulder, leaving her nape bare.

Jared looked down at the vulnerable strip of flesh. Skin that looked like soft pink silk, that never saw the light of day. He felt her tension under his fingertips and knew he was the cause of it. But he knew if he backed down now he would never learn the truth about her past.

"Look at me," he repeated gently.

She glanced upward. Only the slight trembling of her lower lip betrayed her inner turmoil as she stared back with eyes resembling dark purple pansies. Her cheeks betrayed a faint pink flush.

Could ghosts blush? Or cry?

"Why were you still sitting in that chair when I got back?" he asked in a low voice.

"It is a very comfortable chair," she murmured.

"Liar." He was pleased to see a blaze of temper darken her eyes even more. So she wasn't all meek and mild, after all. "Did you honestly think I wanted you to sit there the whole time I was gone? Is that what *he* wanted you to do? Did he want you playing the part of the obedient little puppy, eager to do her master's bidding?"

"I have told you before that I do not think about that time." She vainly tried to free herself again. But he slid his hands to her wrists, which he circled with his fingers. This time when she moved backward, he dropped his hands.

"I am sure you are tired after your evening out," Rachel said, walking toward the stairs. She barely reached the bottom step before Jared moved toward her and grasped her elbow, spinning her around to face him. This time when she tried to shift away from him, she ended up against the wall, essentially trapping herself.

He stood so close to her the toes of his boots brushed the hem of her dress. He dipped his head and breathed deeply. "You always smell like jasmine," he murmured.

Her eyes glistened with tears. "Do not toy with me like this, Jared," she whispered, even as she hated herself for showing any form of weakness toward him. "Please." She hated herself even more for pleading with him and for feeling a strong attraction toward him.

He dipped his head to whisper in her ear. His voice was a silken growl that made her nerve endings quiver with an awareness she didn't understand. "But I do want to toy with you, Rachel." He laced his fingers through hers and rested them by her sides against the wall. "In fact, there's a lot of things I'd like to do with you." His lips rested warmly against the curve of her ear. "Would you like to hear them?"

Rachel could smell the beer on his breath and the harsh tang of smoke that clung to his clothing, but she couldn't detect any hint of perfume. She was surprised he hadn't been with a woman. Not that she had any hold on him. She suddenly recalled the cigars Caleb used to smoke. Ugly smelly things that he thought made him look successful. She'd gagged every time he smoked them.

He had always wanted her after he had been gone most of the night and came back drunk and sometimes belligerent. She'd only felt revulsion.

The man standing before her wasn't drunk. She didn't

sense a need within him to instill fear in her because it made him feel powerful. She felt a darkness in Jared Stryker's soul, but she knew it wasn't the same pitch-black void that had enveloped Caleb. Jared's darkness reached out and wrapped around her, calling to her with a different kind of need.

His words called to a part of her that was tightly curled and was now reacting to the strange sensation uncoiling within her soul. This was something she'd never experienced before. She looked up into his face and even in the dim light could see the answering call in his golden-brown eyes, reminding her of a cat stalking its prey. The fear she'd felt earlier was now gone.

His body stilled as that same sense of heightened awareness that enveloped Rachel sank into him.

"Let's say you're what you say you are. That means all those nights long ago you were here, weren't you?" Jared whispered in her ear, his breath warm against her skin. "At night you must have stayed upstairs in hiding so no one could find you. But you still heard things."

"Yes." Her reply was a wisp of sound.

"And saw things." His lips skimmed along the delicate curve of her neck where it met her shoulder.

Her throat worked convulsively as she fought to find the words to answer him. She knew exactly what he was talking about. He meant what she might have seen and heard the nights he was there with a young woman who was about his own age and seemed to be as damaged as he had been. Rachel kept her gaze on his face as the word finally surfaced with a hint of defiance. "Yes."

His soft devilish laughter seemed to start from deep within him. "Well then, good thing I didn't know I had an audience back in my teen years. There were nights when I had enough performance anxiety as it was."

She shook her head, silently telling him *that* was something she hadn't seen. She believed some things deserved as much privacy as she could give them.

"But you knew what went on here." His words whispered across her skin. "Didn't you? Weren't you ever tempted to creep down the stairs and get a better look? Weren't you ever curious?"

Rachel's eyelids fluttered as Jared's mouth continued to skim along her throat.

"No." She whispered the lie. She had been curious, but feared discovery even more.

"I never knew a ghost could smell or taste so good," he murmured.

Her breathing became labored, as if something surrounded her chest and gently squeezed. "Jared." The only word she could manage to form was his name. She had expected him to display anger. She had expected anything but a gentleness that unnerved her more than any display of violence could. She should have known Jared didn't follow anyone's rules but his own.

"You are a lady with a capital *L*," he murmured, in a soft voice that did strange things to her nerve endings. "What is it they called you back then? A Southern gentlewoman?" He went on without waiting for a reply. "You talk to me with that sexy little drawl and you look at me with those gorgeous eyes, but it's the way you watch me that I love. Do you know how much I like it? Do you know what it does to me?" Her face flamed with brilliant color as he whispered graphic suggestions in her ear. The hardness of his body against hers was further proof of his words.

Rachel's mind raced with possibilities as mental pictures backed up the murmured words. She wanted to tell him he shouldn't say such things to her. She wanted to tell him that things like *that* just weren't done...were they?

But Jared had other plans for her mouth.

When his lips moved to cover hers, she felt her supposedly nonexistent breath leave her body. He probed her mouth with the skill of a man who knew his women well. She felt a melting sensation deep inside as his tongue invaded her mouth the way she wanted him to invade her body. But there was no fear, no revulsion at his action as there had been with Caleb. There was a sense of wonder at the swirls of desire that circled within her. She felt his hands loosen their grip and slide around her body, pulling her against him. Her own arms slowly moved upward to clasp his neck.

Rachel didn't understand the feelings that were blossoming in her. For the moment, she chose not to try to figure them out, but to just enjoy what was happening. Now she felt no hint of Jared's dark side as he seduced her mouth with the same finesse she knew he would use on a woman's body. She'd never experienced something so heady. She felt his arousal against her belly and felt herself swell and soften in response. How could something so very wrong feel so very good?

And why did she have to be dead before she could discover true passion?

"Damn," he groaned against her mouth. "Why you?"

"They all lied about you! You are useless as a woman! The biggest mistake I made was marrying someone who couldn't be a real wife. You're worth even less than one of my dogs! You can't even give me a child! I could have you killed and no one would care!"

A strangled sob escaped her lips as she tore herself out of Jared's arms and backed up the stairs.

"Rachel?" Jared held out a hand as if to stop her, but she

flinched. He winced at her reaction and didn't move another step. "I'm sorry." His stance abruptly changed from seducer to comforter. "I won't hurt you."

She kept shaking her head in denial as she slowly backed up the stairs. She didn't want to tell him that he'd already hurt her. One lone tear made its way down her cheek. That hurt Jared more than any physical action could.

Rachel suddenly whirled around and seemed to literally fly up the stairs. A moment later, Jared heard the door to her room close.

"Damn," he growled, pushing his fingers through his hair. He breathed deeply through his nose in an attempt to ignore his arousal, which pushed painfully against his jeans.

When was the last time just kissing a woman had him this hard this fast? He wanted nothing more than to follow Rachel up those stairs and find out what was under that prim dress she wore. He wanted to banish all the shadows from her eyes. He wanted to lay all her past fears to rest.

She's a ghost, you idiot! What if there's nothing under that dress? How can someone dead all these years actually feel anything? How do you know what goes on inside her head?

And what if she'd run upstairs because what frightened her was him? Jared had figured out enough, and read even more, to know that ole Caleb hadn't treated her kindly.

A soft whine brought him back to the present. Harley sat back on his haunches near Jared's knee and lifted a paw in canine inquiry.

"Go on up to her, boy," he said wearily. "Right now, I don't think I'd be all that welcome."

The young dog immediately loped up the stairs. Jared heard a faint scratching sound against a door, then it opened. The click of Harley's nails on the wood floor was

audible as he entered the bedroom, and then the door quietly closed.

Jared moved over to the couch and flopped onto it. The
names he silently called himself would have shocked Rachel.
He considered them nothing more than the truth.

He was surprised she didn't just walk out of the house.
Then it hit him why she hadn't done that.

*If I try to walk out the door it is as if an invisible wall
pushes me back. I cannot leave the house.*

What if she'd been speaking the truth all along and she *was*
a ghost? What if she was well and truly stuck here?

"You are making enough noise to wake the dead!" Maya
shouted at Jared.

He paused in his work and set down the sledgehammer
he'd been wielding. He pulled off his safety goggles before
he took the mug out of the woman's hands. He smiled at her
as he inhaled the rich aroma of fresh coffee before sipping the
hot brew.

"Since you're already dead, what's the problem?"

She quietly snarled at him.

"Why are you making large holes in the wall?" she asked,
glaring at the wreckage that littered the floor. There was quite
a bit there, since Jared had begun before dawn. "With this big
hole, flies and birds will come into the house. I will never be
able to keep it clean. And what will happen at night with
nothing there to keep animals out of the house?"

"I've got a tarp to cover it up at night," he said. "Any
chance you'll bring me more coffee?"

She sniffed. "I expect you want breakfast, too?"

He grinned. "Sounds good to me."

She narrowed her eyes at him. "You are too cheerful for a

man who must not have slept much last night. Men who drink a lot of liquor and do not sleep usually have heads that hurt." Her black eyes studied him with an intensity that he was positive had her knowing way too much about him. He resisted the urge to curl his lip at her. He knew better than to make her too angry. After all, he hadn't gotten his breakfast yet.

"Must be all that fresh air." He looked at the large hole that used to be a good part of the living room wall. "It gives a man a new lease on life."

Maya stalked back to the kitchen. Jared listened to the less than subtle crash of the frying pan on the stove.

He picked up the sledgehammer and turned back to his project. "She'll probably burn the eggs on purpose."

What was he doing?

Rachel heard a thundering crash below not all that long after she went upstairs and Harley arrived to keep her company. She crept out to the landing and looked down to see a grim-faced Jared standing at the wall and using a large hammer to make holes. She thought he was trying to bring the entire wall down. From her position, she watched him work until dawn peeked over the mountain. Harley uttered a faint whine when she disappeared. After that, she drifted down to the living room and watched Jared from a closer position.

She noticed as she got nearer that he paused in his labor and lifted his face as if sniffing the air. There couldn't be a way he could tell she was there. Could he?

He looked grim and determined as he worked. As the hours passed and the day grew warmer, he stopped to pull off his T-shirt and toss it over a chair. She had seen him with his shirt off before, but she felt something different inside her as she looked at him now.

She noted his skin had deepened to a dark bronze from his days working in the sun. The muscles in his arms and chest were hard from his labors, and the crisp hairs on his chest, along with strands on his head, were bleached a pale gold by the sun.

Jared inspired unsettling feelings inside her. She didn't understand them, but she sensed they were good, because she hadn't felt much in the way of emotion in a very long time.

If she could have, she would have smiled at the byplay between Maya and Jared. She had hoped he would tell Maya what he was doing. She guessed she would just have to wait to learn what he planned to do. It wasn't as if she had anything else to do during the daylight hours....

"Hey, Celeste, we're looking at a real demolition man."

Jared lowered his safety goggles, leaving the heavy strap securing them hanging around his neck. Detectives Celeste Dante and Dylan Parker stood near the foot of the steps. Dylan's grin threatened to split his face. His prematurely gray hair shone with a silver cast under the morning sun.

"You got a problem, Parker?" Jared hefted the hammer in his hand.

"Not a one. I'm just standing here enjoying myself watching you act like one of the guys on *This Old House*." He reached over and covered Celeste's eyes with his hand. "You might want to think about showing some decorum here for the married lady." He nodded toward Jared, who wore only a pair of ragged cargo shorts, a tool belt and work boots. His bare chest gleamed with sweat from his efforts.

Jared grinned. "I don't think she's all that shocked. Are you, Goldilocks?"

"Give it a rest, both of you," Celeste ordered, pushing his hand away. "I'm married, Parker, not dead. Besides, Luc's bare chest is the only one that can tempt me. So, who's your friend?" she asked, stooping down to pet Harley, who ambled up to her and promptly rolled over onto his back. She obliged him with a belly rub. The young dog whined, begging for more.

"That's Harley."

"Original name," Dylan muttered. "What do you expect?" he demanded when Jared glared at him. "You named your dog after your motorcycle!"

"Why are you here?" Jared walked down the steps.

Celeste pushed a stray lock of golden-blond hair behind her ear. "We had to come out this way to interview a witness who claimed to see our invisible shoplifter."

Jared looked intrigued. The bane of the local shopkeepers' existence was a thief who took expensive items that had no rhyme or reason. A top-of-the-line man's silk tie one day. An equally expensive child's toy a month later. To date, no one had been able to get one solid clue on the thief's identity.

"The witness give you anything good?"

"Another dead end. It was just someone else after the reward the local businesses put up," Dylan said with a look of disgust. "So we've pretty much wasted our day."

"Domestic crime that quiet lately that they're sending you out on shoplifting cases?" Jared asked.

"More like store owners screaming for an arrest, so all of us are expected to help out when we can. The mayor is threatening to bring in professionals if the local police can't do their job. His words, definitely not ours." Celeste's disgruntled expression revealed her opinion of the blowhard known as the city mayor. "Since it's an election year we just wasted the last hour discovering the witness had nothing concrete to say. So what are you doing up there besides tearing out part of a wall?" She nodded toward the house.

Jared looked up. "I'm putting in French doors. Thought it would let more light into the room."

Celeste nodded in approval. "I think that will look very nice." She glanced up as if something caught her attention. Her gaze sharpened with interest as she stared at one upstairs window in particular.

When Jared's visitors arrived, Rachel moved upstairs, so she could have a better view of them. She thought the woman was lovely. Even dressed in pants she had a feminine air about her. Rachel floated closer to the window for a better look, then suddenly reared back when the woman glanced up at the window. Rachel swore the visitor could see her, even though she knew it was impossible.

Jared noticed the direction of Celeste's gaze and turned his head to look up.

What did she see up there? he wondered.

"I haven't had a chance to give the windows a good washing, so you can't really see much," he said casually.

"How odd," Celeste murmured, then shook her head slightly. "Maybe it's the idea a violent murder happened here that had my imagination working."

"Like a murder scene is something new to you," Dylan reminded her.

"This one was different," she replied. "It happened over a hundred and twenty years ago, when the wife of the ranch owner was murdered. Her killer was caught right away and lynched. They figured there was no reason to bring the law in, and since the husband was a prominent man in town, no one questioned his actions. Then the husband was killed the next night. All the stories say he was literally torn apart, but no one could figure out how it happened."

"Did you ever think about taking up a more interesting

hobby than memorizing old crime records?" Dylan asked her. "Knowing details of crimes committed decades ago doesn't necessarily help us now."

"You never can tell," she said. "Besides, the murders of Rachel and Caleb Bingham were big news back then. Prominent citizens and all that. Plus, his killer, at least, was never caught."

"You act as if you don't totally believe the stories about the murders," Jared said, still watching her closely.

Celeste shrugged. "Reading the sheriff's reports of the murders was more illuminating than reading the newspaper accounts. A lot of the information was kept from the public. The sheriff back then wrote he was afraid the townspeople would panic at the idea of a killer running free. Plus, it was an election year for him, so he was doing everything he could to cover his own butt. The stories in the newspaper were graphic but still kind of sketchy. The sheriff even wrote something, his thoughts about a local witch being involved. There were rumors she was Caleb's mistress, but it was something no one liked to talk about."

Jared felt ice trail down his spine. Rachel had talked about a witch being there the night she claimed she was killed.

"It just goes to show you never can tell," he said casually.

Celeste shook her head. "The stories never added up. That's one case I'd love to solve. Then there's the husband's murder. You'd almost think it was revenge for his wife's death. If he had a mistress who practiced the black arts, who isn't to say someone had the means to avenge Rachel's death?"

"Hard to believe there could have been crimes of passion back then. Have you seen pictures of the women who lived around here? Most of them were, well, less than attractive," Dylan said, more tactfully than usual.

Celeste shook her head. "This is why you're divorced and women with brains don't want to date you," she pointed out.

Jared noticed Dylan's expression change from its usual laid-back look to something more sad and secretive.

"Yeah, probably why," Dylan murmured.

"Anyway, we just thought since we were in the area we'd stop by to see how you were doing," Celeste said. "It's not the same around the station without your dark brooding presence."

Jared grinned. "You guys actually miss me? I'm touched." He laid his hand over his heart.

Celeste dug her elbow in Dylan's side when he opened his mouth to offer his own opinion of exactly how Jared was touched.

"By the way, have either of you heard about any new meth labs cropping up in the area?" Jared asked.

Celeste shook her head.

"Just the usual, it seems," Dylan said. "They close one down, three more show up elsewhere. Lately, they've been found outside the city limits, so it makes them the county's problem, not ours."

Jared chuckled. "Are you sure you getting him as your partner wasn't some kind of punishment?" he asked Celeste.

"I think they were hoping I could whip him into shape. No one realized just how big a project that was," she said, tongue-in-cheek.

"Hey! I'm standing right here," Dylan grumbled. "I can hear every word you're saying."

"Time to feed my little pet. He always gets cranky when he's hungry," Celeste confided.

"You know, people figured you two would get married," Jared said, walking them back to their unmarked vehicle.

Celeste laughed. "And break up the perfect partnership? That would have been the worst idea around."

"Yeah, Beauty and the Beast," Dylan muttered, climbing into the driver's seat.

As Celeste started to get into the car, she paused and looked up at the window again.

"Something wrong, Goldilocks?" Jared asked, then immediately regretted his sharp tone.

She turned back to him. For a moment, she studied his cautious expression.

"No. Nothing. It was probably a shadow," she said lightly. "Or perhaps a ghost. How many have you come across since you moved in?"

"If you've got the bumps and shrieks in the middle of the night going on out here, we should have our Halloween party at your place this fall," Dylan said, switching on the engine. "Think what a wild time we all could have if you could get the local ghosts to come out and howl at us."

Jared watched the car drive off. He grinned and lifted his hand over his head in a wave when he heard a short burst from the siren before the vehicle rolled out of sight. Once they were gone, he turned around and looked back at the house. His gaze rose upward until it reached the window Celeste had been staring at.

His bedroom window.

"Are you up there, Rachel?" he murmured. "Were you watching us?"

For a moment, he thought he could smell jasmine, except he knew it wasn't possible, since there were no jasmine bushes around the house. And if Rachel couldn't leave the house's interior, there was no way for the fragrance to reach him.

That morning, he'd taken the precaution of gathering up

all the paperwork that had to do with the house, especially anything that mentioned his connection to Caleb Bingham, and tucking them in the cabinet's locked drawer. He knew he'd have to get a desk sometime, but the drawer would work for now. He didn't want Rachel to come across the papers and learn he was a direct Bingham descendant. He knew he'd have to tell her sometime, but he'd rather do it his way. He had a feeling it could cause trouble between them.

He made his way slowly back toward the house.

"I suppose you now want something to eat." Maya stood on the porch with her hands planted on her hips.

"I'm surprised you didn't come out earlier." He climbed the steps. "Meet my..." What would he call them? Friends? Co-workers?

She sniffed. "Did you want them to think you had a woman living here with you? I believe you have enough worries without rumors. Besides—" she looked down her nose in a haughty stare "—you are not my type."

Jared bit his cheek to keep from bursting out laughing. He guessed that Maya had been making use of the television during the day.

"You can go on with your work. I will call when your food is ready." She disappeared through the kitchen door.

Jared stared at the large hole he'd made and thought of the French doors he had waiting for him at the building supply store. He'd promised to pick them up before the end of the day. He was lucky they had just what he needed.

"Never mind cooking," he called out. "I've got to go into town and pick something up." He unbuckled his tool belt and allowed it to drop to the floor. He picked up a T-shirt that had been hanging on the railing and pulled it over his head. "I'll get something to eat while I'm there."

The woman suddenly appeared in the doorway. The gleam in her eyes warned him she had a specific request.

"You will bring me a cheeseburger and fries? And a large chocolate shake. And perhaps those onion rings?"

Jared chuckled. "I've corrupted you to fast food. Okay, I'll bring back some lunch for you."

Maya remained on the porch, watching Jared climb into his truck and drive off. She turned her head and studied the destroyed wall. A slow smile warmed her normally stern features.

"Ah, *niña,* for all we know he could find the key in the wall."

Chapter 8

The first thing Rachel noticed that evening when she regained her form was a rich aroma of tomatoes and exotic spices filling the air.

"What did Maya cook for dinner?" she asked herself as she descended the stairs.

She was hesitant about seeing Jared again after the events of the previous night, but she decided to blame it on his drinking. The one thing she couldn't blame on that was her response to the feel of his aroused body against hers and the way his mouth had seduced her. She suddenly shivered as if she were cold, but the last thing she felt was chilly.

When she entered the kitchen she was surprised to find the table set and a large flat box sitting in the middle.

"I tried to time it with sundown," Jared said.

She looked across the room, where he was pulling a bottle of wine out of the refrigerator.

"You can drink wine, can't you?"

"I…guess so. What is this?" She gestured toward the table. She realized the tantalizing aroma came from the box.

He grinned. "It's called pizza. Since I didn't think you'd had pizza before I played it safe and got it with pepperoni and extra cheese."

Her head snapped up. "Does this mean you finally believe me?" She waited for his answer with bated breath. His gesture told her he must believe her, but she still wanted to hear him say the actual words.

Jared took a deep breath. "You have to understand that my life deals with logic, not fantasy."

"I'm not a fantasy," she argued. "I'm…" *What was she?* She lifted her hands in a resigned gesture. "I don't know what I am. I just know when the sun goes down I feel very real."

He slowly nodded. "I'm trying, okay? Believe me, that's a biggie."

Her lips stretched in a smile, then she looked down at the box. "What is pizza?"

"Something you'll like just as much as you like popcorn." He filled a glass with wine the color of rare rubies and brought out a bottle of beer for himself. "Have a seat. And excuse the fingers, but it's the best way to eat pizza." He opened the box and picked up two slices, placing one of them on her plate.

Rachel looked on either side of her plate. "Where is the knife and fork?"

"You use your fingers." He picked up a slice and demonstrated, biting into his thick piece, which was gooey with cheese and topped with spicy pepperoni.

She looked uncertain as she gingerly picked up her own slice and nibbled on the pointed end. Her expression changed to one of intrigue as she nibbled a bit more. She laughed as a string of melted mozzarella cheese stuck to her chin.

"This is very different," she decided.

"Good different or bad different?" he asked, already guessing her answer.

She took another bite and chewed. In no time, she had finished her piece. "Good different. May I have another, please?"

He grinned at her polite manner. "Have all you want. That's why I got an extra-large pizza." He slid a second slice onto her plate.

By the time Rachel finished her fourth piece of pizza she felt pleasantly full, and mellow from the glass of wine she had drunk.

Jared grinned. "When you feel adventurous we'll try my favorite. Canadian bacon and pineapple."

Rachel thought about the combination for a moment, then wrinkled her nose. "I am not sure I will ever be *that* adventurous. But I like this pepperoni." She picked up her wineglass and sipped. "And this wine is very good."

He leaned back in his chair with one arm draped over the back. He looked about as relaxed as a jungle cat.

"I wish I could figure you out," he said finally.

"I have never been complicated," she replied demurely.

Jared slowly shook his head. "Honey, you've complicated my life since day one. And I don't do well with complications."

She felt a strange feeling in her stomach that had nothing to do with the spicy food she'd been eating. Jared admitted he believed her, but she sensed he still had trouble with her story.

"I am sorry that I cannot leave here and uncomplicate your life," she murmured. "I understand why you feel that way, because complicated sounds exactly like my existence."

"That's not what I meant. It's just…" He paused and shook his head, as if whatever thoughts traveling through his head weren't ones he wanted to speak out loud. "It's just that I don't know what to do with you."

"Maybe one day I will disappear completely and not return when evening falls," she said with a flippancy she didn't feel inside. "I can't believe this will go on forever."

Darkness crept into his eyes. "Obviously there's no hard-and-fast rules on curses. Although I would think there would be a loophole. A way to get out of it. Do you remember anything that was said that night?" He didn't want to say which night and she didn't need to ask. Some memories refused to fade with time.

A furious Caleb shouting at her. Standing next to him was the woman who wanted him, her exotic beauty marred by the hatred on her face. She uttered vicious, obscene words that made Rachel's skin crawl. Then pain exploded through her, fiery hot and unrelenting as the knife descended again and again. The woman had stood over her, her dark eyes shining with an unholy fire as she chanted in an unfamiliar language. As Rachel's world turned black, the woman's words reverberated inside her head and seemed to pull her up into a fiery maelstrom filled with unearthly shrieks and screams. To this day, she had no idea if the screams were her own or merely the imagination of a dying woman.

She licked suddenly dry lips. "I have no idea what was said. I didn't understand the language. All I heard was Caleb insisting he wanted me to suffer forever."

"Do you think it could have been Spanish? Or maybe Russian? I know there were Russians living in the area back then."

Rachel thought for a moment, then shook her head. "I don't think it was either. It didn't sound Spanish and definitely not Russian. We had Mexican workers on the land, so I heard their language a lot."

"Would Maya know where this woman came from?" He

wondered why little had been said about the *bruja*. Had she held that much power?

Rachel shook her head again. "She never said anything to me about it. She felt it was best I not remember everything that happened that night."

"But you still remember some things, don't you?" he probed. "You can't help but think back to that night. You must want to know why it happened."

Rachel picked up their plates and carried them to the sink. "I already know why it happened."

He straightened up. "Oh?"

She carefully washed each dish and set it on the drainboard. After she dried her hands she turned around and leaned against the counter.

"My husband murdered me for several reasons. One, I could not bear his touch. In his eyes, that was bad enough, but that I did not give him any children was a sin. I do not know how long the *bruja* lived here before I came. Many of the workers feared her and no one dared say anything against her. I think she enjoyed the way they cringed in terror."

"And she was the one who cursed you," he said.

Rachel nodded. Fractured memories from that night continued to play in her mind's eye. She wished they could have been erased from her memory as easily as the bloodstains had been erased from her clothing. "I do not want to talk about it anymore." She was proud of herself for not breaking down. She'd cried more than her share of tears decades ago. She'd vowed she wouldn't cry again. To date, she'd kept that promise.

"You've never talked about all of it." His voice had lowered to a soft reassuring tone meant to silently urge a witness to talk. "Maybe you should."

Except Rachel had witnessed not only a murder, but her

own murder at that. For self-protection, she had erected walls even someone as stubborn as Jared would have trouble breaking down.

Her head whipped up. Deep violet eyes shot glittering sparks. "How many times have you been wounded, Jared?"

He thought for a moment. "Shot twice, knifed a few times. Kicked in the ba—ah, I've had my share."

"But you didn't die," she stated. "You did not feel the breath leave your body, or feel your skin grow so cold you never thought you would be warm again, or experience the world around you receding to nothing. You did not descend into hell."

Jared's eyes roamed over her. "I can't imagine you even looking at hell, much less visiting it."

Rachel's smile was a far cry from the sunny one she usually graced him with.

"But you did not live here in the 1880s, did you? You have no idea what life was like then."

"So tell me."

Her brow furrowed. She looked as though she was thinking, but then shook her head. "For now I have said enough." She carefully draped the dish towel over the rack near the sink. "Maya will be sorry she missed eating pizza."

He wanted to argue about her change of subject, but he had a pretty good idea she wouldn't be diverted again. He'd already learned that Rachel Bingham had an incredibly stubborn streak inside that soft Southern belle exterior. The cop in him wanted the entire story, but the man hated to do anything that would hurt her further.

The idea that someone could murder her in cold blood was appalling, even if the subject of murder was nothing new to him. He had no reason to push her about the night of her death.

Did he expect her to readily tell him everything? Did he really think she would recount the experience in clinical detail, as if it had happened to someone else?

Okay, there were times he wasn't the smartest guy in the world. He should have known he had to tread carefully with her.

"I wouldn't worry. She had a double cheeseburger with everything on it, a large order of fries, onion rings and a big chocolate shake for lunch," he told her. " Then she took a nap on the couch. The woman snores louder than the dog does."

A corner of Rachel's mouth lifted upward. "Which proves you do like her."

Jared shrugged. "When the lady asks for a cheeseburger, you tend to honor her request."

Rachel looked off into the distance. "You had visitors today. Are they friends of yours?"

"I guess you'd say that. They were two of the detectives I work with."

"I know women work as police officers because I have seen them on your television, but she is the first one I have seen in person. She is beautiful."

Jared grinned. "We won't tell Goldilocks that. She'll get a swelled head. It would only inflate her ego," he clarified.

"Her name is Goldilocks?" Rachel smiled. "Such as with the three bears?"

"It's just a nickname I call her. Her name is Celeste Dante. Her family has lived here for a few generations and racked up a nice bankroll. She could have been a real social butterfly, but she wanted to be a cop. She and her partner investigate domestic crimes. Family abuse." His tight jaw explained it well enough. "She may look like a cream puff, but she's pure steel inside."

"You admire her a great deal," Rachel said softly.

"Yeah, I guess I do, but I wouldn't say that to her or her husband. Celeste and Luc are used to my tough-guy image."

Rachel nodded. "What are you doing to the wall in the parlor?"

"It's called a family room now," he reminded her. "I didn't like the wall and decided I needed a new one."

She shook her head at his flippant answer. "But with it open, I would think you would worry that animals could come in at night."

"I covered it tightly with a plastic tarp," he said. "It should keep any late-night visitors out."

Rachel started to say something else, but her gaze skated past the window as a faint flicker of light caught her attention.

"What's wrong?" He noticed the change in her expression.

"I see light out in the barn." She leaned over the counter to get a better look through the window. "Jared, there's someone out there!"

He was out of his chair in a flash to peer through the window. He muttered a curse and ran out the door.

"Your gun!" she shouted after him, but he was already gone. "You cannot go out there unarmed!"

Rachel ran back to the kitchen counter and leaned over it, almost pressing her face against the glass so she could see better. Her breath caught in her throat as she watched Jared run toward the barn, with Harley on his heels. The young dog's excited barks were clearly audible.

"Be careful," she whispered.

Rachel rose up on to her tiptoes when she saw Jared stealthily approach the barn. He paused near the door, then moved faster as a faint, ominous light appeared. With the light, she could only see shadows, and worried that none of it looked good for Jared. When he disappeared into the barn she started to fear the worst. She was positive he shouldn't be out there by himself, even with Harley.

"No!" She pushed herself away from the counter and instinctively ran for the doorway. She had barely reached it when she was rudely bounced backward as if someone had roughly pushed her. She squealed with fright as she fell onto the floor with a painful thump. "Jared!" she cried, feeling helpless and frustrated at her inability to help him.

As he ran for the barn, Jared heard muffled sounds from inside the building. He put a hand out toward Harley and was amazed when the dog immediately slowed down and stopped barking, but remained at his side.

Jared mentally chastised himself for leaving his weapon inside the house. He felt the comforting weight of his knife in the sheath tucked inside his boot, and was relieved he wasn't completely unarmed.

"Can't you get that thing to light?" he heard one man growl.

Jared's blood ran cold as he easily guessed their intentions. If they set the barn on fire, it would be easy for a spark to reach the house. He wasn't worried for himself, but what would happen to Rachel and Maya if the place caught fire? He crouched down and crept along the side of the large building.

"What about his bike? We're not going to leave it in here, are we?" The voice sounded familiar. "That's a sweet ride. I wouldn't mind having it."

Jared's lips lifted in a silent snarl. *You touch my bike and we're going to do some serious talking.* He moved faster.

When he looked around the door, which had been left ajar, he saw two men standing in the shadows of a stall. One held a lighter, while another was hovering over Jared's Harley. Both men wore ski masks.

"How many times were you kids told not to play with matches?" he drawled, sauntering across the barn's threshold. "That's a good way to get hurt. Now give them over before you burn yourselves."

The two men swiftly turned around.

"Oh, I see, masks. Sorry, guys, Halloween is some months off," Jared continued. "Next, you'll be hanging toilet paper over the house. Now why don't you two run along home before someone gets hurt." Steel crept into his voice. "And it won't be me."

The man standing by Jared's motorcycle turned to his friend as if asking him what to do. The other one slowly circled, so they were on either side of Jared. The one standing by the motorcycle seemed to make up his mind and suddenly rushed forward.

"I should have known you'd do that," Jared muttered, burying his fist in his attacker's stomach. Air rushed out of the man's mouth and he dropped to his knees. When the second man made his move, Jared turned off all emotion and just fought, down and dirty. He ignored the pain in his skinned knuckles when they connected with one man's face. Harley grabbed hold of that assailant's jeans and hung on as the other man stumbled to his feet and ran off. A moment later, Jared heard the rumble of a motorcycle. He turned back as the first man struck the dog with a stick, to get him to let go.

"You really don't learn, do you." Jared grabbed the stick and, when the man lashed out at him, knocked him unconscious. He was breathing hard as he reached down and pulled off the ski mask. He wasn't surprised to see it was one of the men he'd caught teasing Harley. The young dog growled as if he remembered that day, as well.

"No way I can leave you out here. Your buddy might decide to come back." Grunting, Jared grabbed hold of the man's legs and started pulling him out of the barn. When he reached the house, he dug out a rope and tied the man to a post at the base of the steps. "Don't worry about getting home," he told the still unconscious intruder. "I'll have someone pick you up."

Rachel sat on the floor and thought of the curses Jared shouted when he dropped the hammer on his foot. She wanted to shout them herself and was ready to do just that and rush the doorway again when the door opened.

"Those idiots just made it way too personal," Jared growled, stalking into the kitchen. He stopped short at the sight of her sprawled on the floor. "Rachel, why are you on the floor? What happened? Are you okay?" He held out his hands and pulled her to her feet.

"You are all right!" She threw herself into his arms. She leaned back for a second to study his face, gasping at the sight of a rapidly blooming black eye and abrasions on his cheek, and on his chest where his T-shirt was ripped. "No, you are not!" She gently touched her fingertip to the bruise around his eye. She winced the same time he did. "I tried to go outside," she cried. "But I could not!"

"It's okay, baby. I'm fine," he assured her. He smiled gently and brushed her cheek with the back of his knuckles, then pressed a kiss against her forehead. He reached around her and grabbed up his cell phone from the kitchen table.

"What happened?" she demanded, running her hands over his chest as if she needed to convince herself he was still in one piece. "Who was out there? What were they doing?"

"Two lamebrains tried to set the barn on fire," he said grimly. "One of them got away, but the other is outside waiting for his ride to jail. I know I've seen this guy before. He was one of the goons I chased off the property for teasing Harley. I'm going to assume his friend was with that gang, too." He punched out a series of numbers. "I may have to put the county sheriff's office on speed dial," he muttered. He kept one arm around her shoulders.

"It's Jared Stryker out at the Diamond B Ranch up on Cypress Road," he said into the phone. "I've got a prospective arsonist available for pickup." He chuckled. "He may not be gift wrapped, but he's definitely tied up with a nice fat bow.... Okay, thanks." He tossed the phone back onto the table, then looked down at Rachel. "I have to get back outside. I've got this guy tied up just outside the door, but I don't want to take any chances on his getting loose."

She clutched his shirt at the idea of his being out there alone with a man who'd tried to hurt him and another still running free. "What if his friend comes back and attacks you again?"

"If he's smart, he won't. But this time I'll be better prepared if he does show up again." Jared walked into the other room and unlocked his gun cabinet. He pulled out his Glock and checked it. When he walked back through the kitchen he paused long enough to capture a stray curl and tuck it behind her ear. He gazed into her eyes. "Are you all right?"

She smiled at his evident concern. "Other than feeling scared, yes, I am all right. But that needs to be cleaned." She lightly touched a cut bisecting his eyebrow.

"Later." He took her hand and kissed her fingertips. At the sound of a siren, he grimaced. "I hate to say this, but you might be better off to go upstairs and stay out of sight."

The smile that had bloomed when he kissed her fingers dimmed just as quickly.

"It would be hard to explain you," he said swiftly. "If they think you're a witness they'll want to question you, and the first thing they'd do is ask for your ID. You don't have any."

Rachel looked confused. "ID?"

"Identification. It usually means a driver's license or social security card."

"Oh." She nodded. "You are right, I will go upstairs."

Jared stayed long enough to make sure she did so before he headed outside. A county sheriff's patrol car pulled into the yard and a woman wearing a khaki uniform stepped out. Short dark hair peeked out from under her neatly aligned hat.

"Are you Stryker? I'm Deputy Sheriff Wright."

"Yep." He kept his hands in sight with his detective's shield held high in one hand so she could easily see it. "I've got my weapon on me."

She looked him up and down. "I've heard about you." She sounded as if she liked what she'd heard and definitely appreciated what she saw. She looked past him toward the unconscious man tied to the porch railing. "I understand you have a present for us."

Jared nodded. "I checked for ID but couldn't find any. Does he look familiar to you?" He purposely didn't say he'd seen the man before. He wanted to keep that information to himself for a little while. At least until he could figure out what was going on.

She took her flashlight from her belt and shone the beam on the man's face. He stirred and moaned. "No, but I wouldn't be surprised if someone at the station doesn't know who your little friend is. You said this was arson?"

Jared nodded. "I discovered that he and his buddy, who got away, were getting ready to start a fire in my barn. Luckily, the rags they used were damp, so it didn't do much more than smolder. They didn't like that I interrupted their fun and games. I also noticed the smell of chemicals on his clothing. Chemicals that have nothing to do with fires."

She nodded in understanding, since she'd busted more than her share of meth labs found in the area. Because they didn't need a lot of space, they were usually found in mobile homes or abandoned buildings. "Still, it's a good thing you saw the fire. They might have tried to help it along, since it wasn't going the way they hoped." She raised her flashlight and shone it on his face. "Looks like they got a few licks in before you got the best of them."

"I wanted them to feel manly." He grinned, a fact he promptly regretted when the torn skin at his eyebrow burned.

Deputy Wright untied the man and expertly snapped handcuffs on him. "Come on, Sleeping Beauty," she crooned. "We have a lovely room in our dungeon set aside just for you."

"Okay if I wait until morning to come out and sign the complaint?" Jared asked.

"Sure. He won't be going anywhere." She managed to wrestle the groggy man into the back of her vehicle. "So you're living out here full time now?" She looked up at the torn-up wall covered with a heavy plastic sheet.

"Yeah. I thought I'd fix up the old place and start acting like a landowner." He grinned.

She looked at her back seat. "Can you do us a favor and not have all your little friends over at once? We like it quiet out here," she said.

"You don't need to worry about me. I'm living the life of a monk."

The deputy sheriff looked skeptical at his flippant remark. She drove off with her punch-drunk prisoner sprawled in the back seat.

Jared remained outside until the patrol car's taillights disappeared from sight.

He thought of the two men he'd encountered at the barn. He was positive at one point he'd heard Rachel's voice inside his head, and had turned, barely avoiding a nasty crack to the skull from one thug going after him with a shovel. Jared was positive this time around he'd left more damage on them than they had on him. He just wished he could have caught the other bastard.

As he neared the kitchen door he recalled the sight of Rachel sprawled on the floor when he had walked in. She'd told him before that she couldn't leave the house, yet even so she'd tried to run out to help him.

He shook his head. "There has to be a way to break that curse."

But what would happen to Rachel if the curse was broken? Would she disappear for good?

He didn't want to think of that possibility.

Jared was the first to admit women weren't something he knew much about. The females who had passed in and out of his life may have been all-woman, but they didn't have the innate femininity that Rachel, Lea and Celeste displayed.

A part of him wanted to protect Rachel. He wanted to give her the security she had sought in her marriage and never received. Another part wanted to strip off that old-fashioned dress and show her something else he guessed she'd missed out on. He'd bet everything he had that she'd never experienced true physical pleasure. He only had to see the pictures of the grim-featured Caleb Bingham to figure out the man would have only sought his own release in bed, with no interest in pleasing a partner.

Rachel was different from any woman he'd been with before. As the days went by he couldn't imagine a future without her.

"You're lucky you're dead, Caleb," he muttered to himself. "Otherwise, you'd think whatever was done to you back then was a picnic compared to what I'd do to you now."

He walked into the family room and looked up the stairs.

"It's okay, Rachel. You can come down now."

She appeared at the top of the stairs and looked down. "The police are gone?" she asked in her soft voice.

"Our uninvited guest has been picked up by the local taxi service."

"Is that your way of saying the man has been arrested?" she asked.

He grinned. "Most definitely. He won't be bothering us for a while."

As he looked up at her, he felt an aching in his chest. The light on the landing created a golden aura around her slender figure. She disappeared into the bathroom, then came out holding a cloth, and descended the stairs with her gliding step.

"An angel," he murmured.

"You could have been badly hurt," she told him, pushing him none too gently into a chair. Then she carefully wiped his face with the warm wet washcloth. "There were two of them against only one of you."

"Those odds weren't all that bad. I've taken on more than two and made it out in one piece." He raised a hand with the intention of gently but firmly pushing her away and informing her he didn't need to be looked after like some kid who came in off the playground with skinned knees. He normally didn't like women fussing over him, but it felt different when Rachel was doing the fussing.

At this rate, I'll soon be getting those warm fuzzy feelings and walking around with an idiotic smile on my face.

He looked up and saw concern etching faint lines across her forehead and around her eyes.

"I'm okay," he said softly, placing his hand on her arm to halt her ministrations. "I've had much worse."

Her lower lip trembled, then firmed as if she struggled to contain her emotions.

"I know."

Her whisper might as well have been a shout.

Jared's body stilled. "Of course you do," he whispered, as much to himself as to her. "At night you would have been hiding somewhere upstairs anytime someone broke into the house. The kids didn't go upstairs because they figured the ghosts were up there. They all bragged they were coming out here to find Caleb's ghost, but they didn't do anything that would press their luck. They felt they'd already done their part just by breaking into the haunted house. Lots of initiations went on out here." He kept his eyes on her face. "Face down the ghost at the Bingham ranch. Light candles and say old Caleb's name three times. Scare your girlfriends and make them think you're protecting them. Or…" his smile grew dark "…come out here to a house that might supposedly be haunted, but where you still felt safer than you did in your own house. Even facing down old Caleb wouldn't be as scary as the devil in your family."

"You were nine or ten," she whispered as an old memory surfaced. "Your pants were torn and so was your shirt. You had a bruise on your cheek and your nose was bleeding."

His jaw looked as if it had been carved from granite and his eyes deepened to a dark shade of gold as old memories attacked him. His hand dropped from her arm as if it had been burned. She was forced to step back as he stood up.

"I guess I asked for that." He looked down at her with a black expression that hinted at his own long buried emotions.

"You have memories you don't want resurrected, just as I have mine. Perhaps now you understand more why I feel the way I do. Why I prefer keeping some things to myself." She still had the cloth clutched in one hand. She turned away. "Good night, Jared."

He watched her slowly climb the stairs.

He thought of calling her back. He thought of going up after her.

But then what? He had to remind himself that she wasn't real. That for all he knew she wouldn't be there tomorrow night because the curse would somehow be lifted.

The army had taught Jared to make an orderly life for himself. There was nothing fancy and nothing that held any surprises. He didn't consider the homicide cases he investigated surprises. That was something he understood. Someone was murdered. He combed through evidence and clues. If he did his homework, he found the murderer, and if the courts did their job, the murderer was brought to justice.

As he thought, no surprises. All in order.

Except Rachel Bingham was an unexpected force in his life.

He'd never believed in taking the easy road. It seemed lately that he'd been climbing a pretty high mountain instead of driving a nice flat highway. Everything that had gone on lately was proof of that.

To make matters worse, he had fallen for a woman he could never have.

Chapter 9

Jared used his T-shirt to wipe the sweat from his face before he picked up the water bottle he'd set on the railing. He looked at the brand-new French doors, which looked as if they had been there all along.

"They make it seem too easy on television," he muttered. He glanced down and sighed. "Harley, stop that digging!" The dog looked up from his efforts, then returned to his job as canine earthmover. "Damn dog is going to dig holes all over the yard. You better not dig any holes after I put grass in or you're going to find yourself inside your very own personal fenced-in yard," he threatened.

The pup didn't look too worried about his master's idle threat.

"You are doing this for my *niña,* are you not?"

"I only do things for myself." He glanced at Maya as a thought occurred to him. "Have you been drinking my beer? The bottles sure seem to disappear a lot more lately."

She made a face. "Modern beer is not as strong as the beer in my time. It does not do as well in my stews as I would like, but I do what I can."

His jaw dropped. "You put perfectly good beer in stew?"

She looked smug. "You said my stew is the best you have ever had. That it always tastes wonderful."

"Sure, it tastes good, but it can't be because you put beer in it."

"I say it is." She turned around, then froze. She quickly walked down the steps and stopped at the base. She bent down and fingered the fragrant jasmine bushes that Jared had planted on each side of the steps that morning. When she looked up, her eyes glistened. "The hole you made in the wall now looks very nice with the fancy doors, but you made a lot of dust I had to sweep up. But I forgive you because of these." She touched a glossy green leaf. "You did all of this for my *niña*, Rachel." A sense of wonder and emotion thickened her voice.

Jared was surprised by her emotional reaction. He wasn't used to the older woman revealing her inner feelings. The idea of tough-as-nails Maya getting emotional frankly scared the hell out of him.

She climbed the steps and stopped in front of him, cupping his cheek with her work-worn hand.

"You have a good heart, Señor Stryker," she said in her rough voice. "You are a gift from the gods."

"Does that mean you don't want to cut it out today?" He hoped to stave off any threat of tears.

She smiled slightly. "You are spared for another day." She moved away and went back into the house.

Jared shook his head in bewilderment. "No wonder they say women can make a man nuts. You never know what they're going to say or do next."

He turned back to his task. His day had started early with a trip to the county sheriff's department, where he gave his statement. He wasn't surprised to hear the man he'd captured had a lengthy record that included assault and battery, robbery, drug dealing and arson. Rumor also had it that he was associated with thugs suspected of running a meth lab.

While he liked Deputy Wright's no-nonsense manner, he decided he didn't like Sheriff Mills at all. He easily saw that the pompous man preferred to hide behind his deputies' good work and take the credit when it was due and blame them for his own mistakes.

Jared was grateful to leave the tiny sheriff's station and return home.

He looked down to see Maya outside again, crouching by the bushes. She carried a pot in one hand and carefully poured water around each bush.

"They need water," she scolded.

"I need to get back to police work," he told her. "It's a hell of a lot easier."

"You need to find the other man who hurt you and discover why he wanted to burn your barn. Then you can return to your police work."

Jared watched the old woman tending the bushes. "Tell me something. Do you see things at night the way Rachel sees things during the day? She says she feels as if she's in a cloud."

Maya shook her head. "My time at night is a sense of nothingness. The first thing I saw this morning was your face. Not that anyone could hurt it more. Also, do you realize when those big fancy doors are open we will have flies coming into the house as if they were invited?"

"She gives with one hand, smacks me upside the head with

the other," he muttered, then chuckled at her outrage. "That's what screens are there for. Welcome to the twenty-first century." He carefully closed the doors and opened them. A squeaky hinge was taken care of with a squirt of oil. He rolled his muscles, feeling the aches and pains along with the fatigue from too little sleep. After Maya went back inside the house, Jared wondered if it might not be good idea to sleep on the couch with his weapon close at hand. He'd hate to have anyone try to break into the house.

He walked inside and tried the doors again. The difference was incredible, with more light in the formerly dark room and a sense of the outdoors.

He looked up when a familiar patrol car slowly rolled up the drive. He muttered a few choice curses under his breath. The last thing he wanted was more uninvited company.

Deputy Wright climbed out of the car. She stooped to pat Harley, who had ambled up to greet her.

"Where was your guard dog last night?" she called out.

"I put him in the house when I called the station," he replied. "I didn't expect to see you again this soon."

She shrugged off his less than polite greeting. "I meant to say something when you were in the station. I thought I'd take a look at the barn. See if I could pick up any prints. Have you been in there since last night?"

"Only long enough to make sure they hadn't touched my bike," he replied.

"Then you don't mind if I look around in there?"

"Not at all. Go ahead." Realizing she was focusing on his bare chest a little too much, he casually picked up his T-shirt to slip over his head, until he realized it was too grimy to put back on.

"Engle refused to give up his buddy," she told him. "He

claimed he was working alone. He said you must have been drunk if you thought you saw two men in there. Then he asked for a lawyer. He's going to be arraigned tomorrow. I guess you know he's pretty ticked off at you. If he makes bail, he and his friend just might come around again to even the score."

"And here I was going to invite them to the housewarming," he said lightly.

She didn't smile. "The next time it might be your house, and they'll be sure not to use damp rags."

"I'll make certain there's always fresh batteries in my smoke alarms," he told her.

She looked around, noted the new French doors and the bushes planted nearby. She turned back to him. "Don't you ever sleep?"

"I only have so much vacation time before I return to work, and I wanted to get as much done as possible. If you find out anything more, will you let me know?"

"Sure thing." She cocked her head. "Stories say there's a treasure hidden somewhere out here. Maybe they were looking for that, although I guess if they were doing so they wouldn't have tried to burn down your barn."

"Considering how old it is, they probably thought they were doing me a favor. As for treasure, the only thing I've found out here are rusty nails and ancient horse droppings. I always figured it was another story, along with the ghosts," he said easily.

"No wonder we always had to roust kids off the property," Deputy Wright said, looking up at the house. "At least with you living out here, that should be one less headache for us."

"We can hope," he agreed.

She nodded, climbed back into her vehicle and drove around the house toward the outbuildings.

The next time they might try burning down your house with you in it.

Icy fingers of dread traveled down Jared's spine at the deputy's ominous words. He wasn't worried about himself—he knew he could make a run for it. But what about Rachel and Maya? Rachel was literally imprisoned within the house. Would burning it down destroy her completely? While Maya could physically leave the building during the daylight hours, would she be able to escape during the night, when she was invisible the way Rachel was during the day?

He knew he had no experience in this area. He doubted even a ghost hunter could tell him what was possible.

"Thanks, Wright, for pretty much ruining my morning," he muttered as he picked up his tools and put them to one side before he went into the house.

He winced at the headache-causing sound of pots and pans clanging in the kitchen. And winced again when he realized the television was set to a morning talk show, where women were candidly discussing the lack of sex in their relationships, with no holds barred when going on to say where the men went wrong.

"That's a hell of a lot more than I wanted to know." He looked into the kitchen. "I guess you would tell the women to put some nasty mojo on their men."

"What is mojo?" Maya rolled the word around in her mouth as if she was experimenting with the way it sounded.

"Voodoo." He realized she wasn't familiar with that word, either. "Black magic."

She looked horrified. "Dark magic is never good. It will consume you until you are as dark and horrible as the magic you think you control. Except it controls you until you are nothing more than an empty shell."

Jared tipped his head to one side. "So that's what happened to Caleb? He went over to the dark side?" He made a mental note to dig out his *Star Wars* DVDs. He had an idea Maya would enjoy the science fiction adventure films. He noticed she'd avidly watched all the *Lethal Weapon* movies.

The woman lifted her chin in a haughty manner Jared was becoming all too familiar with. For a moment he felt as if he was facing the queen of an ancient land or perhaps the priestess of an even more ancient religion.

There was something in her expression that had him thinking of Rachel. Not that it took much for him to think about her.

"What did you do to Caleb, Maya?" he asked softly. He knew Rachel could sense people around her, but he wasn't sure how much she could hear, and this was one conversation he didn't want her eavesdropping on.

For a moment the woman's eyes shone, hinting at the secrets within. For the first time, she unnerved him.

"There can be punishment exacted against those who deserve it," she said in just as soft a voice. "No one deserved it more than Señor Caleb. I asked my gods to avenge what he did to Señora Rachel. They did as I asked."

He could feel his stomach tightening. He was finally hearing more of the real story. "The article in the newspaper back then said he was literally torn apart."

She smiled. "He was not a good man. He was a demon who had to be destroyed. Someone like him could not have been allowed to live. Even before my Rachel came here, he took many young women to his bed and he enjoyed hurting them. He whipped anyone who talked bad about him. He liked to see people in pain, because he thought that made them fear him. And if they were afraid of him, they would work even harder, praying he wouldn't hurt them anymore." Her nostrils flared as she spoke. "He deserved what happened to him." Every fiber of her being showed that she didn't regret the score she'd settled in a horrific way so many years ago.

Jared sensed the scars Maya carried were physical as well as emotional.

"Maya, my love, I'm glad you're on my side. I'm going up to take a shower." He was halfway up the stairs when he paused and looked over his shoulder. "When you're…wherever you go at night, do you…?" He feared he looked as uncomfortable as he felt voicing the questions in his head.

Maya looked suspicious. "Do I what?"

"I take a lot of showers at night and—"

A corner of her mouth lifted. "I told you before. You are not my type."

"Right. Sure." He pointed his finger at her. "Okay, I'm going to clean up." He started back up the stairs.

"That does not mean that Rachel might not look when you bathe in the daytime."

Jared promptly tripped over his feet. He swore loudly as he caught himself and ran up the stairs to the sound of Maya's laughter.

Since Jared moved into the house, Rachel had made sure to be in one of the upstairs bedrooms when sundown came, just as she now ensured she was alone at sunrise. The only time she'd erred was that one morning when she'd stayed up all night with Jared.

She took care not to let it happen again.

She wondered what he had been doing the past few days. He'd worked like a man demented as he destroyed almost half the wall. She'd hovered in the room those days, watching him work. She especially enjoyed watching him after he took his shirt off.

Rachel thought that Jared had a body better than any picture of a Greek god she'd seen. The hard muscles in his arms and chest had her thinking of a man meant to protect a woman. Not hurt her.

If I cannot find the key inside the house, he might be able to find it outside, niña. He could have been sent to us to help.

Over the years Rachel had come to the conclusion that the key and the treasure were two more fabrications of Caleb's. He'd enjoyed his cruel jokes, and the idea that she would spend eternity looking for a nonexistent key would have amused him to no end.

She stopped in front of the mirror and took down her hair to brush it and put it back up in a loose knot. She'd been grateful when, one day, she'd found a brush and comb sitting on a small chest. The brush wasn't silver with boar bristles like the one she'd had before, and the comb seemed smaller, but she discovered they did what she needed. She knew Jared had left them for her, and that made the gift all the more special.

She studied her reflection in the mirror set up on the chest. She looked as she had more than a hundred twenty years ago.

As a child she had wished for eyes like everyone else's. The children she'd grown up with had all had blue or brown eyes. She remembered a few with green eyes, but she knew no one else who had eyes the color of dark violets. She'd once asked Pastor Davis and his wife the color of her mother's and father's eyes. The saintly couple had looked horrified at the question and urged her to never voice it again. They'd informed her in cold tones it was best she not even think of the people who had created her. It was best she think of making her life a righteous one. After that, she'd never asked again. What little she gleaned from unashamedly eavesdropping on conversations during the Ladies Missionary League meetings held in the church basement had her believing her parents had consorted with the devil. The few young men who showed interest in her never came courting after their fathers informed them they were better off not romancing a girl who had no proper family. When Pastor Davis told her her Christian duty was to do the right thing and become a teacher, she gladly took the position in hope of saving enough money to leave Atlanta and go to a place where no one knew her and she could have a fresh start.

Rachel always thought it ironic that while the townspeople didn't think she was good enough to marry their sons, she was good enough to teach their children.

Perhaps that was why she'd jumped at the chance of marrying Caleb. For once a man wasn't put off by her lack of family history. Instead, he'd woven tales of a land where an individual mattered more than family background. What she didn't know was that the minister and his wife, people who supposedly deplored lies, stretched the truth more than a little by spinning a tale about a poor orphaned plantation owner's daughter who'd lost everything during the War of Northern Aggression. They'd told him about a young woman of good breeding who taught because she wanted to work with children until she married and had a large family of her own. Rachel saw her marriage as her chance for a new beginning. She just didn't expect a deadly ending to it.

She smoothed her hands down the front of her dress, ironing out nonexistent wrinkles. It had been a long time since she'd wished she had something else to wear. While she never suffered from feminine vanity, the idea of wearing a pretty dress appealed to her as it hadn't in years. But she knew it wasn't to be. While Maya's gods granted her a bloodstain-free dress for eternity, they hadn't thought to give her a change of wardrobe.

She decided it was time to forget about herself, and picked up one of the three books lying on the chest.

Property of Sierra Vista Public Library was stamped on the inside cover.

Sierra Vista—Its Past and Present.

Faded photographs from her time period stared back at her.

A sense of loss washed over her as she looked at pictures of a town once familiar to her, until Caleb decided she wasn't allowed to go visiting. She closed the book and put it back, noticing the other two books also dealt with local history.

She knew Jared had left these for her, too.

When she'd first sorted through his reading material, she'd found only magazines about guns or motorcycles. Lately, magazines meant for women, as well as history books, had shown up. She smiled at his thoughtfulness.

Rachel felt an awareness of Jared that puzzled her. She had read enough magazines to understand that after the way Caleb treated her, it would be understandable for her to feel fear around men.

She had been wary of Jared in the beginning because of the darkness she felt that surrounded him. That he had the ability to rein in his temper impressed her. She understood that while Jared had the look of a man who lived with violence, he didn't embrace it as Caleb had.

Over time she'd dropped the habit of thinking of Caleb Bingham as her husband. She knew a husband wouldn't have treated his wife, the woman he had promised God he would love, honor and cherish, the way Caleb had. He wouldn't have brutally murdered her because he felt she was inadequate. Rachel preferred to think of him as a frightening chapter in her life that was best kept closed.

Especially now, when she was experiencing feelings for

Jared that left her…unsettled. Feelings that she knew could never be realized, since she had no future to give him.

She didn't think ghosts were supposed to have feelings or experience emotions—unless it was the need for revenge.

It was a shame no one told her that because she had fallen in love with Jared Stryker—even though she knew it was a love already doomed.

"What if there really is a key?" she murmured. "What if there is the slightest chance for me to have what I didn't have before?"

As always, there weren't any answers to the question she had asked so many times.

Jared knew the second when the sun dropped behind the horizon. He had become so attuned to the rhythms of the house that he felt a shift of energy within the building, as if the air itself changed as Maya disappeared and Rachel returned.

He felt a stirring of anticipation at Rachel's reaction when she viewed the French doors for the first time. He'd left them open to allow the cool evening air to flow inside the house, bringing with it the faintest hint of jasmine from the new shrubs. This time, he knew the scent wasn't warning him of Rachel's approach. He could hear her moving around upstairs. He stood at the open doors, looking out onto the drive that led to the road.

A faint electric sensation skating across the surface of his skin warned him he was no longer alone.

"Oh, Jared." Her voice was breathless with wonder.

He didn't turn around, but felt her move to stand beside him. He'd made sure to stand far enough back from the threshold.

He turned his head to look down at her. Tears glittered on her eyelashes. Even with no makeup on her face, she looked beautiful. Gazing at Rachel, he understood the term natural beauty.

"They make the room look larger, don't they?" he said, more pleased by her reaction than feeling pride in his handiwork. "You didn't believe in big windows back then, did you?"

"Glass was too expensive," she murmured.

She reached out as if to attempt to walk through the doors, but drew her hand back before it could be rejected. She suddenly laughed.

"Jasmine! I smell jasmine!" She stood up on her tiptoes so she could look outside, and saw the tops of the bushes planted at the foot of the steps. "But my bushes died from lack of care years ago." Her laughter was a mix between surprise and pleasure.

"The nice thing about nurseries is that they carry all sorts of flowers and plants and bushes," he said. "We have a nursery in town that's owned by a cranky old woman and her son, but she carries a good assortment. She's familiar with the property here. She suggested I might want to plant trees for a windbreak along the drive. Claimed she'd give me a good price." He winced at the memory of Mrs. Crandall's idea of a good price.

Rachel nodded. She looked pensive. "There were trees lining the drive, but over the years they died from neglect, just as my flowers did."

Jared shifted uncomfortably at the idea of planting flowers. Lea's teasing remarks about gardens and white picket fences were becoming all too real.

"But these beautiful doors. This is what you have been doing. This is why you have practically gone without sleep." Her eyes shone brightly. "Thank you."

"You have so little, yet you've never complained," he said awkwardly. "I thought if you couldn't go outside I'd try to bring some of it inside to you."

Rachel practically danced on her toes as she carefully inspected the white painted doors.

Jared winced when she got a little too close to the threshold and suddenly appeared to be bumped backward, as if an unseen hand pushed her. He saw distress shadow her eyes momentarily, then she seemed to shake it off. She lifted her head, threw her shoulders back and pasted a smile on her lips.

"Maya seems to think I'm not very good with plants," he said in an attempt to divert her from realizing she'd never be able to move past the doorway. "She said she'll take care of the jasmine bushes for you."

Rachel nodded. "She has a magic touch with flowers. I would think a plant was truly gone and she always found a way to bring it back and make it bloom." Rachel spun around to face him, her hands clasped in front of her. "Saying thank you isn't enough."

"You already thanked me," he reminded her.

Her smile didn't leave her lips. Joy seemed to bubble up inside her and reach out to Jared. "I did, didn't I?" She moved slowly toward him. "But I still feel that just saying the words doesn't seem enough for a gift this glorious."

Hope rose up inside him. "It doesn't, huh?"

She nodded. She stopped in front of him, the hem of her dress swirling around his boots.

"Maya had the television on this afternoon while she cleaned the room," she told him.

Jared had no idea why Rachel suddenly brought this up, but as he watched her sparkling eyes and smiling lips, he realized he didn't care. All that mattered was that his efforts gave her this much happiness.

"Yes, I see she's discovered talk shows," he said.

"And something else." Rachel fairly bubbled. "So I know exactly how to say thank you."

Jared wasn't prepared for her to grab hold of the front of his shirt and pull him to her. But he wasn't about to object when her lips fastened on his and heat immediately exploded inside him.

What the hell kind of program had she watched that afternoon?

Chapter 10

Jared Stryker didn't believe in not taking advantage of a good thing when it came his way. Especially when the best thing to ever come into his life was kissing him as if her life depended on it. He wasted no time in wrapping his arms around her and pulling her hard against him. She was a perfect fit.

He wasn't sure if the jasmine scent was coming from Rachel or had drifted in from the bushes outside. Then he wondered why it even mattered—as long as Rachel was in his arms and she was kissing him like a dream come true.

She was so slight of build that she felt like a feather resting against him. The heavy cotton fabric of her dress was slightly rough against his palms, but what mattered to him was the woman inside the dress. Out of habit he ran his hand down her back, searching for a zipper, but he only found fabric. That was when he realized he wouldn't find one.

Jared transferred his attention to her face. He cupped it with his hands, his fingers tangling in her hair as he studied her smiling features. He noted the contrast between his sun-bronzed skin and her own luminous pearl-like complexion.

If the guys at the station knew I just compared a woman's skin to a pearl they'd be laughing so hard they'd split themselves open, he thought.

"What are you thinking about?" Rachel asked in a breathless voice.

"You." He liked how her face lit up when he told her she was on his mind.

She rewarded him with another kiss.

Jared smiled at the naive way she kissed, with her closed lips slightly pursed. Her hands rested lightly on his forearms.

"Open your mouth a little," he whispered.

Confusion clouded her eyes. "Why?" she asked, at the same time Jared showed her. A soft "oh!" escaped her lips as his tongue slipped inside.

Puzzling thoughts kept racing through his head.

If Rachel was a ghost, why did she feel so real in his arms? How come she tasted like the best thing to come from heaven?

But she couldn't be a dream because there was no way he could ever conjure up a woman as perfect as her. Plus, if she was nothing more than a dream, would she have come to him like this? Could she have kissed him so sweetly?

Jared didn't think of himself as any prize, but that hadn't stopped women from coming on to him in the past. He knew some chose him because they considered a man wearing a badge a turn-on. Others thought his bad-boy-on-the-road-to-hell image was a real turn-on. But none of those women had ever bothered to look at the man below the surface. None of them cared for more than a night, sometimes two, of hot sex.

And because he knew how they felt, he hadn't allowed himself to feel anything more for them. It was easier to just walk away and not run the risk of being hurt.

But this was different. He sensed that Rachel saw *all* of him. *Into* him. The idea that she had delved below the surface was frightening to him. With good reason, he'd kept a good part of himself hidden away, yet somehow she'd found her way in. As a result, he knew he would do whatever was necessary to keep her safe. But for now, he wanted her to just plain feel.

He heard the moan travel up her throat as his tongue stroked her lips. The soft sound seemed to vibrate across her lips. He tasted surprise and desire there. He felt that same surprise move through her body, and was glad to know he could affect her that way.

She suddenly pulled away and took a step back. Her eyes were wide and a darker purple than usual.

"Oh my," she breathed, staring at him in surprise. She had no idea how desirable she looked with strands released from the neat coil of hair pinned to the top of her head, giving her a slightly disheveled look instead of her usual prim appearance. Her lips were moist from their kisses and her cheeks flushed a dark rose color, while her eyes were ablaze with sensual awareness.

He'd say the lady was turned on and liking it. He'd also bet this was something very new to her, which amazed him because he could see that Rachel was one very sexy lady once she allowed herself to give in to it. He intended to see how far that would go.

"Yeah," he agreed with a broad grin as he reached for her again.

Rachel didn't hesitate in returning to the circle of his arms and lifting her face to his. Jared didn't waste any time in taking up her unspoken invitation.

"Please tell me that Maya can't see anything we're doing," he murmured against her lips.

"She once told me she feels as if she's fallen into a deep sleep until morning arrives." Rachel's smile seemed to imprint itself on his skin.

"Good, because I'd hate to have her smack me come morning because she thought I'd seduced her little darling." He maneuvered Rachel over to the couch until the back of her knees connected with the edge, and she dropped down onto the cushions.

She laughed as her skirt flew up to reveal a lacy froth of petticoats, a hint of stocking and the tantalizing glimpse of a slender foot in a black leather shoe.

"It seems like the TV is turning you into a twenty-first century woman. So tell me what kind of shows you've been watching to turn you into this wild child," Jared demanded, leaning over her with a hand planted on the cushions on either side of her hips.

Rachel didn't look overwhelmed or act wary at his closeness. She placed her hand against the soft cotton of his shirt as if she couldn't stop herself from touching him, which was true. She didn't think she ever wanted to stop touching him.

"I gather they are called soap operas."

Jared laughed. "Soap operas, huh? I've heard they're pretty hot. If I'd known they were giving out these kind of ideas I would have started watching them a long time ago. But I'm happier that you've been watching them." He reached for, and found, the pins holding up the remnants of her loose knot, and tossed them to the floor. Her hair immediately spilled down her back in loose waves. She blushed hotly. He paused, fearing the worst. Was she having second thoughts about him? He sure hoped not, because he didn't want to even think about losing her. But he didn't want to move so fast she'd feel uncomfortable with him. "What's wrong?"

"In my day…" she hesitated, as if she needed to choose her words carefully "…only a woman's husband saw her with her hair down."

Jared combed his fingers through the heavy mass, watching the strands wrap around his fingers as if they were alive. He saw glints of gold and bronze among the toffee-brown color.

"I can understand why. There's something so sexy about a woman with her long hair hanging loose like this," he mused.

She blushed again, but didn't discourage him from playing with a stray curl.

Jared suddenly had a vision of a naked Rachel with only her hair, and him, wrapped around her.

"You don't think I'm too forward?" she asked in a hesitant whisper.

"Trust me, you're not even close." He kissed the curve of her ear. He liked the idea of them stretched out on the couch with her lying in his arms. Any other time when he'd cuddled with a woman like this, it usually ended up with both of them tearing each other's clothes off because they didn't want to take the time to make it to the bed. "In fact, feel free to be as forward as you'd like. Do whatever you want with me. Kissing me the way you did was very—" he punctuated the word with a light kiss "—very nice. You can kiss me all you want. Feel free to take advantage of me."

He fervently hoped she *would,* but he sensed she wasn't ready to go much further. Plus he was enjoying seeing this new side to her.

There had to be a way to keep her in human form all the time.

For a man who didn't believe in commitment, he was putting on a good act—owning a home, having truck payments, a dog and even a woman who had become an important part of his life. The downside was that he only had Rachel after sundown. She disappeared at sunrise and he only had memories.

A complication like that could put a strain on any relationship.

Rachel hadn't smiled and laughed so much for more than one hundred years. She knew if she thought about it, she would realize it was even longer than that. Caleb only laughed when he'd drunk too much whiskey or humiliated someone. She hadn't laughed for the pure joy of it until now.

She wanted to thank Jared for making her aware of her surroundings. In a way, he made her feel alive.

The hours of daylight no longer saddened her as they used to. She still hated that she had no form, but now she had something, someone, to watch during those hours. Even seeing Jared's distant figure when she hovered by a window was better than what she'd had before. Sometimes a tiny voice whispered inside her head that he could still turn out to be like Caleb, but she banished the thoughts the moment they cropped up. Maybe she was too eager to have someone care for her the way Jared seemed to. Maybe she was being foolish. But for once, she was going to take what was offered, and perhaps her life would be restored to her.

She knew Maya enjoyed having household tasks to perform again. The older woman learned to use the washing and drying machines that Jared brought to the house. Rachel smiled at Maya's scorn for the latter, saying that clothing drying in the fresh air was much better, but she admitted it would be nice for cold and rainy days.

Rachel wondered if they would still be here when winter came.

For more years than she could count she had prayed to be released from her hellish nonexistence. She understood why Maya prayed to her ancient gods on Rachel's behalf. The woman had hated Caleb and felt Rachel's death was senseless. At first, Rachel had railed against the fate that would have her existing in such a way for so many years, but her feelings about her situation had changed when Jared moved into the house.

Now she prayed she would find the key and have the chance to become fully mortal again. Maya had said that with the key would come the treasure. For a long time, Rachel had thought the two were one and the same, until Maya explained they were separate yet connected. Rachel still didn't fully understand what the older woman meant, but she knew Maya would never do anything to hurt her. Rachel could only put her trust in Maya's words and believe that everything would turn out all right.

She knew that Caleb distrusted banks and once said he'd made sure he would have funds even if the bank failed. Over the years she had seen treasure hunters go through the house and barn in search of booty, but no one found anything but an occasional skunk or field mouse.

She didn't wish for the treasure for herself. She hadn't grown up with much money and never felt the need for it. She sensed Jared had spent a great deal of cash working on the house and property, and he would probably need even more for future work. She also had an idea that he didn't make a lot as a police detective, though he never acted as if money meant very much to him.

Jared had helped her so much. She wanted the chance to

help him. She wanted to give him something. She only wished she could give him herself.

"What are you thinking about?" His whisper brought her back to the present. She was curled up on the couch with his arms wrapped around her. Not once had he groped her breast in a rough manner or suggested they go upstairs. He seemed content for them to just sit here in this manner. He had called it cuddling. She liked the description.

"I am thinking about how nice this is," she said softly, moving just enough to rest her cheek against the hollow between his collarbone and shoulder. She frowned when she felt a faint ridge under the fabric. She used her fingertips to trace what she knew was a scar. How had she missed this the times she'd seen him with his shirt off? How had he been hurt?

"Knife wound," he explained, guessing her unspoken question. "Kid on too much speed."

"He was fast?"

Jared chuckled. "Speed's also a pretty potent drug. Very nasty stuff."

She slid the flat of her hand down and along his side, where she felt the imprint of a puckered wound.

"Gunshot. The suspect didn't want to be taken into custody," he continued. "He tried to tell us he had no idea why he was being arrested. The trouble was, the gun he used to shoot me was the same gun he'd used to shoot his boss. That was a slam-dunk conviction."

"It appears guns are just as deadly now as they were in my time," she murmured, saddened at the idea that he'd suffered pain. She'd seen him bruised and battered, but she saw this as different. Beatings had a better chance of healing than a bullet wound or knife wound, which could easily become infected. She was relieved he had survived these life-threatening injuries.

"The lieutenant prefers I wear a vest, but I don't like the way they feel, so I only wear one when absolutely necessary."

"A vest?" She pictured one of the fancy embroidered vests Caleb wore under his suit coats.

Jared chuckled. "Another newfangled gadget," he teased. "It's a special garment made of dense material that can stop most bullets. Unless you get shot in the head. Then you're out of luck," he said with dark humor.

Rachel looked up. Her eyes were shadowed with concern. "You lead a dangerous life."

"I do pretty good," he said lightly. "Of course, I didn't realize that idiots who might be running a meth lab would want to tangle with me."

Her forehead crinkled in thought. "What is a meth lab?"

"Meth is methamphetamine. It's a very bad drug that too many people are hooked on." He continued combing her hair with his fingers. "It speeds up your heart rate, alters your perception of the world around you, makes you do really stupid things. And it kills," he said softly. "Too many lives are destroyed by it."

"Then you will have to stop them, won't you?" she said, with confidence in his abilities.

Jared threw back his head and laughed. "Sweetheart, if only it was that easy." He hugged her tightly. "But thank you for thinking I can do it."

Rachel thought of the lights she'd seen in the distance. And then there were the far off voices she'd sometimes heard in the middle of the night. She shivered inwardly as she recalled the men who'd come to burn down the barn. And worried they might return and do worse. She thought back to that night men had left a beaten and battered Jared in the house.

If that hadn't happened, and she hadn't felt the need to care for him, would she have shown herself to him or would she have made sure to hide herself away all these nights?

Before, it had been easy to keep her presence in the house a secret. She never worried about the teenagers, who only stayed for a few hours at most. But Jared lived here.

She was relieved her secret was out. And even more relieved that Jared finally understood.

But she still had a small worry that refused to go away. She felt conflicted, because each morning she turned into something that essentially didn't exist. When the sun peeked over the distant mountains she felt a disorienting sensation flow through her body, right before she was sucked into a nebulous state that allowed her to see the world as if from a blurred distance.

She had a sudden vision of Jared with silver hair, lines carved deep beside his sharp, intelligent eyes. She knew his laughter would still be rich and full. The time would come when he would walk slower, but his mind would never falter. She knew it as surely as if she'd seen into the future.

Except she also saw herself standing near the older Jared Stryker, looking the same as she did tonight.

Unthinking, she buried her face in the curve of his neck. She inhaled the musky scent of shower-fresh skin and Jared himself.

"What's wrong?" he asked, sensing her distress. His arms tightened around her.

She shook her head. She didn't want to tell him that she was afraid of the future. Afraid of losing him.

"You smell nice," she told him.

"Rachel, what's wrong?" He shook her gently.

She lifted herself up and placed her fingertips against his

lips. "I am sure that Maya left us an excellent dinner, but could we sit here for a little while longer?" Her eyes pleaded with him not to ask her again.

"Sure." She breathed a sigh of relief at his reply. "We can sit here just as long as you like."

Rachel rested her head back against his chest, listening to the slow, steady thump of his heartbeat.

If she didn't allow her imagination to run away with her, she wouldn't imagine the steady heartbeat was counting down his days.

Jared knew that Rachel was lying to him, but he couldn't imagine why. Something had upset her, but she refused to tell him what or even admit that she was upset.

He found in talking to her that, while her education had ended more than a hundred years ago, she was eager to learn as much as possible, and picked up new concepts very quickly. She was fascinated with television and enjoyed the books he chose for her at the library. She had told him that during the nights after he went to bed, she would curl up on the couch in the family room with a book or take it to her room to read. Until she began the first history book Jared left her, she had no idea she had so much to catch up on. So many historical events had happened, and there were so many new words for her to learn.

She told him it wasn't just her clothing that was out of date. She herself was an antique.

She asked Jared about things she couldn't understand. Some, he readily explained. Others, he had trouble talking about, and muttered that they were women's issues. He teased her, saying her mind was a sponge that absorbed everything.

Later in the evening Rachel warmed up their dinner. They carried their plates into the family room, where she sat on the couch while Jared sat on the floor near her feet. With the evening still warm he'd kept the French doors open to allow fresh air into the house.

Rachel looked down at Jared. She hadn't realized she could develop such deep feelings for a man, thought Caleb had forced all emotion out of her. She'd felt dead inside for the longest time, and now she felt incredibly alive. She was perceptive enough to know that what she felt for Jared had nothing to do with gratitude. Her feelings were much more complex, touching a chord deep within her.

Except she knew she was powerless to pursue such feelings, which had her blushing every time she thought about them.

She couldn't recall any happy memories from her marriage to Caleb. It had been as if once he'd attained his goal of making her his wife, he didn't need to bother to charm her any longer. All he'd cared to do was remind her of her place and tell her that she was nothing more than a possession, just like the horses in his corrals.

She recalled the morning of her wedding day, when Mrs. Davis had come into her bedroom to speak with her privately. Her adoptive mother didn't look at her once as she explained that men had disgusting urges that women could not understand and shouldn't bother to try. Rachel should just accept it was something women were created to bear. And if God saw her as a willing and obedient wife, she would be blessed with children.

Obviously, Rachel had been neither willing nor obedient enough. Instead, she had been punished.

Jared looked up at her. "What are you thinking?" His grin made her insides flip-flop. "You can't tell me you're not thinking of something because I can hear the gears whirring inside your head."

"I do not have gears in my head," she said primly, but a small smile escaped. "I was just thinking how nice this is, sitting here together. What were you thinking of?"

He looked down at his empty plate. "I was wondering how much of my beer Maya used in this stew." He shook his head in disbelief. "Using perfectly good beer in food."

"She always believed that beer or whiskey was good when cooking meat." Rachel hesitantly touched the collar of his shirt, hoping he wouldn't notice she'd given in to temptation. If he did, he gave no indication.

"So she did the cooking even back then?" he asked.

Rachel hesitated. "No, Caleb preferred someone else to do the cooking."

Jared's jaw hardened at the inference that the man didn't consider Maya's heritage good enough for him. He wondered why Caleb had allowed the woman in the house if he had felt that way. "I get what you mean."

Rachel shook her head. Caleb's notions of what was proper and what wasn't had always bothered her.

Rachel shook her head. "I think Caleb did not want Maya doing any of the cooking because deep down he was afraid she might poison him. He knew she hated him."

"Then why did he keep her on?"

"Because he could," she said simply. "Caleb didn't believe in explaining his reasons for anything. I know Maya's son worked in the barn. He was able to tame horses others were afraid to approach. And I think, in the beginning of our marriage, Caleb was willing to do anything to keep me happy, which was how I was able to keep her as my personal maid."

"The guy was scum," Jared muttered, standing up. He took her plate out of her hands. "You sit here. I'll load the dishwasher."

"It is easier to wash the dishes than put them in that machine," she protested.

"Not the way I see it." He disappeared into the kitchen. Harley was fast on his heels in hopes of snagging some leftovers.

Rachel got off the couch and walked over to the open French doors, making sure to stand a few inches back from them. She could hear the sounds of the night and inhale the heady fragrance of jasmine coming from the bushes Jared had planted for her. For a moment she fancied that her world was the way it should be. The way she wanted it to be. That she was a normal woman living in a normal world.

Without thinking, she stepped forward with the intention of going outside. The moment her foot reached the doorway she felt the barrier.

For the briefest of seconds furious thoughts flew through her head. *It's not fair! Jared made this for me! I should be able to do this for him!*

But she was still rudely pushed backward. This time she didn't fall, but her feet skidded a little. She threw her hands out to the sides to help keep her balance.

Tears pricked her eyelids. She could have sworn that the resistance in the doorway had been less than she'd encountered before.

Or perhaps it was wishful thinking on her part.

"Rachel?" A hand touched her shoulder. She looked up.

"I tried to go outside," she murmured. "Is that not silly? After all these years, that I would still try something like that?"

Jared wrapped his arms around her and pulled her close against him.

"There's got to be a way," he murmured, cupping the back of her neck with his palm as if warming her skin with his touch. He gently rubbed her neck. "We'll find it, Rachel. I promise we will."

She shook her head, inadvertently rubbing her nose against his shirtfront. "It's a curse, Jared. It's not meant to be broken. Because I wanted to leave the house that night, because I wanted to leave him, he intended to make sure I never could."

"But it still can't go on forever," Jared grumbled. "You said Maya pleaded with her gods to save you. If they were merciful enough to do so, they must have had something in mind that would eventually free you. We just have to find out what it is and break this curse or spell or whatever you want to call it."

Rachel inhaled the warm scent of his skin. "You are a very stubborn man."

"Damn straight." Keeping one arm around her, he guided her to the couch. "Stretch out, relax." Once he was assured she was comfortable, he walked over to his collection player and rummaged through his CDs until he found what he wanted.

"I love that you can have music all the time," she said when the rich tones of Faith Hill floated through the air.

He flopped back down next to her. "There's an even better reason for having music all the time. It's great for making out," he growled.

"What is mak—?" Her question was cut off by his mouth pressing against hers. A dazed part of her brain pointed out that she should have known Jared preferred to show her instead of explaining.

She enjoyed the showing part. And apparently, so did her body. She could feel it warm and soften under his roaming touch. He fingered the tiny covered buttons at the front of her bodice.

"You women must have been a real challenge to men back then," he teased.

"I think you would have handled any challenge you faced if you lived in my time," she told him with a hint of a smile.

He brushed aside a stray lock of hair and kissed the curve of her ear. She shivered under his touch.

He shifted on the couch, rolling over with her now lying on top of him. He shifted her until she sat squarely in his lap. He laughed at the stunned look on her face.

"You are teasing me!"

"No, I'm just showing you what it's like if you're in charge." He settled her more firmly, and knew the exact second she became aware of his arousal nudging her bottom. There was no missing the bright flush of color blooming on her cheeks. But he didn't care. Even with their clothes on she felt so damn good against him.

"You are a very wicked man." It was clear she sensed what he was thinking.

"Then you'll just have to reform me." He grinned, showing her that wicked side.

"I do not think you want to be reformed." Even blushing hotly, she didn't move from her position.

"I might. If you were the one doing the reforming."

"Except if I tried to reform you, you would be too occupied trying to do the opposite to me." She rested her hands against the middle of his chest.

"Just giving you a taste of the modern man, darlin'." He picked up one of her hands and brought it to his lips. He drew one of her fingers into his mouth, sucking on it gently.

Rachel's eyes darkened. As if an invisible thread pulled her, she leaned down until her lips were close to his. Her kiss was tentative, as it had been before, but there was an eagerness that touched something deep inside him.

"What the hell?" he muttered, as his hands tracked her middle.

"Jared, you really need to watch your language," she scolded.

He sat up. "I can't believe I missed this before. What is this you're wearing? Some kind of cage? And then there's this thing back here." He touched her bustle. "Talk about a torture device."

Rachel blushed and batted at his exploring hands. "Ladies don't speak of such things to gentlemen," she chided primly.

"Then it's a good thing I'm no gentleman. What is this thing?" He grabbed for her again, but she scooted across the couch, out of his reach. It wasn't easy with her full skirt and petticoats hampering her movements.

"It's personal." She could feel her cheeks heat up further. She could tell he wasn't going to back down. She looked at her lap as she whispered an explanation.

"What?" He leaned forward.

"It's my corset," she said a little louder. She glanced up, with her chin held high. "It's what ladies wear—corsets and bustles. It's all the fashion."

"Not these days, they aren't." He frowned as he rested a hand against her waist. "How do you breathe wearing this thing?" He realized his mistake the moment he said it. "I guess more like how *did* you breathe in this thing? This isn't a corset, it's a cage."

She had to smile at his discomfort, even if his interest in her clothing was much more personal than men in her time period had ever displayed. Proper etiquette dictated that gentlemen didn't show an interest in what a lady wore under her dress. All Caleb cared was that she showed a proper lady's figure, and that meant a suitable corset even if the one he wanted her to wear was more structured than the new ones that had come out then. By evening, she always had marks etched in her flesh from the constricting garment.

"We weren't expected to breathe. We were just meant to give the appearance of a proper lady," she explained.

"It feels as if it's made out of sticks." He was still frowning. "Like some kind of torturous cage."

"They used to be made from whalebone," Rachel explained. "Fashion dictated that the smaller the waist, the prettier the woman."

He shook his head at such an idea. "There must have been a lot of fainting women back then, because I don't see how a person could breathe wearing this thing. I don't know how you can even sit comfortably."

She chuckled. "Breathing wasn't always easy. Especially if the laces were pulled too tight. But we managed."

He looked off in the distance, his brow furrowed in thought. "Even now I don't see how it can be good for you," he muttered.

"You are doing it again."

"Doing what?"

"Showing what a kind heart you have." She smiled.

Jared grinned again. "Maybe it's a good thing you don't know anyone at the police station. They'd laugh themselves hoarse if you said that. I told you, Rachel. I'm the bad ass around there." He took her hand and idly played with her fingers.

Rachel opened her mouth to argue with him, but a familiar rumbling sound alerted them something wasn't right. Harley roused from his nap and headed for the French doors.

"Harley!" The harsh command caused the dog to skid to a stop. Jared jumped off the couch and ran for the doors, quickly closing them and securing the lock.

"What is it?" Rachel raised herself up on her knees and looked over the back of the couch.

He rushed to the cabinet and unlocked it, pulling out a shotgun and retrieving ammunition from a drawer.

"Jared?" Rachel's voice grew more fearful as the rumbling sounds became louder and more ominous.

His stark features could have been carved from stone. "We might be having company."

"And this company is not someone you want coming here?"

"Definitely not," he said grimly.

"Do you think it is the men who were here before?" she whispered, as if she feared she might be overheard.

"I don't know, but we may find out soon." Once the shotgun was loaded and cradled in one arm, he hurried back to the doors. "Installing bulletproof glass might have been a good idea," he muttered.

"Bulletproof glass?" Rachel's voice squeaked with fear. "But you do not have that! Bullets can break the glass and hit you!" Panic swamped her. "Get away from the door, Jared!" She started to get up. "Please! You could be hurt!"

"Stay there, Rachel!" His harsh order was firm enough to freeze her in midmotion.

"But they cannot hurt me and they can hurt you!" she argued, wringing her hands.

He looked over his shoulder. His eyes glowed in the low light. "Turn off the lamp."

She scrambled to the other end of the couch and switched off the lamp, plunging the room into darkness.

Jared cocked his head to one side, listening intently. "Five, maybe six bikes," he muttered. "And one needs a tune-up real bad."

"Where are they?" she whispered.

"They're circling us," he said in a low voice, looking out the glass door. "They don't have their headlights on, so we can only hear them. This is their idea of scare tactics. You can hear them, but can't see them. Makes it more frightening that way."

Rachel dug her fingers into the back of the couch. "They are doing an excellent job of frightening me. Should you not call the sheriff? He would come out and arrest them."

"The problem is they're not doing anything illegal," Jared explained. "Since they're not close enough for me to make out any details, I'd say they're right outside the property line, so I can't accuse them of trespassing."

Rachel's stomach clenched painfully. She had no idea how long the siege went on, only that the horrible rumbling sound was constant. She watched Jared stand by the door, his body like a statue as he stood guard. Harley stood by him, fairly quivering with the urge to go out and chase whatever was upsetting his humans.

Unable to stay on the couch any longer, Rachel crept over to Jared's side. Not wanting to distract him, she wrapped her skirt around her legs and sat on the floor. She could see the outline of his head as he glanced down, and his lips curved in a faint white flash of a smile.

"You're a stubborn woman, Rachel Weatherly Bingham."

She smiled back. "And you know how to make an evening interesting, Jared Stryker."

He looked back through the glass, even though he couldn't see anything in the darkness. "You know, there's nothing worse than people coming over uninvited. What if we weren't home?"

"You are right. They should call on the telephone first," she said, sharing his dry humor.

Jared grinned. His grin faded as he looked toward the table, where his cell phone rested. He silently cursed himself for not snagging it on his way over.

"You've seen me use the cell phone," he said. "So you know what to do if you have to."

Her stomach clenched again. Why did he sound as if he wouldn't be able to use it himself? She didn't want to think about the possibility of him ending up badly hurt. Or worse. "Jared—"

He shook his head. "Listen to me, Rachel. I don't know what these guys have planned. Sure, logic tells me you're safe, but the rest of me isn't that logical, and, well, I'll do whatever it takes to *keep* you safe. Can you get over there and grab the phone for me? If things start getting crazy, I want you to punch the numbers 911 and tell whoever answers to get out to the Diamond B Ranch. Tell them a police officer is under fire. And if something happens…" he paused "…just say 'officer down.' Got it?"

She nodded and immediately crept over to the table, picked up the phone and carried it back. She sat on the floor again, cradling the small instrument in her lap.

"Do you know why they are doing this to us?" she asked in a low voice trembling fear. "You had to call the sheriff when they broke into the barn."

Jared thought it probably had more to do with the night he'd been pulled into a van and pounded to a pulp.

"Could be they know I'm a cop and don't like it. Could be they just don't like me. Doesn't make sense, since everyone knows I'm a real likable guy."

"Perhaps they do not like likable guys." Rachel rested her shoulder against the wall. "We can hope they will make a mistake so you can arrest them."

He grinned. "Sweetheart, you can be on my team anytime."

* * *

Hours later, when the motorcycles sounded as if they were finally moving away, Jared still didn't relax his vigilance. His eyes burned from lack of sleep, but he kept his senses attuned to the surrounding area as he waited. He sensed Rachel in her curled up position just behind him. That she stayed close by was a comfort to him. For the first time, he didn't feel alone.

With their visitors finally gone, he found the silence almost as unnerving as the rumbling of the motorcycles had been.

As he looked outside, he could see the night sky just start to lighten to a pale pink.

"I guess everything's okay now," he said, looking over his shoulder.

At that exact second, his cell phone dropped the short distance to the floor. Just like that, Rachel was gone.

Chapter 11

After that night, Jared refused to take any more chances. He knew he needed to check a few things out, but he didn't like the idea of leaving the house unprotected even if the two women occupying it didn't truly need any physical protection. He realized he didn't have to worry once he familiarized Maya with handling a modern shotgun.

"Just don't try to blow me away when I come back," he told her as he walked out the door.

"Then do not surprise me!" she called after him.

Jared's first stop was in town. Once he finished his errands there, he drove on past the ranch and took the winding two-lane road up into the hills. He hoped his truck with its tinted windows wouldn't arouse suspicion among the residents. Thanks to the four-wheel drive, he was able to get off the paved roads and check some of the outlying area.

Memories of days roaming these hills were still strong. Of

nights when his old man had had too many beers and Jared had slipped out of the mobile home, always heading for the empty ranch house. Now he understood why he considered it a refuge. How had he missed not seeing Rachel back then?

He stopped near a rocky ledge overlooking a meadow.

"Rachel would love this," he murmured, looking at the large grassy area with trees in a half circle around it. For a moment he imagined driving her up here. Maybe even bringing a picnic basket. He thought she would like coming here for a picnic. Days like today were perfect for spending the afternoon outside. Then a sharp pang of realization hit him. Rachel would never be able to come out here and have a picnic in the meadow.

Jared's frustration was twofold. One part was that he couldn't find what he was searching for—he didn't even know what it looked like. The second had to do with Rachel.

He knew if she couldn't leave the house, then she would always be there. She would always look the way she did now. And each day he would grow older. He never thought of himself settling down, but what if he completely lost his mind and found someone? What if he got married? How would he explain to a wife that two women lived in his house and, by the way, the ladies were ghosts? That he'd fallen for one of them big time, but it seemed there was no future for them?

Not an ideal situation for newlyweds.

As if he could even consider being with another woman after knowing Rachel.

An afternoon wasted, with only his troubling thoughts for company. He ignored the lengthening shadows as he drove out of the hills. He didn't bother going back to the ranch. With the way he felt, he knew seeing Rachel just now wasn't a good idea. Instead, he headed for the only other place he felt comfortable in.

He knew Lea would sense something was bothering him, but she wouldn't pester him with questions. She'd wait for him to tell her. He doubted he would be talking about Rachel to anyone else anytime soon.

Rachel couldn't stop herself from glancing out each window for a sign of Jared's return even if she couldn't see anything in the darkness. Earlier in the day, she had watched him drive away in his truck. She'd spent the hours moving through the rooms, watching Maya worry over nonexistent spots on the windows and specks of dust on the furniture.

After the night they'd spent listening to the men trying to terrorize them, she felt the strong need to see Jared. She needed the comfort of being with him. The longer he was gone, the more worried she became. She thought back to when she'd sensed the sun setting.

"I sense your eagerness, *chica,*" Maya had chuckled. The words barely left her lips before she disappeared in the blink of an eye and Rachel appeared.

Rachel pressed her hand against her stomach now. What if Jared was waylaid on the road? What if he was badly hurt and he couldn't get help? She knew he carried his small telephone with him, but what if he was so badly hurt he couldn't use it? What if he was lying in a ditch somewhere? Or worse?

She stifled the whimper that threatened to crawl up her throat as horrifying images of an injured Jared flashed through her mind.

Anything could have happened to him and she was powerless to help him. There was no way she could go to him.

An uneasy Harley remained at her heels as she walked through the house, pausing every few minutes to look out a window. She had even tried to open the French doors, but found them resistant to her pulling on the knobs no matter how hard she tried. Upset and angry, she spat out a curse she'd heard Jared use, and kicked one of the doors. She welcomed the pain that radiated up her leg because it made her feel alive.

"Where is he?" she cried out, resisting the urge to kick the door again. She wondered if it would open if she kicked it enough times. She settled for stamping her foot. "Dammit!"

"Ah-ah-ah! Ladies mustn't swear."

She spun around at the sound of the gently mocking voice.

The front door stood open, with a dark-visaged Jared standing there, radiating danger.

As he stepped inside, she could see the sparks in his eyes and the wry twist to his mouth. This was a Jared Stryker she had never seen before. She knew she should be afraid of him in this precarious mood, but strangely, she felt no fear.

"I was worried about you," she said.

"You don't need to be concerned about me. I've been taking care of myself all these years without too many problems. But I guess you feel the need to worry about something, don't you?" He pushed the door shut with his shoulder, then secured the dead bolt. "Since you don't need to worry about yourself."

"What do you mean?" She wasn't sure where the conversation was taking them, but she didn't think she liked the direction.

He shrugged. "You're a ghost." Rachel flinched at the harsh way he spoke the word. "You're already dead, so you can't die. You've looked like this for the past hundred plus years, and you'll look just like this a hundred years from now. Maya will have one of my descendants to boss around. And you..." he paused "...you'll stand there looking beautiful and defenseless, making another sucker fall for you. He'll be a goner before he comes to realize that time will pass and he'll grow old but you won't. You'll be the same as you are now and as you were all those years ago."

If his words were meant to draw blood, he made a direct hit. Her eyes suddenly snapped with purple flames.

"Yes, I will look the same, and even then I will be a prisoner!" she retorted, waving a hand to encompass the room. "I'll know nothing but what is inside this house. But in another hundred years who knows what will happen? Perhaps by then the house will no longer stand and I will not exist except as part of a legend." Her voice trembled, but this time with anger and not fear. "Your descendants will have a chance to truly live. To *feel,* to experience everything life has to offer. While even then, I will only discover what is brought to me. So tell me, Jared Stryker, does that sound like an existence anyone would choose? Is that what you would want? Spending an eternity as a prisoner! An eternity as nothing more than a supernatural *thing!*" Her voice rose with her agitation.

He walked toward her with the loose-hipped grace of a predator. The dark light in his eyes was a warning she was too angry to acknowledge.

He caught her wrist and brought her up against him.

"Funny, you don't feel like a thing." His whisper flowed across her skin with almost lethal overtones. Except Rachel didn't feel threatened by him. Instead, she felt as if something wild and free had been released within her.

She lifted her chin and looked him square in the eye and saw the hint of a smile on his lips.

Everything about Jared screamed *Danger!* but she didn't move a muscle. An instinct long-buried over the years told her that if she stood her ground, she would discover something new and thrilling.

He lowered his face until his lips almost touched hers. She

knew she only had to close that last small gap to feel them on hers, but she didn't. She waited to see what he would do next. With his body so close to hers she felt the heat of his skin surround her. No matter how many years she existed after this night, she would never forget the warm musky scent of his skin.

"I knew you were trouble the second I saw you," he murmured.

"You were badly beaten. You could not have known very much," she dared to say.

Was that glint in his eye approval for her standing up to him?

She showed no fear when he raised his hand to caress her cheek with the back of his fingers.

"You look real," he muttered. "You feel real, so I don't think I'll wake up in the morning and discover all of this was some crazy dream. But if it is, I might as well take advantage of what I've got here right now." He lowered his head that last scant distance and kissed her with a hunger he hadn't displayed before.

Rachel's head spun at the onslaught of sensations that raced through her. She felt as if she'd been thrown into a volcano. She could only grip his arms and hang on.

Jared raised his head. "Let's see just how real you are." He scooped her up into his arms and headed for the stairs. He didn't take his eyes off her face as he ascended to the second floor. If he thought she might protest, he was in for a long wait.

Rachel sensed she would find out just what she'd missed all those decades ago.

Before, she'd only been in his bedroom in her daytime state. This time, she was carried over to his bed and lowered onto it. Her skirt billowed upward, showing a froth of lace-trimmed petticoats. The only light in the room was the moonlight streaming in through the window.

Jared bent a knee, resting it on the mattress. "I've been curious to see what's underneath that dress of yours." He fingered the top button of those trailing down the bodice. He loosened it and moved to the second one.

"Wait!" Rachel grabbed his hand, stopping him. Panic had taken over. "What if—" She suddenly felt as if she couldn't breathe. "What if something terrible happens?"

He kissed the corner of her lips. "And what if something doesn't? I wouldn't let anything happen to you, Rachel. You know that." He kissed the other corner.

Her fingers relaxed and dropped away. With each button released, her lace chemise was slowly revealed.

"We need to talk about modern clothing, darlin'." He eyed the bustle fastenings with male confusion. "No wonder you women had maids back then. It was the only way you could get undressed. Good thing zippers were invented." He pressed another kiss against the hollow of her throat.

Rachel still worried that lightning would strike or worse, but she showed Jared how to unfasten her bustle. He muttered curses at the wire used to create her bustle and her corset. More curses followed when he tried to unfasten her shoes with their dozen buttons. But with the loss of each item of clothing she felt lighter and strangely freer. She saw the dark glitter of desire in his eyes, which was much more than lust. More than the need for possession that Caleb had showed her. Jared didn't want to possess her as a thing. He wanted her as a woman.

"Silky skin," he muttered against the hollow between her breasts. "You are so beautiful."

Rachel felt the same need to see him. Her fingers fumbled as she pulled at his T-shirt and wrestled with his jeans. He took pity on her and pulled off his boots and socks before shucking his jeans to reveal a very bare, very male body. She sat back on the bed in her chemise and petticoat, staring at him with wide-eyed, undisguised awe.

Her mouth went dry at the sight of the hard, muscled body before her as her eyes traveled downward to where his skin was paler. His sex was heavy with an arousal she knew was for her. She gave in to temptation and leaned forward to press her hand against his chest. The wiry hairs prickled against her palm.

"Perhaps you are the one who isn't real," she whispered, lifting her face. "It might be me waking up in the morning and discovering this is all some incredible dream."

Jared moved back onto the bed and over her. "Then let's make sure we make it a dream we'll never forget."

She parted her lips for his invading tongue. He left her only long enough to pull her chemise over her head before he returned to kiss her with a raw hunger that couldn't be denied. She was hazily aware of her petticoat sliding down her body and her stockings being rolled down her legs, with him kissing every inch of skin on the way.

"By the time I get through there won't be one bare inch of you I won't know," he murmured against the back of her knee.

"I…" Rational thought disappeared as he nipped her inner thigh, then soothed the skin with his tongue. "Are…" She swallowed. "Why…" Now she suddenly found it hard to breathe as his mouth moved closer to the part of her that arched up under his seeking mouth. She looked down at the top of his head. "Is this right?" she finally managed to squeak, knowing she sounded as amazed as she felt.

He looked up and grinned in that way that always turned her stomach upside down. "Trust me, darlin', this is very right." Then his mouth settled fully against her.

Rachel's own mouth widened in a shocked, then pleasurable, "Oh!" Any thought of dissuading him disappeared as her body responded. She seemed to be stretched so tight she thought she would snap in two. The heat that started at her center now radiated outward, and she felt as if flames were licking at her skin. She tried hard not to move against the seductive pressure of his tongue and teeth on her flesh, or cry out, but the need to do so was overpowering.

"Come on, baby," he whispered, nipping her tender skin. "It's okay. Show me what you like. Tell me what you like."

"Everything!" she moaned, allowing her hips to rise up. "Don't stop!"

He chuckled and obeyed.

Rachel closed her eyes, thinking it would hold off the tightness coiling inside her, then opened them because she needed to see him. For a moment she was afraid she would be twisted up in that same coil.

As if sensing her need for even more, Jared raised his head and moved up her body. His mouth came down on hers at the same time he drove into her. Rachel was so close to the edge that it took only two thrusts to push her over.

She instantly spun out of control, the dictates of her body taking over completely. Jared arched upward, his own body convulsing before he collapsed on top of her, spent. Mindful of his weight on her, he rolled over onto his side but kept an arm around her, drawing her against him.

It could have been minutes, it could have been hours before they each caught their breath.

"If I didn't know better I'd swear fireworks shot off around us," Jared said once he'd regained his breath. His chest still rose and fell sharply.

Now Rachel felt safe enough to close her eyes and savor

the moment. She idly ran her hand down his chest, feeling the damp skin.

"I think they did." She couldn't stop smiling. She had no idea it could be like this! Before, she had always thought the act degrading, somewhat painful and messy. Jared had changed her mind all the way around. In fact, she wouldn't mind doing it again. Still smiling, she ran her hand lower.

"Whoa, baby." Jared laughed softly, grabbing hold of her wandering fingers. "With a hot little woman like you, a man needs some time to recover."

Rachel rolled over onto her stomach and lifted herself on her elbows. "I had no idea!" Her voice was filled with awe. "This was so wonderful."

His gaze centered on her breasts. Needing to do more than just look, he lifted his head to kiss a dark pink nipple, which instantly tightened at his touch.

"I think I've wanted to do this since that first moment I saw you."

"You mean you wished this even when you thought I was trouble?" She arched an eyebrow.

"Yep. I wanted to see those gorgeous eyes widen just for me." He smirked. "And they did."

She shocked herself that she didn't feel embarrassed at lying naked in bed with him. Then again, after what had happened, she decided lying naked here wasn't all that shocking. "I thought if you took off my clothing I would disappear for good," she said softly.

He grinned. "Instead, I gave you a memorable night." Jared stroked her midriff, wincing at the visible dents in her skin. "No more corset," he insisted. "You're so thin you could blow away. You don't need one." He tapped her open lips with his forefinger to quash her argument. "You'll still be a lady even without it. In fact, I'm going to make sure you don't have to worry about it again." He carefully put her from him and rolled off the bed.

Rachel sat up, holding the sheet against her chest. She watched him snatch up her corset from the floor and walk over to the open window.

"This is outta here!" He tossed the corset out the window.

"Jared!" She started to protest his actions, then burst out laughing as the corset seemed to bounce off an invisible wall and flew back to slap him in the face.

"Damn thing can't even be thrown out," he muttered, dropping it back on the floor. "I don't care. You're not wearing it again," he told her as he returned to the bed.

"Yes, Jared," she said meekly, but he noticed a spark in her eyes that hadn't been there before.

"Hot damn, I've created a monster." He settled down next to her, gently pulling the sheet away. He bent down and dropped a kiss on one perky nipple.

"Is that a good thing?"

Jared tugged her back to him, enjoying the magical sensation of her soft, scented skin against him. "Trust me, it's a very good thing." As she molded herself to him, he realized he wanted to show her just what she meant to him.

He reluctantly moved away and climbed out of bed once more. Walking over to his chest of drawers, he picked up her hairbrush, lying next to his wallet and keys. He resisted the urge to strut back to bed when he found her gaze centered on his nude body.

Settling down among the covers once more, he placed Rachel in front of him, then slowly ran the brush through the long, heavy waves of her hair. Rachel closed her eyes and tipped her head back as he accompanied his brushing with kisses along the delicate line of her jaw and featherlight touches against the side of her breast.

"Just like satin," he murmured when he'd set the brush to one side, then draped the strands of hair over one shoulder so he could place a kiss on her skin. Not content with one, he trailed more along her shoulder and up the side of her neck to her ear.

"Jared." Her voice was a breathy sigh.

"Hmm?"

"No one has ever kissed me the way you do."

"Good," he whispered, reaching around to cup one breast with his hand. His thumb teased the nipple with a pleasing, raspy touch.

"Or done that." She tipped her head back farther until it rested against his shoulder.

"What about this?" His fingers traveled down to circle her belly button, then moved lower. A slight hitch in her breath sounded at the same time as he reached his objective. He smiled at the dampness that met his fingers. She was so responsive he felt humbled by the trust she offered him.

She started to turn to him, but he quickly moved his hands to her waist to halt her. "This is all for you, darlin'," he murmured in her ear. "Just relax and let yourself feel." He dropped his hand back to her center, stroking the swollen petals.

"How am I supposed to relax with what you are doing?" Her chest rose and fell faster, even as his strokes became slower and more languid. She shifted her hips in an attempt to intensify the sensation going on inside her. She blindly reached down to grasp his arms, her fingernails digging into his skin. With each stroke of his invading fingers, she felt the tension coil even tighter inside her. "Jared?" She gasped his name, unable to understand what she was feeling.

"Just let yourself go, Rachel," he whispered, not letting up as he found the nub that sent shock waves through her body. "Feel me." As he stroked harder, his teeth gently sank into her earlobe.

Rachel's eyes flew open as she felt herself shatter into a million pieces. The sheer pleasure sent her flying, lost in myriad sensations.

This time, when she turned, he didn't hold her back. With a soft cry, she covered his face with kisses and settled herself on his lap, easily taking him inside her.

Jared's eyes glowed a deep golden-brown as he looked at Rachel, her features luminous with passion.

He thrust upward, feeling her muscles tighten around him. In moments like this he felt as if they were truly one. He watched her eyes dilate, her skin glow and her lips part. Unable to resist, he leaned forward and kissed her deeply, his tongue thrusting inside. She moaned softly, seeming to melt into him.

Jared gripped her hips, his movements faster as they raced to completion together. Rachel cried out his name at the same time he growled hers. When she collapsed against him, he wrapped his arms around her and buried his face in her hair.

He thought of the woman who'd come into his life in the craziest way imaginable and managed to change it in more ways than he could count. Now he couldn't envision what it would be like without her. And he didn't want to even consider how barren his life would have been if he had never known her.

At that moment, he would have gladly given up his life if it meant Rachel could have a full existence.

I love you. Since they were words he wasn't used to saying, it was easier to speak them inside his head than to say them out loud. At the moment, he would continue to show her how much she meant to him.

Jared was half-awake when the sky outside started to lighten. He heard Rachel utter a sleepy murmur of protest just before the pleasurable weight on his chest disappeared, as if removed by an invisible hand.

The contentment he'd felt disappeared right along with her.

"Some morning we're going to have breakfast together," he murmured.

He didn't bother rolling over and going back to sleep. It just wasn't the same now. He smiled as he smelled jasmine.

"Good morning to you, too," he whispered.

It had definitely been a night to remember. The breathy sounds of her sighs when he'd thrust into her softness. The tightness of her center as it clenched around him. The way she'd wrapped her arms about him.

If there was a dark spot in the night it was the awareness that dawn would come too soon.

At one point, he'd climbed out of bed, picked up her corset and marched downstairs, throwing the offending garment into the trash and actually stomping it down into the trash basket with his foot.

When he'd gotten up in the middle of the night, he'd tripped over the damn thing, lying on the floor by the bed. Rachel's giggles had mingled with his muttered curses.

He realized he would have stood on his head and done everything possible to keep her laughing like that. Instead, he'd returned to the bed and coaxed another, more physical, reaction from her.

"You do not intend to sleep all day, do you?" Maya's strident voice drifted up the stairs. "Your dog will eat your breakfast if you do not come down in five minutes!"

Jared grinned when the scent of jasmine seemed to stroke his face.

"Yeah, I know, she means well," he muttered, climbing out of bed. "But we both know she'd feed the dog if I was thirty seconds past her deadline."

He looked around him, hoping to see even a trace of Rachel's presence. All he had was the elusive scent.

"Stay out of trouble, sweetheart. I'll see you tonight." He headed for the shower. He suddenly grinned as the scent seemed to follow him. "And no peeking!"

Chapter 12

He'd bought her a dress.

The moment she materialized in her bedroom that night she saw a splash of dainty flowers on the bed.

She walked over to it and reached out hesitantly, afraid to touch it for fear it would disappear. But she couldn't stop herself from fingering fabric that felt light as air.

The pale cream color had tiny violets scattered across the surface. It was pure spring compared to the dark purple, two-piece, heavy cotton dress she had been wearing for an eternity.

Rachel picked it up, holding it against her. It wasn't like many of the dresses she had seen on television. The calf-length dress was an A-line design, with tiny purple buttons down the front. The V-shaped neckline had a tiny ruff of lace to keep it from appearing too improper in her eyes, even if the sheer sleeves ended at her elbows. She immediately fell in love with it.

She wanted so badly to put the dress on, but she still feared the idea of completely discarding her old clothing. Jared taking her clothes off to make love to her was one thing, but what if she took off her dress with the intention of never wearing it again? Would she be punished for wanting to completely banish the past?

But the new dress called out to her and her vanity won out. She wanted to wear something pretty that was from Jared's time. Even more, she wanted to look pretty in his eyes.

Plus, he'd picked the dress out himself, with her in mind.

She struggled to unbutton her bodice and release herself from her skirt.

"You could see fit to put me back in my clothing this morning, but you could not find a way to help me tonight?" she muttered to the powers that be as she slowly dropped her petticoats. As they touched the floor she wondered if this would be the moment she disappeared for good, but nothing happened. She released the breath she had been holding and quickly picked up the dress.

Jared's breath caught when Rachel came into the room.

The dress was a perfect fit. While it showed off her slender curves, it covered up enough of her for her to feel comfortable in the modern clothing. She had done something different to her hair, putting it up in a loose knot, with a few tendrils hanging down to highlight her cheeks and the soft nape he loved to kiss.

He noticed the brighter color highlighting her skin, adding a new sparkle to her eyes.

"Do you like it?" she asked, hesitant because he hadn't said a word yet.

Instead of telling her, he walked over to her, framed her face with his hands and lowered his head to cover her mouth with his in a kiss that said more than he could ever vocalize. With his kiss, he told her she was more beautiful than he ever could have imagined. He told her that giving her a dress was nothing compared to what she had given him. He told her just how much she meant to him. His kiss told her he was in love with her.

Her eyes were large and dazed when he finally lifted his head.

"You'd think I'd know better than to pick something that had a million buttons," he said wryly, spanning her waist with his hands. "Glad to see you left your cage off."

"It did not go with the dress," she said. "This is beautiful. Thank you."

He looked at the joy on her face and knew his panic and unease in the boutique had been worth it. Once the salesclerk had helped him figure out Rachel's size, and he saw the dress that he knew was meant for her, he'd paid for it and fled the store, feeling as if he was escaping with his life.

He'd gladly do it again just to see that smile on her face.

He glanced down at her feet, now bare.

"Sorry I couldn't figure out what size shoe you wore, but I found something that should work." He walked over to the table and picked up a box. "They sort of stretch."

Rachel discovered the cream-colored, silky ballet-type slippers fit her just fine.

"I feel brand-new." She spun in a circle with her arms held out. She stopped and ran her hands down the front of her dress. "I have never felt anything like this before."

"No corset, no bustle, no high button shoes. Just you."

Rachel's laughter was music to his ears.

Jared wrapped an arm around her waist and twirled her around. He didn't consider himself much of a dancer, but with Rachel following his moves, it didn't matter.

He vowed to do whatever it took to keep her laughing like this. And one day, to dance with her outside.

It was her cries of passion that lifted him up the most. All it took was a certain smile from Rachel and he was hard as a rock.

He knew what he wanted to say would wipe away her sleepy, sated smile, but he needed to ask.

"Tell me everything you know about the curse," he said quietly. When she started to move away from him, he tightened his hold. She finally settled back in his arms.

"I finally realized I could no longer live with Caleb," she said softly. "A woman could not seek divorce then and no proper woman left her husband. But I didn't care. Maya helped me by hiding a bag of my clothing near the ranch entrance and arranging passage on a stagecoach to San Francisco, then a boat to Los Angeles from there. I was so desperate to leave I didn't care where I went."

"Didn't you have any friends in town who would have helped you?" he asked.

She shook her head. "I wasn't allowed to make friends. Caleb wanted his wife to be above everyone else. I was here as someone for his friends to envy, and to bear him the sons he wanted for his dynasty."

"And what did you get in return?"

"His name," she murmured. "Caleb had very little education, but he understood horseflesh. He could look at a foal and know if he had a winner or not. He envied men with book learning, even if he never let on."

"And wives with book learning?"

She sighed. "I was a teacher when Caleb met me."

"When exactly were you born?" He rubbed the top of her head with his chin.

"I was born in Atlanta, Georgia in 1865," she said primly. "My parents were not married and I was raised by a local minister and his wife. They felt I should do something useful with my life and so I was trained to teach. Caleb had come to Atlanta to buy a stallion that belonged to one of the church deacons. I met him when he accompanied the deacon to church one Sunday."

"And the walls didn't fall down on him?" Jared muttered.

"I am sure that would have happened later on," she whispered.

He felt the immediate tension in her body. He ran his hands down her arms in hope of relaxing her. "Tell me."

Rachel took a deep breath. "Caleb started accusing people of plotting against him. I think that's why his mistress was able to control him so easily. She had him believing he would be wealthy beyond his dreams and would have everything he ever wanted."

"But she was a *bruja*," Jared recalled. "A witch."

Rachel nodded. "I knew Caleb had a mistress and I was relieved because that meant he left me alone." She blushed. "Maya said she was a dangerous woman. She refused to mention her name. She insisted the woman practiced black magic and should not be spoken of or to. But I heard that she wanted to be Caleb's wife. I thought it was nothing more than native superstition, since others were so afraid of her."

"Until it was too late?"

With each word she spoke her tension increased. "Only Maya knew of my plans of leaving."

"Someone probably followed her into town and watched her making your travel arrangements," he murmured.

"Yes, that is what happened. Except this woman made Caleb believe I was leaving with a man." Rachel momentarily closed her eyes as if gathering her courage. "I thought he was at a neighboring ranch for a poker game and it would be a safe time for me to leave. But as I was getting ready to go, he stormed into the bedroom and demanded to know the name of the man I was leaving with. He refused to believe me when I said there was no one." She burrowed closer to Jared. "He hit me." She stopped and took a deep breath.

"It's okay, Rachel." He brushed a kiss across her brow. "He can't hurt you any longer."

"I was so scared," she whispered. "She was with him and had this look on her face, as if she knew she had won. She told him I should be punished, and all he did was scream at me that I could not leave. He had a fearsome temper to begin with and she kept telling him to hurt me. Then he brought out this knife." Rachel's breath hitched as the memory returned. "He told me I would never leave this house, that I would be here until the end of time. She…she said words I could not understand, and then I heard and felt this wind around me. That was all I knew until I woke up. At least, I thought I was waking up. Maya was there. She explained to me what had happened and that she'd appealed to her gods on my behalf. She said they'd exacted vengeance on Caleb and the woman. And that I would only have human form from sunset to sunrise. Maya would be here for me, but she would have her human form from sunrise to sunset. That day was the last time I truly saw her," she murmured.

"But what about a chance of you coming back again?" he asked. "Nothing about that? Magic words? Fairy dust?"

"A key," Rachel said flatly. "Supposedly there is a key that will release me from my half existence. But it was never said what the key looked like."

"Snow White and Sleeping Beauty had it a lot easier," Jared mused. "There was no description of this key? Where it might be? What exactly it's supposed to do?"

She shook her head. "All Maya said is that I will know when I find it. She once said it was within. For nights I searched this house, from the attic to the floorboards downstairs, but I did not find a thing. I do not know if it was part of the legend or merely lost over the years."

"Maybe it's with the treasure," he joked.

"Caleb did not trust banks. He once said he would bury all his money because then he knew it would be safe. I would think any money he hid was found years ago," she said.

"Nowadays, Caleb would have been locked up in a psych ward." Jared ran his hands up and down her arms in a soothing gesture.

"You mean an asylum." She shivered at the thought. "He once threatened to put me in one. They are horrible places."

"If he used that kind of threat he deserved everything he got." He angled his body so he could look at her face. His first thought was to banish the shadows from her eyes. "Okay, enough scary stories for tonight. We don't want nightmares, do we?"

"No," she murmured. "But you have your own scary stories."

"I called the sheriff's department today," he said. "They're going to check out a trailer I found up in the hills. There's nothing like a good meth lab bust to make a cop's day."

"And meth is bad." She smiled, remembering what he'd told her about the dangerous drug.

"Definitely. It brings property values down." He rolled over onto his side, facing her. "Enough talk about things we don't want to worry about, lady. I'd rather talk about you. You're naked and in my bed."

She smiled. How could she not when he looked at her like a wicked little boy? "Yes, I am."

"And I'm naked in my bed." He easily lifted her up onto him until she was seated on his hips.

"Yes, you are." She wiggled a bit until she found a comfortable position. She couldn't help but notice what her wiggling did to his anatomy.

He narrowed his eyes at her. "And you're absolutely positive Maya doesn't know about anything we do at night?"

"Yes."

"Because she gave me a funny look this morning."

"I thought you said she gives you a funny look every morning." Rachel stretched out her legs until she lay flat on top of him, with her arms resting on his chest. Any hint of shadows in her eyes was now gone.

"We're going to find the key, Rach," he said softly.

She was quiet for a moment. "What if doing so means I'll completely disappear?" That idea no longer appealed to her, as it had for so many years.

Jared shook his head. "I don't think that's the case. Why would whatever Maya begged to save your life basically take it away, just because you discovered what would save you?"

"Is this what detectives do?"

"Solve puzzles? Definitely." He ran his hand across her shoulder, enjoying the feel of her skin. "That's how we catch the bad guys. Or in your case, find that magic key to unlock the dungeon door."

She smiled at him. "My knight in shining armor."

Jared wrapped his arms around her. "Oh, honey, not even close. Not close at all," he whispered.

He was a goner. Jared Stryker had done the unthinkable. He had fallen in love with a woman who couldn't give him more than nighttime hours.

But he felt his luck might be changing, which could mean that Rachel's luck could change, too.

"It was a meth lab, all right." Deputy Wright had called him that morning with the news. "Thanks for backing me up, Jared. I told the sheriff I felt the lab was up there and he told me no way. He was even trying to blame it on The Renegade."

Jared stiffened at the idea of Lea being hassled by the law when she didn't deserve it.

"So you set him straight?" he asked.

"The bust did. Plus your chief of police." She chuckled.

"Wright," he said, lowering his voice. "Do you think your boss might be dirty?"

"More than once, but I haven't been able to find anything against him. The guys we busted are blaming you. They're convinced you used the ranch as a cover so you could stake them out. We don't think they'll make bail, but you never know."

"They never did have an ounce of brains between them," he chuckled. "Thanks for the call, Wright."

"No problem. If there's anything I can do for you, just let me know."

"Same here."

Jared clipped his cell phone on his belt loop. "Always did like having a target painted on my back," he muttered, getting back to his work.

He'd spent the morning looking over the property, trying to think where the key might be hidden. He had even dug out the deed and description of the ranch, in case it mentioned an old well or shed.

"Any reason why your gods can't give someone a description of a damn key?" he growled at Maya.

The woman didn't turn a hair at his bad mood. "The time will come soon, and she will know when it is right."

Jared glared at her. "Do you know what the key looks like?"

She shook her head. "I only feel it here." She placed her hand over her heart. "Just as *la niña,* Rachel, will."

"I'm one of the most logical men you can find," he said. "So even talking about some magical key is not something I ordinarily do."

"But you believe in it." Her black eyes gleamed with understanding.

"So what do I do to find it? Slay a dragon? Throw an evil witch in an oven?"

Maya shook her head. "She must do it," she said softly. "She will understand what she must do and she will do it." She appeared to take pity on him. "You are in love with Rachel."

He didn't bother to admit the obvious. "I don't understand love. I didn't see much of it as a kid."

"Love is in the heart and in the soul," she said.

He considered her words. "So love is the key? What if Rachel falls in love with me? No…" He swiftly backed off. "Not me. She deserves someone better than me." He felt a strange pang in the vicinity of his heart.

Maya moved closer to him. "Love understands what is right and what is wrong. Love will make everything right," she said cryptically.

"If love makes everything right, how did someone like Rachel, with so much capacity to love, end up with Bingham back then?" he demanded. "How did someone who only wanted to love and be loved end up dead by her husband's hand?"

She slowly shook her head. "Things happen that we do not understand," she murmured. "I do not know why she suffered."

"But you have a theory," he guessed, seeing a familiar gleam in her eye. "You think you know why," he added.

She nodded. "I think my Rachel was born too soon. And I think that who was truly meant for her hadn't been born yet."

She eyed him closely. "Since a mistake was made, something had to be done to put things right."

"You're making it sound like some kind of fairy tale," Jared pointed out. "I never believed in fairy tales."

"Maybe you need to," Maya said.

He stared at her, waiting for more, but he should have known better. Whenever he wanted answers, she kept her mouth shut. When he didn't want any, she talked his ear off. He sighed heavily. He really hated giving in to her!

"There has to be more to it," he argued.

She smiled as if she knew he would say so. "You cannot worry. You go out and do your work. Everything will be fine." She picked up a large pot. "I will make stew."

"I'll be outside," he told her, not having a clear idea what he'd be doing there. He just wanted to get out in the sunshine. He had already planned on waiting until cooler weather before he started painting inside. The idea of Rachel helping him choose colors for each room was appealing.

"You could dig up the garden," Maya suggested. "We should plant vegetables."

"You mean *I* should plant them." He already envisioned an aching back with a dictatorial Maya directing him. "And leave my beer alone!" He walked outside. Frustration already stirred a tempest inside him. Seeing Harley in the middle of the former garden, digging a hole while carrying a beef bone in his mouth, merely added to it. "I mean it, Harley! No more holes!"

As if afraid his prize would be taken away from him, the young dog ran around the side of the house.

Jared glared at the holes the dog had already dug. "Maybe I should have let him keep on digging. That way, most of the work would have been done for me."

As he walked off, he glanced upstairs at his bedroom window. He imagined the curtain stirred. Feeling lighter at heart, he smiled in that direction, then headed on. He was already counting the minutes until sundown.

Looks like you've got two choices. Either you find the key or you'll still be doing this fifty years from now.

The idea that Rachel would still be with him in fifty years was good. The idea that Rachel would look as she had the night before, and that the day could come when he would have to leave her forever, was downright depressing.

"There are two little old ladies in town who I know would love to talk to you," Jared said. He was pleased to see that Rachel was once again wearing the dress he'd gotten her. He vowed to find a few more. "They run the local historical society." He showed her the Web page on his laptop computer. They sat on the couch together as he showed her pictures the society had posted. "They have newspapers dating back to the very first issue printed in town, some diaries written by local ladies, and furniture that's as old as you are," he teased.

Rachel wrinkled her nose at him. "Yes, but I look very young for my age." She entered into the play, then sobered. "They know about me and Caleb?"

He nodded. "It seems not too many people liked him back then. It's just a hunch, but I think you could have found someone to help you."

She placed her hand on his. "I did find someone." Her eyes glowed.

He leaned over and kissed her softly. "Maya said some things are meant to be. So maybe I'll be the one to find the key to free you. Hey!" He used his thumb to wipe the lone tear that tracked down her cheek. "No crying, okay?"

"I did not expect you," she confessed. "I did not expect to feel the way I do. And that makes me afraid."

"Afraid, why?" He had a sinking feeling in his stomach. Even with everything Rachel and Maya had told him, he still had no idea how the curse worked or what it truly entailed. As if he feared she might suddenly disappear right in front of him, he wrapped his arms around her. She laid her head against his shoulder and snuggled closer.

"That I do not deserve this," she said softly. "No matter what happens, Jared, I want you to know that you have given me something very special and I will always cherish these memories."

Jared dropped a kiss on her forehead and tightened his hold on her, but she didn't protest.

With his chin resting on her hair, he stared unseeing at the wall as thoughts raced through his head.

He had grown up without knowing what affection was. The only positive note in his life had been Lea.

As an adult, he'd seen himself growing old without a family. It never bothered him before. His solitary lifestyle was fine with him and he didn't miss a thing. Then Rachel had entered his life and he realized what he wanted.

He wanted this woman. He even wanted kids with her. The idea of having a child scared the hell out of him; he hadn't had the best role model for fatherhood. But Jared figured he knew what not to do.

Now all he needed was to bring Rachel fully into this world. He knew there would be some tricky details to iron out, but it wasn't as if he didn't know what to do to bring a nineteenth century woman into the twenty-first. After all, he was a cop with access to pretty much every database in California. And he knew of a few forgers who were artisans in creating false identification papers. Jared was positive he could provide Rachel with a brand-new life.

Another troubling thought that plagued him was the idea he would have to tell her he was related to Caleb. She was still afraid of a man long dead. At least the paperwork revealing the relationship was still safely locked away.

Jared was a stubborn man who was determined not to give up the best thing in his life.

Chapter 13

"You are in love with him, *niña*," Maya talked as she busily polished the furniture until it shone from the lemon oil she used. "And it is very obvious that he loves you."

Love shouldn't hurt. It should make you feel joyful and excited. So why do I feel so sad?

Rachel knew why she was sad. For the first time in decades she felt free and happy. She felt as if she had something very extraordinary in a special someone. It wasn't just the time they spent making love, but the way they curled up in each other's arms and talked about anything and everything.

But something he'd said to her that first night they made love always remained in the back of her mind. Jared had told her the day would come when he would no longer be here. The thought of losing him hurt her more than anything she'd experienced before.

Maya paused in her task of polishing the coffee table.

"With love must come trust, *chica,*" she said softly. "With love and trust, you will have everything. But you must be brave enough, and strong enough, to allow them into your heart."

She's talking about the key again. Why does she still believe it's out there? And why talk of love and trust? I feel love for Jared and I would trust him with my life, if I still had one! But it has nothing to do with the key. If it existed we would have found it by now. It's gone, Maya. It's not here, just the way Caleb's alleged treasure is nothing more than a story. A legend, like you and me.

"He never puts anything away," Maya grumbled, stacking together papers that were strewn about near Jared's laptop computer.

Rachel couldn't see clearly, but she saw well enough to note that the letterhead on the top sheet of paper was from a lawyer's office. She remembered that Jared had sat there earlier in the day writing something on the computer. When he'd heard Maya scolding Harley for digging more holes, he'd left the computer and must have forgotten what he had been doing before he was distracted. As Rachel looked at the paper, Caleb's name sprang out at her.

What is this about?

For the rest of the day, Rachel counted the seconds until sunset. She hoped the papers would still be there, so she could look at them more closely. She knew she would have a chance when Jared went upstairs for his shower, although he usually tried to tempt her into taking it with him. That was one temptation she always succumbed to without an ounce of guilt.

Tonight, she stood her ground and sent him upstairs alone. The moment she heard the water running, she hurried over to the table and picked up the papers. She wasn't familiar with some of the legal language that indicated the paperwork was the deed to the ranch, but the accompanying letter told her everything else. She felt an icy cold lump settle in her stomach as she realized that the reason Jared had inherited the property was because he was a direct descendant of Caleb Bingham.

"No." She refused to believe what she'd read and reread. She hadn't imagined it. She felt as if she was encased in ice.

Jared was descended from Caleb's brother.

Rachel had only met the man once and thought him as cold and evil as Caleb himself had been.

She'd never really stopped to question how Jared had obtained the property. He'd mentioned he'd inherited the ranch from his mother, but Rachel hadn't realized that he was a Bingham descendant. Caleb had once explained that the property could only be handed down to the eldest son of the owner. She'd thought the property had changed hands over the years and left the Bingham family, altogether.

"And to think Maya always believed in Jared," she whispered to herself. The fear she hadn't felt for a while came back with a vengeance as she heard his footsteps on the stairs.

"Rach, what's wrong?" He walked downstairs, wearing only his jeans, his hair still damp from his shower. His smile faded when he saw the expression on her face. "Rachel?" His voice sharpened. He glanced at her hand. She still held the papers, but what bothered him was that her hand was trembling.

"You…" She swallowed the lump in her throat. "These papers say that you are descended from Caleb."

"You knew I'd inherited the ranch." He was puzzled by her calm manner. With the revelation, he'd expected fireworks. He knew how she felt about Caleb. That was why he hadn't wanted to tell her just yet.

She shook her head. "Yes, but I did not realize you were a

direct descendent of Caleb's. Or perhaps I did not want to realize it."

Jared started toward her, then froze when she backed away.

"Just because I'm somehow related to that old bastard
doesn't make me any different than I was five minutes ago,"
he said harshly. "Or does it?" he demanded when she remained silent. "Answer me, Rachel!"

She flinched.

"Caleb made me believe I could have a house and a family," she whispered, still refusing to look at him. "I didn't realize the price I would pay. He felt as if he'd been cheated
because I couldn't give him children. He didn't want anyone
to know that I wasn't the perfect wife he'd led people to believe I was. I was to let them think we had a wonderful marriage. My clothing could hide the bruises. When he killed me
I thought I was finally free. Instead, he found another way to
imprison me."

Jared looked incredulous. "And you think I'll turn into a
sadistic monster like him?" he demanded. Pain crossed his face.

She gazed down at her clasped hands. "You have a dark
nature, Jared. Perhaps it is because of your work, I don't
know. But what if it overtakes you? What if something happens that you can't control?"

"If that was the case, it would have happened years ago.
My God!" He looked as if he was ready to tear his hair out.
"Rachel, the property came to me through my mother. There
wasn't one mean bone in her body. That's why she left my
old man. She left him because she couldn't take his abuse anymore. The problem was, she left me, too, and I don't know
what I did to deserve to be left behind. Maybe she thought I'd
end up like him. Maybe she didn't love me, so she left me the
property as her way of getting rid of her guilt for abandoning

me. I *don't know*. But I learned long ago that if I didn't want to end up in a prison cell like my father I'd have to find a way to control my temper. And I did," he told her. "The last thing I would ever do is hurt a woman. I'd cut my hand off first. You should know that by now."

He tried to reason with her, but for some reason she refused to listen. She kept shaking her head.

"Dammit, Rachel! What—are you afraid I'll kill you?" he shouted, feeling the frustration build up.

Realizing he wasn't getting anywhere, he turned away.

"Fine, you want to believe the worst because it's easier for you." He headed for the open French doors and went outside, an agitated Harley following him.

Jared didn't know *what* to do. Why did Rachel have to be so stubborn?

"Quiet, Harley," he ordered when the young dog started barking. "You're not chasing rabbits or whatever you think is out here."

The words barely left his mouth when the memory of a sound he'd heard before finally made sense.

"A bike that needs a ring job!" he whispered. Blinding pain exploded across the back of his head and he fell to his knees.

"You had to stick your nose in our operation, cop," the man snarled. "Big mistake!"

Rachel! Her name bounced around inside his head just as his world turned dark.

Rachel walked over to the open doors and looked outside just as a man crept up behind Jared and hit him on the back of the head. She screamed his name but realized her warning came too late. She instinctively ran to help him, but was violently thrown back.

"No!"

As she looked outside she saw the man who'd struck Jared now look up at her. The cold, feral smile on his face sent a chilling fear through her body. She had no doubt he would kill Jared, then come after her. And before he tried to kill her she knew even worse things would happen.

She stood frozen to the spot as the man started walking toward the house with his gun held loosely in one hand.

"That cop thought he'd mess with our lab and we wouldn't find out? Undercover cops are like snitches. They deserve to be dead," he said in a rough voice as he advanced toward her. "Nice to see I'll be getting something extra."

"I'm homicide, you idiot, not a narc!" Jared snarled as he got to his feet and jumped at the man's back. Except his head injury affected his balance and he couldn't hold on as well as he wanted to.

The two men tumbled into the house, both fighting for a grip on the gun.

Rachel screamed when gunshots echoed inside the house and a bullet buried itself in the wall near her head.

She knew immediately that one shot had found its target when she saw red blossom on Jared's chest. With a last burst of energy, he wrestled the gun from the attacker's hands and managed to shoot him in the knee. His assailant dropped to the floor, screaming in agony, while Jared also fell backward. The gun slid across the polished planking.

Rachel's hands shook violently as she ran over and picked up the gun before making her way to Jared. She winced along with him as she carefully lifted his shoulders so she could hold him against her.

"Keep the gun pointed at him," he wheezed.

"You need a doctor," she cried. Fear gave her the strength

to tear a strip off the bottom of her dress. She folded it into a pad and pressed it firmly against the wound on his chest. She looked around wildly.

"My phone's in my front pocket," Jared gasped. "You've seen me use it. Just punch 911 and tell whoever answers that a cop is down." He lifted his hand and caressed her cheek. "Trust me, sweetheart, they'll know what you mean."

"You're going to die, cop!" the man screamed at Jared.

Rachel's heart thumped wildly at his words.

"Yeah, well, you'll be walking with a limp for the rest of your life. Nothing like a cripple in prison," Jared retorted in a weak voice. The hand he'd used to touch Rachel's cheek now lay limply on her arm.

Rachel tried not to jostle Jared too much as she pulled the cell phone from his pocket and followed his instructions.

Afterward, she talked to him incessantly.

"Stay awake, Jared," she pleaded. "Please, do not close your eyes." She stroked his forehead even as she made sure to keep the gun trained on their prisoner. At one point, her gaze turned cold as she stared at the man. "If you move even a finger, I will kill you." She knew he was aware she made no idle threat. She glanced down at Jared. "They said someone is coming right away. I love you so much," she whispered against his ear. "Do not leave me, Jared."

"By the time they show up he won't need a doctor. He'll need the coroner," the man laughed.

Rachel didn't think twice; she raised the gun and pulled the trigger. The bullet left a hole in the floor a bare inch from the man's hip.

"I promise you the next time I will not miss," she said coldly. Her head snapped up when Harley started howling in accompaniment to a high-pitched wail that grew louder by the second. Another siren sounded, coming from another direction.

"Cavalry's a little late." Jared laughed weakly.

Vehicles skidded to a stop and Rachel soon found herself flanked by two men, while the woman deputy she'd seen before ran in with her weapon drawn.

"Please, help him!" Rachel begged the paramedics. One of them helped her to her feet and gently put her to one side as the second briefly checked the other man, then came over to Jared.

"Hey, I'm shot, too!" the man growled.

"Doesn't look as if anything important was hit," the deputy said dispassionately. "You should have aimed a bit higher, Stryker." She glanced curiously at Rachel, then back at the man as she crouched down next to him. "While I know you know your Miranda word for word, I don't earn my pay unless I repeat it to you." She fastened handcuffs on him as she recited his rights to him.

"We've got a collapsed lung and looks like internal bleeding," one EMT reported. "We need to get him in now."

Rachel watched them carefully maneuver Jared onto a gurney.

"What are you doing?" she asked.

"We're taking him in to the hospital, ma'am," one of the paramedics told her, as he set up an IV line.

"Hospital?" She felt her breath leave her body. Memories of the hospitals more than a hundred years swept over her. People died in hospitals!

She felt helpless as she watched the paramedics load Jared in the ambulance, while another ambulance arrived and paramedics settled Deputy Wright's prisoner inside the vehicle.

"If you want to go to the hospital I can arrange for some-one to take you in," the deputy offered gently, sensing Ra-chel's distress.

She felt like crying, but adrenaline had run through her body so fast she couldn't find the energy for any more tears.

"No," she whispered, feeling the lump in her chest move upward. She had no idea her face was a picture of raw anguish.

"He'll be fine," the woman told her, obviously puzzled by her refusal. "He's a tough guy. Look, I've got to go. If you want someone to take you to the hospital, just call the sher-iff's station. Someone will pick you up and take you over there." She ran out to the ambulance and climbed inside with her prisoner.

Rachel saw the rapidly fading taillights of the first ambulance. She looked down and saw smears of blood on the front of her dress. While she never saw the graphic evidence of her own death on her clothing, Jared's blood remained on the fabric.

Worse than the horror of her past was the terror of not being with Jared when he needed her the most. The idea that he could die alone filled her with a panic that threatened to overtake her.

"No!" she screamed, with a fury she had never felt before. *"It is not right!"*

She didn't think twice as she ran to the doorway. She only knew she wasn't about to be denied what she wanted most.

Rachel felt herself pitching forward and she fell hard onto the veranda.

She feebly batted an excited Harley from her as she slowly stumbled to her feet. She felt as if her long-starved senses were on overload. She heard the steady drone of night insects, and looking up, saw the black canopy of the night sky instead of a beamed ceiling. Even the rich scent of jasmine in her nos-trils seemed stronger. Disorienting.

She stared with shocked disbelief at her surroundings. Tiny spots of light danced before her eyes.

"I am free," she whispered, stepping forward. A rush of cold air hit her face just before her world turned black.

Nothing felt right. Or sounded right.

What was that beeping sound? And why did she hurt all over?

Rachel kept her eyes closed as she took mental stock of herself. All she knew was that her head hurt and that there were strange sounds around her.

Did I finally die and go to heaven? Does heaven have all these strange noises?

"Baby, I'd feel a hell of a lot better if you'd open those beautiful eyes of yours for me." A familiar voice caressed her ears.

Her stomach tightened. *Did Jared die, too?*

Then she remembered. She'd somehow managed to escape the house, but everything after that was a blank.

Rachel opened her eyes and slowly turned her head in the direction of the voice she loved so much.

An unshaved Jared sat in a wheelchair by her bed. His normally bronze skin was pasty. She could see the heavy bandages that were wrapped around his chest and his features starkly etched from the pain he must have suffered. She knew immediately he should be in bed.

"Jared," she whispered.

He leaned forward, grimacing in pain and covered her hand with his. He brought it up to his mouth.

"You've had me worried, darlin'," he said in a low voice. "You have no idea what I've gone through the past few days, waiting for you to wake up. You scared the hell out of me."

She looked around the room, noted the strange-looking boxes by her bed and the even stranger sounds they made.

"What is this?" She looked down at the tubes attached to the back of her hand.

"You're in the hospital." He grinned, but concern still shadowed his eyes. "I had to do some major begging, but they took pity on me and put you in the room next to mine."

She wanted to tell him it didn't look like any hospital she'd been in before. She started to move her head, then pulled back when white-hot pain streaked across her forehead.

"What is this?" she whispered, nodding toward the machines.

He smiled. "Monitors. They measure your blood pressure and heart rate."

"Heart rate? Blood pressure?" Now she was truly confused. "But how? And how did I get here?"

"It seems you fell off the porch and hit some pretty hard dirt. Maya called 911. Paramedics joked that they spent their entire shift out at the ranch. That old witch was with me after I got out of surgery." He grinned wryly. "I've got to say she wasn't exactly who I wanted to wake up to. You've been unconscious for the past four days, sweetheart. You suffered a head injury. The doctors think you tripped on something when you left the house, and I'm letting them go with that theory. Which brings us to something very good." He looked at her lovingly. "You do realize you're now outside of the house, don't you?" he murmured.

Rachel thought back to those moments before she'd stormed through the doorway. At the time, all that mattered was reaching Jared.

She looked past him to the window. A window through which she could see the bright light of day. It was past dawn and she was not only still in mortal form, but she was away from the house.

"You were so badly hurt and I was afraid you would die in

the hospital," she murmured. "And I did not want you to be there alone. I wanted to be with you and tell you how much I love you."

"Then whatever you did worked, because I'm still here." He kept her hand imprisoned in his. "And so are you."

"So I'm…" She gestured toward the monitor. She still didn't understand what had happened.

Jared nodded. He kept his eyes on her as if afraid she might disappear at any moment, even if it was long past dawn.

Rachel felt long-buried emotions start to rise up inside her. After so many years of solitude, the idea of freedom was slow to come to her. She opened her mouth to speak, but instead of words coming out, tears streamed down her cheeks.

"Oh, Rach, no," Jared groaned, holding her hand as carefully and as tightly as he could. He leaned forward, taking her into his arms, mindful of the IV tubes. "Don't cry, Rachel. Please, don't cry," he begged.

She nodded her head as if agreeing she wouldn't, but the tears continued to fall.

"I never thought I would be free," she sobbed against his shoulder. "I did not think I would ever be free again."

"But you are," he soothed, stroking her tangled hair back from her face. "You found the key, Rachel."

She shook her head. "But I didn't find anything. All I knew was that I needed to be with you."

"And you are with me," he assured her, kissing the tears from her cheeks. "You're not disappearing from me again. I'll do whatever it takes, even if I have to tear the house down to make sure you'll always be safe." He pressed his lips against her forehead, then the tip of her nose, before moving down to her lips.

She touched his battered face with her fingertips as if she

still couldn't believe he was real. That this wasn't some sort of dream. The dampness she found against her fingers told her more than she expected.

"You are crying," she said with a sense of wonder.

He smiled. "What you're seeing is relief," he told her. "These days have been pretty long while I waited for you to wake up."

She continued touching his face with her fingertips. "It is all too much."

"Information overload," he agreed. "All you need to worry about now is getting well."

Fear still lurked inside her. She had been cursed for so long. The idea that she was free was overwhelming.

"When I woke up after my surgery, Maya was standing by my bed. She told me you had been brought in with a head wound," he explained. "She also said I didn't have to worry about anything happening to you when dawn came. It didn't help that I couldn't get out of bed to see for myself, but then I realized it was the middle of the night and Maya was standing there." Jared framed Rachel's face with his hands, his thumbs brushing away the last of her tears. "No more tears, darlin'," he murmured.

She smiled at his gentle command. "I am so glad you are all right."

He moted at the expression in her eyes and sighed. "Aw, sweetheart, you can't look at me as I'm some knight in shining armor, because my armor is more than a little tarnished." He took a deep breath. "Rachel Weatherly Bingham, I love you more than life itself. When I heard you'd been brought in here with a head injury and they thought you weren't going to wake up, I thought I'd die myself." The stark anguish on his face betrayed his feelings. "I know I'm no prize. I forget myself in my work sometimes. I'm land rich and cash poor. I don't really have a lot to offer you, but I can promise you that I will do everything in my power to make sure you never cry again. I will do everything I can to keep that beautiful smile on your lips and hear you laugh. You're my other half, Rachel." He stopped talking, fearful of her response.

She reached out and stroked his whiskery cheek. Before her sat the disreputable man who'd stolen her heart from the beginning. This was the man she had fallen in love with. "And you are the other half of me," she admitted softly.

"Of course, we'll have to do something about getting you an identity," he said with a smile. "Don't worry. I have contacts in low places who can handle that for me. In no time, you'll be Rachel Weatherly to the world, even if it will be only for a short time, since I intend for you to become Rachel Stryker. How does that sound?"

"I say yes," she said with a breathy sigh.

He felt a lightening in his heart he had never known before. "Is that yes to everything? To a preacher and a gold ring and forever and ever with me and a dog who will dig holes in the garden I know you want to plant?"

She nodded, happier than she'd ever imagined she could be. "Yes to everything."

Jared didn't waste any time in sealing the proposal with a kiss that soon turned explosive.

They were so lost in each other they didn't see a familiar figure standing in the doorway. Maya's normally stern features were relaxed in a broad smile as she overheard them place their hearts in the other's keeping.

She moved off, aware that a new chapter for the couple was just beginning and that the last remnants of Caleb Bingham's evil hold on his wife and land were gone—forever.

"All right, handsome, you've been on the loose long enough." A willowy woman wearing angel-print medical scrubs walked into the room. She took one look at Rachel and started taking her vitals. "I thought I told you to alert us immediately if the lady woke up."

Jared didn't take his eyes off Rachel. "She woke up and she's agreed to marry me."

"Congratulations, or maybe I should offer her my sympathy, since you've been nothing but trouble since you were brought in. Now it's time for the doctor to check out Miss Weatherly and time for you to go back to bed." She took hold of his wheelchair and turned him around.

"I'll be back once I can lose the warden," he promised over his shoulder as he was wheeled toward the door.

"Do we need to tie you to the bed?" the nurse mock threatened him.

He grinned at Rachel as he answered her. "Sorry, beautiful, I'm an engaged man. I only let Rachel use the handcuffs."

Rachel fell back against the pillows. She didn't know whether to laugh or cry, so she settled for both. The nurse smiled when she returned to her side.

"That man has been in here more than he's been in his own bed," she said. "I'd say you are one lucky woman." She handed Rachel a tissue.

Rachel mopped her eyes and blew her nose. She thought of everything that had led up to this moment. She knew she would endure it all again in a heartbeat as long as it meant she would have Jared in the end.

Her smile was brighter than any sunlit day. "Yes, I am."

"Jared Stryker, you are supposed to take it easy!"

"I am taking it easy." Jared kept a tight hold on Rachel's hand as he pulled her outside. Harley ran alongside, jumping at them and barking in pleasure at having company. "That's why we have to wait before I can carry you over the threshold. I can't afford to pop any stitches with that extra weight." He grinned at her.

"Jared!" She playfully smacked his arm. "I am not that heavy!"

"I don't know. All that hospital food seemed to have put a few pounds on you," he teased, twirling her around him. He enjoyed watching her calf-length skirt swirl around her legs. One of the first things he had done once they were both released from the hospital was to take Rachel clothes shopping. For a man who hated to shop for himself, he greatly enjoyed watching Rachel take another step into the twenty-first century. "Look at us, Mrs. Rachel Weatherly Stryker," he whispered. "We're outside at—" he glanced at his watch "—ten o'clock in the morning." He twirled her around again.

"You are both crazy!" Maya called from the top of the stairs.

"Any reason why she had to come with the deal?" Jared wrapped his arms around Rachel and pulled her up against him.

Rachel felt her spirit fly with the joy she felt. She found she couldn't stop smiling, and she'd been doing a lot of that lately. Especially since Jared had not only found a way to make her a real person in the eyes of the state of California, but to arrange a quick marriage, too.

"Are you kidding? The entire judicial community will turn handsprings to see me married and respectable," he had told her when she asked him if that was possible.

She kissed him because she loved hearing him say the word *married*. And because she just plain loved kissing him.

"Maya is like a member of the family," she reminded him.

"I have some mother-in-law jokes for you then."

All Rachel knew was that she discovered what it meant to

love someone so much it hurt, and Jared learned that love filled the void that had been inside him for far too long.

"With you, I have the entire world," he told her, feeling the need to share with her all he felt.

She looked up at him, the sunlight glowing on her up-turned face. "We have everything."

Barking diverted them for a moment.

"Dammit, Harley! I told you no more digging!" Jared shouted at the dog, who was again furiously digging in the middle of a dirt patch set aside for Rachel's flower garden.

The dog lifted his head from the hole he'd dug, then slowly backed up, his teeth fastened on something. He kept backing up as he dragged it out of the ground.

"What do you have?" Jared asked, crouching down to the dog's level. He held out his hand. "Come here, boy."

Harley made his way toward them, dragging a small bag he'd pulled out of the earth. He dropped his find in front of his owner's feet.

Jared looked down at the bag, then at Rachel. She gazed at it, then at him. Both could see the leather was old and scarred, and just under the tattered flap of the bag something metallic caught the sun and glittered brightly.

"Do you think—?" They spoke simultaneously.

Harley nudged the bag with his nose, and a few gold coins slid out, falling to Rachel's feet.

Maya stood on the porch above them and just smiled.

* * * * *

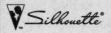

I N T I M A T E   M O M E N T S™

Bounty hunter Ike Walker needed his ex-wife,
Lindsay Hollis, to help prove her brother was
the victim of a cold-blooded murder.

But would working together to resolve the
heart-wrenching crime take them down
passionate—and deadly—paths they
wanted to avoid at all costs?

Deadly Reunion
by
LAUREN NICHOLS

Intimate Moments #1374, June 2005

Visit Silhouette Books at www.eHarlequin.com

SIMDR

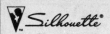

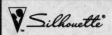

INTIMATE MOMENTS™

The second book in
the thrilling new miniseries

A few hours can change your life.

Truth or Consequences

(IM #1373, on sale June 2005)

by DIANA DUNCAN

Sexy SWAT rear guard Aidan O'Rourke
makes the rules...and aspiring journalist
Zoe Zagretti breaks them. When Zoe's
search for the truth—and Aidan's desire
to keep her alive—get them into grave
danger, the unlikely lovers fight for their
lives and lose their hearts in the process.

***Don't miss this exciting story—
only from Silhouette Books.***

Available at your favorite retail outlet.